The Game Is a Footnote

ame

Is a

Footnote

A SHERLOCK HOLMES
BOOKSHOP MYSTERY

Vicki Delany

CROOKED
LANE

NEW YORK

Published in the United States by Crooked Lane Books, an imprint of The Quick Brown Fox & Company LLC.

Crooked Lane Books and its logo are trademarks of The Quick Brown Fox & Company LLC.

Library of Congress Catalog-in-Publication data available upon request.

ISBN (hardcover): 978-1-63910-145-0
ISBN (ebook): 978-1-63910-146-7

Cover illustration by Joe Burleson

Printed in the United States.

www.crookedlanebooks.com

Crooked Lane Books
34 West 27th St., 10th Floor
New York, NY 10001

First Edition: January 2023

10 9 8 7 6 5 4 3 2 1

To Isla Gail Webb,
who has many years of reading
ahead of her

Prologue

Despite being the oldest house in West London, Massachusetts, Scarlet House has led a quiet, peaceful existence. Robert and Julia Scarlet came from England in 1640 and laid the foundations for the house in 1648. Descendants of their seven children lived there for generations: a long line of farmers; some teachers and doctors; and a couple of lawyers, civil servants, and small-town politicians, along with numerous children, various in-laws, and the occasional stray relative. The number of servants working and living inside the house, and farmhands laboring outside, increased and decreased as the family and the town prospered, or failed to. Additions were added to the main building and adjacent property purchased as money permitted and needs required. James Scarlet represented Massachusetts at the Continental Congress of 1776, and various Scarlet boys fought for their new country while wives and daughters worked the farm. In 1825, Theodore Scarlet went to sea on a whaling vessel and made enough money to thoroughly renovate the house, build a substantial extension onto it, and buy the neighboring farm. On Theodore's death, the property was inherited by his first-born son, Jeremiah. Theodore's eldest child, a daughter, Josephine, had earlier scandalized the family and the community by moving to New York City and becoming a newspaperwoman. The second son, Edward, joined the state department and served in Europe from 1854 until 1861, when he was killed in an accident caused by a horse frightened by a crash of thunder as he returned to West London after abruptly resigning his post. Earlier that year, the three sons of Jeremiah had eagerly joined the Union Army, and they came home to all appearances unscathed. Jeremiah himself died shortly after seeing his sons off to war, when his heart gave out while he was attempting to work his fields by himself. Jeremiah's two eldest sons had little interest in remaining on Cape Cod or in running the farm, and so it was taken on by the youngest, George. George himself had no children, and on his death in 1896, his aunt Josephine, who had earned a fearsome reputation as a reporter in New York City, returned to West London to take control of the farm. Josephine had no descendants either, and the members of the now-dispersed family had no intention of taking up the lives of farmers. And so the house passed out of the hands of the Scarlets on the death of Josephine in 1914.

The new owner, Mr. Harold Hastings, age twenty-one, intended to work the farm, but he left for the war in Europe in 1917, the moment he was called up. Harold did not return, and his wife, Abigail, was left to raise their son, Harold Hastings Jr., on her own. To do so she rented out the farmland and took boarders in the main house. Abigail eventually married the neighboring farmer, Ralph Goodman. By all accounts the marriage was a happy one, and they had a son and a daughter. When it came time to enlist for the next war, Harold Jr. was exempted because he was needed on the farm; the Goodman daughter went to Europe as a nurse; and the younger boy worked in a government position he was not permitted to discuss with anyone. Neither of Ralph's children wanted to return to Cape Cod after the war, but Harold Jr. and his only child, Imogen, worked both farms until 1955, when the properties, situated on prime land close to the town and overlooking the ocean, were sold to accommodate the needs of the burgeoning town of West London. The family kept only the house, still known as Scarlet House, along with a much-reduced farm. In 1956, Miss Imogen Hastings married Harold FitzRoy, a high school teacher, and over the years she worked the small plot to provide for the family's needs and to sell the vegetables (considered by many to be the best grown anywhere in the vicinity) at local markets. She also cared for a few pigs, chickens, and goats who were almost like pets—until slaughter time, of course. The daughter of a farmer, Imogen Hastings FitzRoy had little sentiment when it came to animals. In due course, Harold and Imogen's children left Cape Cod for the bright lights of New York or Los Angeles or Dallas. Harold lived to see the millennium in, but not the collapse of the twin towers. Imogen died at age eighty-five, the result of a fall sustained while attempting to wrestle a stubborn pregnant pig into the barn. Imogen's children had no interest whatsoever in the old house or the small-scale hobby farm, and immediately put it up for sale. The residents of West London, horrified at the idea of losing such an important part of their history, gathered together to form the West London Historical Society and managed to raise enough money to buy the property, which included the house, the barn, and an acre of arable land. Two years of additional fundraising enabled them to tear out most of the modernizations to the buildings and return the property to the state it would have been in during the mid-eighteenth century. Recently, a fire in the house destroyed some of the original furnishings and much of the carefully restored interior, but the house itself was saved and, yet again, the West London Historical Society set their highly efficient fundraising machine in motion. Restored and accurately furnished, the property is once more open to visitors as an important historical site.

In the three hundred and seventy-five years since the first logs were laid for a one-room house by Robert and Julia Scarlet, there has never been a whisper of crime or scandal or even minor irregularities touching Scarlet House or any of its residents. The recent fire was an accident, a burning candle unnoticed when the museum closed for the day; it caused no loss of life, and nothing structurally critical was damaged. In an old house, in an old town, no one has ever sensed any paranormal forces at work.

Until now.

Chapter One

"Surely you don't believe that," I said.

Leslie Wilson shrugged. "I don't know what to believe, Gemma. The witnesses aren't known as people of particularly vivid imagination."

"In the words of Mr. Ebenezer Scrooge, 'a bit of overdone potato' perhaps? Or more likely, more than a bit of potato distilled into vodka?"

"Apparently not." Leslie Wilson put down her teacup. "All I'm telling you, Gemma, is what I was told. I wasn't there."

Leslie's daughter, Jayne, nibbled on a cucumber sandwich. "I fail to understand what this has to do with us—with Gemma, I mean."

Leslie picked up her cup again and stared into its depths, as though attempting to read the tea leaves. "I . . . uh . . . reminded the board that Gemma had been helpful dealing with what happened at the auction." Mrs. Hudson's Tea Room had catered the major fund-raising event in support of rebuilding efforts following a fire in the museum. The afternoon had not gone entirely as planned.

"*Helpful*," I said, "might be the word. I solved two . . . no, make that three murders. Which is beside the point. I am not a consulting detective—"

"As you've said before," Jayne pointed out.

"And even more to the point, I'm not a paranormal investigator."

"It wouldn't hurt for you to come and have a look, Gemma," Leslie said. "I . . . uh . . . sorta told them you would."

I leaned back in my chair and cradled my own teacup. It was four PM on a Friday in January. Jayne Wilson, half-owner and head baker of Mrs. Hudson's Tea Room, and I, also part owner of the bakery, as well as part owner and manager of the adjacent business, the Sherlock Holmes Bookshop and Emporium, were having our daily partners' meeting in the cozy window alcove of the tearoom. Our partners' meeting is as much a girlfriends' chat and gossip session as a business meeting, so Leslie Wilson had no hesitation in joining us.

Jayne and her mother sat across the table from me, both of them watching me. Except for the fine lines radiating from the corners of Leslie's mouth, the circles under her eyes, and the gray in her hair winning its battle with the natural blonde, they could be twins. Perfect skin, heart-shaped faces, pert noses, cornflower-blue eyes. Jayne had pulled her hairnet off to take a seat in the restaurant, and her long hair was pinned up into a messy bun; Leslie's much shorter hair still showed evidence of the wool hat she'd pulled off when she came inside. They were both slim and petite, and substantially shorter than my five foot eight. I've never been considered petite, and my dark, curly hair tends to look like an overused mop, particularly toward the end of the day.

The Game Is a Footnote

They regarded me with identical expressions.

At our business meetings, we take advantage of any leftovers from afternoon tea service, and today we enjoyed dainty cucumber sandwiches prepared with a sprinkle of curry powder, along with lemon tarts topped with freshly whipped cream, and Jayne's marvelous scones, made in the true English fashion.

"Tell me again," I said, "what happened."

Leslie let out a long breath. "The board sent me here as an advance scout, so what I have to say is secondhand. If you want further details, the museum members who were there will talk to you."

I leaned back in my chair, closed my eyes so I could mentally visualize the scene, and waved my right hand in the air, telling her to continue. Leslie shifted and cleared her throat. I heard the tinkle of fine china as Jayne poured herself another cup of Darjeeling and stirred in a few grains of sugar. Befitting the name of the restaurant, Jayne does a proper afternoon tea with china tea pots and cups and saucers, linens, silver cutlery, flowers in glass vases, three-tiered stands, and little pots of butter, jam, and clotted cream. The tearoom closes at four, and I could hear Jocelyn and Fiona, the assistants, going about their end-of-the-day tasks. From the Emporium next door, I heard the sound of the door opening and Ashleigh, my full-time salesclerk, ask if she could be of help before the sliding door joining the two businesses was closed and the lock twisted. Outside, traffic moved steadily down Baker Street, but not many pedestrians were out today. It was the middle of January: few if any tourists were in town. Christmas shopping was finished for another year, and the post-Christmas sales over. The town of West London would now fall into a pleasant, welcome slumber for a couple of months until the first days of spring saw the return of the tourist hordes and eager shoppers streaming (I hoped) through our doors.

The slow season, finally time for Jayne and her fiancé, Andy Whitehall, to get on with it. Jayne wanted a "small, simple" wedding, which I figured would be just about impossible for her to pull off, considering the vast number of friends she had, as well as her mother's all-encompassing social network—not to mention Andy's huge extended family, the loyal staff at his restaurant, and his own friends. Finally, the date had been set for a year from now, a winter wedding, when things were quiet in all our businesses. The church had been booked, and the restaurant where the reception would be held arranged. I'd been asked to be the maid of honor and had joyously accepted. The wedding wasn't for a year, but time would pass quickly. I'd hoped we could get started on some further planning today.

Instead, I'd been asked to investigate a "haunting."

"Scarlet House has been continually occupied," Leslie began, "from 1648 until 2010. It was empty for a couple of months when the Historical Society took it on, but that means empty of people living there, not really empty, as they started work on it almost immediately. In all that time, from what we know, there has never been the slightest suggestion that the house is haunted. It's possible, of course, that the residents didn't want to mention it, but you'd think such a thing would get out."

"Particularly in the old days." I heard the scrape of a butter knife as Jayne scooped up butter to spread on the second half of her scone.

"No one stays in the house overnight anymore," Leslie said, "but it's always busy during the day—tourists in the summer, school visits and the like in the winter, children's programming all year round."

"Is it open every day?" I asked.

"We don't have visitors every day, no, but the farm needs tending every day, even in winter, and the volunteers who work in the barn are allowed access to the house, to have their lunch if the weather's poor and to use the restroom, etcetera."

"Does everyone and their goat have a key to the house?"

"No. The board chair, Robyn Kirkpatrick—you remember Robyn, Gemma?"

"Oh yes. I certainly do."

"She and the head of the volunteer committee, who is currently me, and the treasurer have our own keys. A rotating key's exchanged between the docents and the farm volunteers, and a spare is kept hidden under a plant pot in the garden, in case the volunteer forgets their own."

"Therefore," Jayne said, "in Gemma's words, everyone and their goat has a key."

"Precisely," I said. "Any one of them could have had a copy made; anyone who lives with them, or even anyone simply dropping in for a nice cuppa or to fix the plumbing, could have taken it to have a copy made. Anyone who knows about this plant pot has access to a key. Anyone who's looking for a key will immediately think of checking under a plant pot. I hope you don't have your own keys hidden in such obvious places, Leslie."

I heard Leslie shift uncomfortably. I had no doubt she'd be scurrying home after this meeting to relocate the spare key to her house.

"Now that we've established that those known to be in possession of a key is irrelevant," I said, "continue."

"It started a couple of weeks ago. Brenda, one of the volunteers, couldn't find the rolling pin she uses to make pies as part of the kitchen demonstration. She's known to be . . . shall we say slightly flighty, so no one paid much attention. We simply assumed it would turn up, and in the meantime we asked the woodworker we use to make another period-appropriate pin. The original one did turn up, a few days later, in the airing cupboard, buried in a pile of woolen blankets. People suspected Brenda had had the rolling pin in hand when she accessed the cupboard, and left it there. But then a week later Donna, who is not known to be at all flighty, couldn't find the volunteer record book. It's just a notebook the volunteers leave messages in for the people on the next shift, and where they record anything out of the ordinary that happens. The previous volunteer said she'd made a note in the book that they were almost out of furniture polish, and left the notebook in its regular place in the volunteers' office. Donna searched high and low, and eventually found it in the flour bin."

"Someone's playing a practical joke," Jayne said.

"Maybe," Leslie replied, "but incidents are continuing. An object that was where it was supposed to be one day isn't there the next. Nothing seems to be going missing during the day. Meaning, if someone's working in the kitchen and goes out to the barn for a chat, everything's in place when she returns. But it might not be there the next morning."

"All this disappearing, or rather moving around, of objects is happening in the house only? Not in the barn or other outbuildings?" I asked.

"Only in the house. One of the candlesticks from the main bedroom disappeared for a couple of days, to be later found in the cradle in the nursery. Tucked neatly into the baby's blanket."

"I assume if there'd been signs of a break-in, you would have told me that from the beginning."

"I would. Believe me, Gemma, the board has been over the house with a fine-toothed comb. Nothing."

"What are the volunteers saying?" I asked.

"At first we thought it was one of them playing a practical joke, or some kids fooling around. But some are starting to whisper about a poltergeist."

I opened my eyes and studied her face. "You don't buy the former. I can hear it in your voice."

"We know our volunteers, Gemma. They're our friends, neighbors. Many of them have been with the society since its founding. As for kids, they do silly things, but they get bored easily and soon go on to do silly things someplace else. Kids like to see the results of their so-called pranks. In most of these cases, no one from outside the Historical Society has been around at the time the object was either lost or found."

"And this has happened to several different people?"

"Yes. If it was always Brenda, we might think it was time to suggest she move on. But different people, different days of the week."

"Tell me about what happened last Thursday night."

"You heard about that?"

"Everyone heard about that," Jayne said. "Dave Chase came in here for a coffee on his way home from trying to settle his animals down. You know Dave—he loves to be the center of attention, and he enjoyed having an audience."

"If not for the fact that Dave was summoned from his bed by a neighbor," I said, "I wouldn't have given his story any credit at all, seeing as to how he does think of himself as a master storyteller. I know what he says happened, but tell me again."

"At about four AM, the Scarlet House neighbors were woken by sounds coming from the barn."

"What neighbors? Which house?"

"The one immediately to the east on Harbor Road. The farmland backs onto their property. The animals were in an uproar, the chickens clucking, the pigs squealing, the donkey braying, the sheep baaing."

"I get the point," I said.

"Just painting a picture," Leslie said.

"Speaking of people who like to tell stories," Jayne said, her voice full of affectionate humor.

Leslie ignored her. "They made sufficient racket that the neighbors at first thought the barn might be on fire. They ran out of their house but didn't see anything amiss. No fire. No smoke in the air. No one, as far as they could tell, on the property. All quiet and peaceful except for the animals, who continued to bray or cluck or snort or whatever they do. Their names are Craig and Cassie Jones. The neighbors, not the farm animals."

"We got that, Mom," Jayne said.

"Cassie helped out as a docent over the Christmas season, and she has our contact numbers. They first called the police and then Dave Chase. The police checked the property and found nothing amiss and no signs of anything like an intruder. By the time Dave arrived, the animals were calming themselves down. The police left, and Dave stayed until dawn. We would have assumed a fox was prowling, or something like that, but in light of the other incidents . . . it all seemed of a part, is what I'm saying."

"And then yesterday . . ."

"What I heard—"

I stood up. "I don't want to hear this secondhand, Leslie. I need to hear it from someone who was there."

"Robyn will be happy to talk to you."

"No reason we can't go now."

"Meaning, you'll take the case?"

"Meaning, I believe there might be something to this, although I don't have the full picture. If this was happening to an individual, I'd assume an attempt at extortion, to put a scare into an adversary, to drive someone off their property for whatever ends, and I'd tell you to contact the police immediately. But the West London Historical Society . . .?" I let the sentence trail off. Even the most respectable of volunteer groups can have internal strife. Sometimes, the lower the stakes, the more the animosity. I knew, after the events following the death of a previous board chair, that emotions in Scarlet House could run deep. If someone was creating mischief to get revenge for a supposed insult, all they'd need in order to stop would be to know they'd been found out, and then given a stern warning to the effect that "next time it will be the police calling."

"Uh, Gemma?" Jayne said.

"What?

"Aren't you forgetting something?"

"As I didn't bring my car to work today, I assume Leslie will be driving us, so I don't need my bag."

"The store?"

"The store?"

"The Sherlock Holmes Bookshop and Emporium. Where you work?"

I sat down. "Oh, that store."

"Ashleigh came in for her coffee at nine thirty this morning, so I assume she's leaving at five today. Which is half an hour from now."

"Maybe she'll agree to stay later."

"You can't just assume, Gemma."

I turned in my chair and peered through the sliding glass door that joins the two businesses. Ashleigh was helping a young girl make a selection from our YA section. "I suppose you're right. I'll ask nicely. What do you suppose she's pretending to be today? A fashion influencer would be my guess."

"Maybe she has plans for after work," Jayne said.

My shop assistant, Ashleigh, has what might be called an eclectic wardrobe. I wouldn't be surprised if she rents a separate apartment just for a place to keep all her clothes. She dresses, so she says, as the mood strikes her. Sometimes she's in the mood to be a business executive, sometimes a safari guide, sometimes a Japanese anime character, sometimes a middle-aged garden enthusiast with limited vision. The list is endless. Once she was in the mood to be me. I pretended I hadn't noticed. Today she'd gone to a lot of trouble with her hair, pinning it up in a loose messy bun. Her earrings fell almost to her shoulders in a river of red stones. Her tight, white, ankle-length jeans were fashionably shredded, and her white T-shirt had red sparkles that formed a heart across the front. The outfit was completed with a red linen jacket and short red leather boots with two-inch heels.

I admitted that she might have after-work plans today.

"What about your new clerk?" Leslie said. "Jayne told me you've hired a part-timer. Can you call her to come in?"

"Gale? I haven't taken her through the end-of-day routine yet. If we're not back in time, I wouldn't like to leave her in the lurch."

Leslie helped herself to a lemon tart. "I'll call Robyn and ask if she can see us at nine thirty tonight."

Chapter Two

I closed the door to 222 Baker Street at 9:29 PM, daring to risk a complaint—yet another complaint—to the Baker Street Business Improvement Association by my nemesis, Maureen McGregor, owner of Beach Fine Arts, located across the street at number 221.

"Now remember," I said to the shop cat, perched on the top of a bookshelf, "I'm leaving my livelihood in your capable paws. See you tomorrow."

Moriarty narrowed his eyes and hissed. Several years ago, my great uncle Arthur, founder of the Emporium, found the abandoned kitten in the alley and brought him inside. You'd think Moriarty would be grateful to us for giving him a home. Instead, I sometimes think he hates me. I try not to take it personally.

I locked the door behind me as Leslie Wilson pulled up to the curb. Jayne was in the front passenger seat, and I hopped into the back. Jayne, who starts work at five AM on winter mornings (four in the busy season), had gone home for a nap and to change into jeans and a heavy cardigan prior to our outing.

"We're expected," Leslie said. "Do you need to see to the dogs first?"

"Not necessary. I called Mrs. Ramsbatten and told her I'd be late tonight, so she gave them their dinner and let them out." Mrs. Ramsbatten is the elderly neighbor who helps with my dogs when Uncle Arthur's away and I'm busy at the shop.

"That's nice of her." Traffic at this time in the winter was light; streetlamps threw a yellow glow through the bare branches of the stately oaks and maples lining Baker Street. "Speaking of Mrs. Ramsbatten," Leslie said, "did you know she's begun volunteering for us?"

"For you where?" I asked. "You have to be more specific, Leslie. You're on the board of half the organizations in West London."

"She's right about that, Mom," Jayne said. "And for the half you're not on the board of, you're still involved."

"I mean Scarlet House. Mrs. Ramsbatten sits in a rocking chair by the fire and knits. At the moment, she's working on what will probably be the longest scarf in New England, if not the entire Eastern Seaboard. Maybe all of—"

"Okay," Jayne said, "she knits. What else does she do?"

"My point," Leslie said, "is that she knits, but not well. I don't think she knows how to cast off, thus the scarf will never end."

I chuckled. "Sounds like her."

"She talks to the school kids about families making their own clothes back in the day, and how prosperous houses, such as Scarlet House, were passed down through generations. How the old people stayed in the house until they died, surrounded by their children and grandchildren."

"I bet they think she was a sweet little farm housewife," I said. Less than five feet tall, Mrs. Ramsbatten probably only hit the hundred-pound mark on the scales if she was dressed in her winter clothes and carrying a sack of potatoes. She had a halo of gray curls and sparkling blue eyes. These days she peered at the world through thick lenses and needed the help of a cane to get around, but she was as sharp as she must have been in her youth. Rather than a life spent knitting and raising grandchildren on the family farm, Mrs. Ramsbatten had been a computer pioneer. She'd worked with the legendary Admiral Grace Hopper in the development of COBOL before joining the late Mr. Ramsbatten at Microsoft to work on the beginnings of the personal computer.

"She's active in the garden club," I said. "Probably needs something to get her out of the house in the winter."

I'd been to Robyn Kirkpatrick's house before. The chair of the board of Scarlet House and her husband lived in the nearby town of Chatham, on a pleasant, heavily treed street of large houses with double garages and immaculately maintained gardens, now put away for the winter. Lights glowed from over porches and inside houses, and we could see the occasional blue flicker of a television. One or two dog walkers were out, but otherwise all was quiet.

"I'm sorry for calling so late," Leslie said once we'd been admitted to the Kirkpatrick home. "But as you know, Gemma has her store to run."

"Perfectly fine." Robyn was a short woman with a slim, gym-toned body, expensively styled, dyed, and highlighted blonde hair, subdued makeup, and light pink polish on her manicured hands. Tonight her smile didn't touch her eyes. I'd upset a lot of apple carts at Scarlet House when I'd last been involved with the goings-on there, and she was still wary.

Three people waited for us in the living room. The men got to their feet, and Leslie introduced us, but I knew them all. Ben Alderson was the board's vice-chair; Dave Chase looked after the farm animals; and Sharon Musgrave served as treasurer and bookkeeper as well as a house docent. Glasses of wine were on side tables and a cheese board rested on the coffee table. The glasses were less than half full; the cheese and crackers, decimated; paper napkins, crumpled into balls and tossed aside. I was precisely on time, a bit early even as traffic had been light, and I hadn't gone home to tend to the dogs. Quarter to ten in the evening wasn't a normal time for volunteer groups to discuss business. Clearly, the members of Scarlet House had wanted to talk over a few details before speaking to me. Get their story straight was the phrase that came to mind.

If I saw any signs that they were attempting to manipulate me, I was prepared to walk out the door.

"Can I get you a glass of wine?" Robyn asked.

"Nothing for me, thank you," Leslie said, "I'm driving." Jayne and I accepted, and we took our seats.

The men were of much the same age—in their seventies. Ben, tall and lean, sharp bones and gray hair cut short; Dave, broad-shouldered, heavily built, ruddy-faced. A retired veterinarian, he cared for the farm animals at Scarlet House and played farmer for the benefit of visitors. His hands were large and calloused, a small amount of dirt caught in the cuticle of his right thumb. The index finger on his left hand was missing the top joint. He was neatly dressed in beige trousers and an oatmeal sweater. His black shoes were clean, but a light splattering of mud marked his trousers from the knees to mid-calf. He'd dressed for this meeting, but he'd stopped at the barn on his way over, putting on boots to go inside.

Sharon Musgrave was about the same height as Robyn but considerably plumper. She wore a black calf-length skirt, a red pullover that was pilling badly, and clunky black shoes over black socks. Her round cheeks put me in mind of a chipmunk, and she had the sort of jittery energy that puts everyone around her on edge. Tonight, her eyes glowed and her fingers twitched with excitement. She might have had a glass or two of wine more than was good for her, but she was also, I thought, thrilled at being caught up in a "mystery." I'm well aware that, as Sherlock Holmes said, "it is a capital mistake to theorize before one has data," but I was prepared to theorize right now. If Sharon wasn't directly responsible for whatever was going on at Scarlet House, she would do her absolute best to make the most of every minute of it.

"It was my idea—mine and Leslie's—to ask you to look into this," Ben said. "You have a reputation, Gemma, for being able to figure things out. Even before the police do."

I lifted one hand. Robyn put a wineglass into it, and I thanked her. I put the glass down. "First, let's get some things straight. I'm not here in place of the police, or as a substitute. So far, I've heard about nothing criminal, apart from possible break and enter, going on at Scarlet House. The moment that changes, if it does, I'll tell you to call the police, and I'll return to my own affairs."

"Fair enough," Dave said. "On our part, let me say that Robyn was reluctant to involve you."

"To put it mildly," our hostess said. "If an organization has a problem, that organization must handle it."

"But," Ben gave Robyn a respectful nod, "I pointed out that any organization, when confronted with problems outside their area of expertise, consults further afield."

"Right," Dave added. "When I had my veterinary practice, I didn't fix the plumbing myself."

Robyn snorted, politely of course. I decided to hear what they had to say and then take my leave. This was an iffy idea anyway, and I wasn't going to do anything if the chair of the board didn't want me involved.

Sharon bounced on the edge of her chair. She gave me a huge smile. "That's what I said! You were so helpful to us at the time of . . . that other incident, Gemma. And we were so grateful, weren't we, Robyn?"

That took me by surprise. What I'd learned about Sharon was that she was a minor embezzler with a drinking problem, as well as a woman who had such a limited personal life that volunteering at Scarlet House *was* her life. Perhaps that was it, she wanted me back in her life to provide some excitement.

I don't care to be used.

I looked at Dave. He picked up his wineglass and swirled the deep red liquid in the bowl. He was not smiling, and he was not perched on the edge of his seat in excitement. "You're worried about the animals," I said.

"Yeah, I am. Nothing happened to them the other night, but something had them in a state."

"A fox?"

He shook his head. "I checked in the daylight and could see no signs of one, or anything else prowling around the barn. We're situated in a residential area, near the middle of town, but we still get cats or escaped dogs as well as the occasional wild creature sniffing around in the night, looking to see what's on the menu. My animals might get restless if they sense something outside, but they know they're safe in the barn." He shook his head. "It would take a good deal more than a passing fox to cause that sort of commotion."

"The people who called you—the Joneses, is it? They didn't hear anything else, other than the noise in the barn?"

"That's the thing, Gemma. No. If kids had been making mischief, they would have set up a racket, shot off firecrackers or guns, if they had them, to deliberately wake the animals. Our barn gets regular visitors, so it's tidier than the barn of any genuine working farm, but it's still a farmyard. The police searched for footprints or other signs of intruders, and I watched them. The ground is naturally churned up most of the time, and they found nothing that couldn't be explained."

"Something," Sharon declared, "disturbed the animals in our barn that could not be heard by human ears."

"Don't leap to conclusions," I said. "'Did not hear' is not the same as 'could not hear.'"

"I'm an educated man," Dave said. "A doctor. An animal doctor anyway. I've been around a long time. I worked in Mozambique for a number of years, training vets, visiting cattle and goat farmers."

"That must have been interesting," Jayne said.

"It was, and when you have a couple of hours free, I'll tell you about it. Meanwhile, what I'm trying to say, in my own awkward way, is I've seen animals do things you wouldn't credit if you didn't witness it with your own eyes. They have much stronger, and often vastly different, senses from ours. You have dogs, right, Gemma?"

"Two. I also have a shop cat who appears to be an excellent judge of character." *Except for his judgment of my character,* I didn't add.

"You know something of what I mean, then. But in this case I mean . . . I don't always know what I mean, but I've seen animals do things I can't explain. React to something that's not only hard for me to see, but something I know is simply not there."

Jayne sucked in a breath. Sharon tittered. Robyn shifted uncomfortably in her seat. She crossed her legs. A stiletto-heeled shoe dangled from her right foot.

"Dave knows what he's talking about," Ben said. "Which is why we're not dismissing what happened out of hand."

"Just so we're clear what we are talking about here," I said, "you think something in the realm of the supernatural frightened your animals?" I took a sip of my wine and almost spat it out again. Robyn appeared to have money. She could afford a half-decent bottle. Clearly, she didn't bring out the good stuff for her Scarlet House guests.

Dave didn't seem to mind. He downed the rest of his wine in one gulp.

"Yes!" Sharon said. "That's it! You might not know this, Gemma and Jayne, but I've made an extensive study of Scarlet

23

House and its history. In the early days, the time of the pilgrims, people simply believed that the supernatural was part of life."

"Far too many unexplained things," Leslie said, "were placed at the feet of innocent women and men, who died because of ridiculous, unfounded accusations. Things that we know today have perfectly sensible explanations."

Sharon waved that trifle away. "Yes, but people got on with life, didn't they? All I'm saying is they accepted that there were forces in the world beyond their understanding."

Robyn snorted. "And they treated common illnesses with leeches. I trust we've gone beyond that."

Sharon's face tightened. "Surely respect for the history of Scarlet House includes respect for the traditions and—"

Dave interrupted before the women could get into a verbal battle. "Strange things are happening, for sure. We're not frightened, none of us are. *Concerned* might be a better word."

"Mildly concerned," Ben added.

"Wondering," Leslie said.

"Determined to get to the bottom of it!" Sharon glanced out of the corner of her eye at Robyn, seeking the other woman's approval. But Robyn was looking at me.

"Tell me what happened yesterday," I said.

"I was there and—" Sharon began.

"Robyn?" I asked.

She took a deep breath. "Shortly after noon, Sharon and I were in the house. Dave was out in the barn. We had several school visits scheduled for the day. We wore our costumes, as we do when we're on duty. Sharon was demonstrating cooking techniques. Mrs. Ramsbatten was also there, knitting by the kitchen fire."

"Is that normal?" I asked. "You're the board chair, Robyn. Do you often act as a docent?"

"Not often, no. I enjoy it, but I can't donate as much time to it as I would like." Her eyes shifted away from me, and I knew she was lying. Robyn didn't like the hands-on part of the museum work. She likely didn't care all that much for the history of the house, or history in general. To her, being on the museum board, and now chair of the board, was a position of importance in the community, and it gave her the prestige she craved. Thus the conflict between her and Sharon, to whom the sanitized version of history they presented at the house was the entire point of the thing.

"Our regularly scheduled volunteer had gone to visit out-of-state family," Robyn said. "She gave us no notice of her intention. We're open limited hours and run scaled-down programming from New Years until Memorial Day, so we don't need anywhere near the number of volunteers as over the holiday season and in the summer. No one else was available to step in at the last minute, so I offered to fill in." I hid a smile. Robyn had clearly not been happy at having to fill in. "She, the traveling docent, will not be invited to return, I can assure you of that."

"Three of you in the house," I said. "Dave in the barn. Ben, were you there?"

"No."

"Ethan was working in the kitchen," Robyn said.

"Ethan? Who's Ethan?" Why had no one mentioned this person earlier? Sometimes trying to help people is heck of a lot of work.

"Ethan Evanston's a student at Yale," Leslie said. "He's completing his PhD in American history. His thesis has something to do with the lives of Cape Cod farm families in the eighteenth and nineteenth centuries, so he's been doing some research at the house. We have little in the way of documents or letters from the Scarlet family; most of those were destroyed or taken away when the farm was sold, but Ethan says the feeling in the kitchen as we go about our tasks is conducive to his work."

"How long has he been doing this?"

"He arrived a couple of days ago," Robyn said. "He asked if he could spend some time in the house. *Soaking up the atmosphere,*' he calls it."

"He says it's a perfect example of the houses of prosperous farmers of the period he's interested in," Sharon said. "We're thrilled to have him."

"I, for one, am not thrilled," Robyn said. "I find it inconvenient in the extreme. Sitting there tapping away on his computer when we're trying to demonstrate farm life in the eighteenth century."

"To be fair," Leslie said, "he usually puts the computer away when visitors come through."

"*Usually* being the operative word," Robyn replied. "I've told him—. Anyway, that's neither here nor there. To return to yesterday, Sharon was working in the kitchen, as she normally does on Thursdays, and my role was to show visitors through the rest of the house. House tour, kitchen demonstration, then out to the barn. That's our usual routine." She stopped talking, shivered ever so slightly and took a deep breath before continuing. Not as calm as she pretended to be. "I had a group of third-graders. Twelve of them. The best age for showing the house to, as they find everything fascinating. We were climbing the stairs to the second floor. I led the way, accompanied by one of the mothers, and the teacher brought up the rear, to make sure no children wandered away. At the top of the stairs, I saw . . . something at the end of the hall. A woman. Wearing a floor-length brown dress. Homespun by the looks of it, simply cut, with no adornment. White cap, white apron."

"Can you describe her?" I said. "Age, height, weight?"

"I thought at first it was Sharon, or maybe one of the other docents had come in without me noticing and gone upstairs. Her face was . . ." Robyn struggled for the words. "Indistinct. Only later did I realize I couldn't put a description together. I can't say if she was small or large, tall or short, young or old. I can describe the clothes—not the person wearing them." Her composure cracked, and she stared at her hands. I was reasonably confident Robyn was telling me the truth, as she believed it. She wasn't embellishing her story; she wasn't trying to create high drama. She wasn't watching the others, waiting for their reaction, but speaking almost to herself.

She gathered her composure and continued. "It was extremely cold at the top of the stairs. I was about to ask her if she'd left a window open, when one of the children tripped on the stairs and cried out. The other children started to laugh, and the teacher snapped at them to behave themselves. I turned to see what was going on, for a fraction of a second, and when I looked again, the woman was gone. I gave my head a proper shake and continued with the tour."

"You said one of the mothers was next to you? Did she say anything about seeing this woman?"

"No. And I didn't ask. To be honest, it happened so quickly, and then she was gone. At first I didn't give it much thought other than wondering who'd come to work without me knowing and where she'd gone so abruptly. But the more I thought about it . . . The house isn't large; it's not the sort of house where you can go in one door and out another without being seen."

"Did you find the open window?"

"A window in the master bedroom had been opened, and I shut it. But the hallway began warming up even before I did that. The press of the children's bodies, I supposed, although . . . such an abrupt change of temperature has never happened before."

"Is there a second staircase?"

"Yes, there is. At the end of the corridor, what would have been the servants' stairs. She might have gone there, but I didn't hear the door either opening or closing. After my section of the tour finished, when we were in the kitchen, I asked Mrs. Ramsbatten who'd been upstairs. She said she didn't realize anyone other than my group and I had been there."

"I was making cookies," Sharon said. "The children love watching me cooking over the open fire. I'd made a batch earlier for them to try. After I finished my demonstration and the children went out to the barn, happily munching on their cookies, I might add, Robyn asked me who was working upstairs today and why. In the summer, when we're busy with drop-in tourists, we station a docent on the second floor and one in the parlor to keep an eye on things, but in the winter, with supervised school groups, that's not necessary. I told her no one, and no one came in through the pantry."

"Does the pantry access the servants' stairs?" I asked.

"Yes," Robyn said.

"Why didn't you go back upstairs if you thought it was one of your volunteers? Once the group was in the kitchen, it doesn't sound as though they needed your supervision."

Robyn focused a direct, unblinking stare on me. "I was needed downstairs. Rambunctious children and open fires do not mix."

As well as Robyn, four adults had been in the kitchen: the teacher, the parent, Sharon, and Mrs. Ramsbatten, all of whom would have been watching the children. Robyn was lying again, but I didn't think that significant. She'd been frightened and was too proud to admit it.

"Perhaps I shouldn't have told Ben and Dave," she said. "They're making far more of this than it warrants. One of our ladies made a mistake in her calendar and came to put in a shift. When she realized she wasn't needed, she went home."

"Without stopping in the kitchen to say hi?" Sharon said. "Without being seen? Unlikely."

"But possible," I said.

"Yes," Sharon admitted.

Ben said nothing, but he looked thoughtful.

"I'd say, let it go," Dave said. "Put it down to a trick of the light. An open window, a flight of imagination. Except for the other incidents. The things moving around? Or being moved around? The behavior of my animals in the night?" He shook his head. "Something's not right."

I agreed with him. Put all the incidents together, and something was not right. I didn't know what Robyn had seen, but I had no doubt she thought she'd seen something. As she talked, her face had turned pale under her perfectly applied makeup, and her hand shook when she reached for her wineglass.

Something was not right, but whatever it was, it had absolutely nothing to do with me. I stood up. "I thank you for your faith in me, but I don't know what I can do other than give you some advice you've probably already received. First, change the locks on the doors and control the distribution of keys. Hire a security company to spend a few nights keeping an eye on the place. Resume your summer staffing schedule, if you can, so you have more people around when visitors are in."

"That's it?" Sharon said. "That's all you have?"

"I'm not going to pull a rabbit out of a hat," I said.

"Paid security is expensive, and we don't have extra money," Robyn said. "What about Leslie's idea?"

"What idea?" I turned to Leslie. She gave me a crooked grin, identical to that of her daughter, and said, "I sort of . . . uh . . . suggested to Ben and Robyn that maybe you and Jayne. . . Or you and Ryan could—"

"Not involving Ryan," I said firmly. Ryan Ashburton is not only the man in my life, he's also the lead detective at the WLPD. He'd kill me (rhetorically speaking) if I tried to drag him, professionally or otherwise, into this.

"We could do what, Mom?" Jayne asked, before I could stop her.

"Spend a night in Scarlet House," Robyn said.

Chapter Three

I don't quite know what happened, but I'd found myself agreeing to spend Saturday night at Scarlet House, on the alert for wandering ghosts. I walked to work Saturday morning in a glum mood, cursing myself for being manipulated.

Maybe my mood wasn't entirely because of the prospect of sitting up all night in a drafty old house without central heating, but the weather. So far this winter had been warmer than usual. That's not always a good thing. Instead of lovely clean snow and bright winter sunshine, heavy dark clouds hung low overhead, and we'd been promised cold rain moving in later this afternoon.

On the other hand, maybe my mood had to do with missing Ryan. He'd been away for a week, in Florida fishing with his dad. Ryan had confessed to me that he'd rather not spend his valuable vacation time with his father, but his dad was finding the damp winter difficult, and his mother was finding having a grumpy husband underfoot all the time difficult, and so Ryan suggested the trip. They'd arrived back in the early hours of this morning, too late for him to pay a call on me.

Not that I usually care what time Ryan pays a call on me. As I thought about him, I realized I was walking faster now, and a noticeable spring had appeared in my step. Ryan and I had a complicated and sometimes difficult relationship. We'd been on the verge of getting engaged at one point (and the less said about that disastrous evening the better), but he'd reconsidered the idea and fled to Boston. A couple of years later he came back, we reconnected (over a murder at a hotel, as I recall), and found that the spark between us hadn't faded in the least.

As usual, I made a stop at Mrs. Hudson's before going to the Emporium to start my day. The sliding door between the two businesses was open, meaning Ashleigh had arrived. Hoping for a moderately busy day, and enough time to myself to get some work done on the accounts, I'd scheduled my new part-time helper, Gale, to work this afternoon. I'd hired her for the holiday rush and found her to be keen and hard working. A long-divorced woman with adult children who'd moved away for university and never returned, Gale had recently retired from teaching and was looking for something to do between bouts of volunteer work at the hospital. She didn't want a full-time job, and it suited us both for her to act as Ashleigh's backup during the slow off-season.

At Mrs. Hudson's the breakfast rush was over and the lunch crowd yet to arrive, so I didn't have to wait in line to place my order of a large tea and a blueberry muffin.

"Busy morning?" I asked Fiona, behind the counter dressed in a black blouse and skirt under a long white apron adorned with the Mrs. Hudson's Tea Room logo of a steaming teacup next to a pipe.

"It has been. We have reservations for an almost full house for afternoon tea today."

"Always good to hear."

Fiona handed me my muffin, and her eyes widened as she caught sight of something behind me. She sucked in a quick breath. "It's her! I've been hoping she'd come in. Oh my gosh, she's coming this way." Fiona was in her early forties, but she squealed like a teenage girl.

I turned to see an excessively thin woman glancing around the tearoom. She wore sunglasses that covered half her face, a puffy black jacket, and a red scarf wrapped several times around her neck. Her jeans were fashionably shredded and stuffed into knee-high boots with four-inch heels that managed to make her about my height when I'm in my bare feet. Her nose was pert, her bones sharp; she had a slight cleft in her chin, and age lines tugged at the corners of her mouth. Her lips were too plump for the fine bones of her face, the result, no doubt, of too many injections.

She might have been cute in her youth, I thought, but that youth was long gone. I'd never seen her before, but I knew who she was.

The branch of the West London Grapevine that passes through Mrs. Hudson's and into the Emporium reported that a former pop star had been spotted around town. Rumor said she'd rented a house in West London and planned to spend the winter. I'd never heard of her before, which wasn't much of a surprise as I'm not knowledgeable of twenty-years-out-of-date American singers.

I stepped to one side as she slid up to the counter.

"Good morning!" Fiona's voice was unnaturally high pitched. "What can I get you?" She gave the customer a radiant smile. Conversation had stopped at several tables, and people leaned close to whisper to each other.

"Large coffee. Black. No sugar." The woman had a Midwestern American accent and a scratchy voice, evidence of too many late nights, far too many cigarettes, and probably too much whiskey.

"Coming right up!" Fiona cried.

I'd turned to go when the woman said, "That place next door. That's the Sherlock Holmes store?"

"Oh yes," Fiona said. "You're in luck, Bunny. This is Gemma Doyle, right here. Gemma, have you met Bunny?"

Bunny—*Bunny?*—lowered her sunglasses and peered at me over the rims. Her eyes were large and a startling shade of green. Fine lines radiated from the corners of those eyes and deep circles, permanent ones, lay under them.

I put my tea into my left hand, held out my right, and said, "I haven't had the pleasure."

She looked down, hesitated just long enough to be rude, and then took my hand in hers. I've felt firmer three-day old fish.

"Gemma owns the bookstore," Fiona said. "This is Bunny Leigh. You know of her, of course, Gemma. Everyone does. Bunny's come to West London for the winter, and we're so excited about that. You're putting a new group together, right, Bunny? She's spending her time here developing the concept for her comeback album."

Bunny's face twisted at the word *comeback*. I know nothing—probably less than nothing— about the pop music industry, but I'd take a guess Bunny's comeback album would not be enthusiastically received by anyone other than her ageing fans. If ever it got produced.

"Here you go," Fiona chirped. Bunny took the cup and mumbled something that might have been thanks.

"The Emporium's open," I said. "If you're wanting to have a look around."

"I will. Thanks." She walked away.

Middle-aged women watched her, open-mouthed, while the younger ones exchanged "who was that?" looks.

"Oh my gosh." Fiona sighed. "I cannot wait to tell my friends I made a cup of coffee for Bunny Leigh. She was *soooo* big when we were in high school. We all *adored* her."

"A badge of honor she cherishes, I'm sure," I said.

When I went into the Emporium, Ashleigh was behind the sales counter, ringing up a stack of books as high as Moriarty for three laughing women. Other customers were browsing the games and puzzles table or checking out the nonfiction and Holmes pastiche sections while Gale shelved newly arrived books. Bunny Leigh stood in the doorway, next to a life-sized cardboard cutout of Benedict Cumberbatch and Martin Freeman as Sherlock and Dr. Watson (personally signed by Benedict himself, I might add), clutching her coffee cup and watching Ashleigh as though she needed assistance but was too shy to ask for it.

I smiled at her. "Can I help you find something?"

"No," she said.

The women left with bulging shopping bags, and I said to Ashleigh, "How was your night out last night?"

"How'd you . . .? Oh, right. I keep forgetting—you know things, Gemma."

I smiled at her.

"It was fine, thanks. I went for a quick dinner and then a movie with Wanda Barrington, who works at the shop in the fish market. She's nice. We had a good time."

The chime over the street door tinkled, and one of our regular customers, a woman in her early thirties who was a civilian clerk at the police station, headed straight for the new releases shelf. She gave us a wave.

"I see Lisa's back with her husband," I said in a low voice.

"I hadn't heard that. Who told you?" Ashleigh asked.

"No one told me. I observed. I am observing now." Immediately after her husband left her for another woman, Lisa had fallen into a state of low-level depression. Her hair hung lank around her shoulders, her skin turned pasty, and she put on weight so suddenly that her clothes fitted badly. "Her hair's been styled a different way. A younger, bouncier look. Fresh makeup. A dress so new, she forgot to take the sales tag off the back. She's had her engagement ring cleaned; it was looking very grimy. Most of all, she smiled when she waved to us."

"Okay," Ashleigh said. "I guess I can buy that. Anyone would have noticed those things, Gemma."

"Yes, but anyone didn't. It won't last, though."

Ashleigh peered across the room at Lisa, who was reading back-cover blurbs and putting aside the books she wanted. "How can you tell that by looking at her?"

"I can't. But her husband was in the other day. He bought a gaslight book. Lisa doesn't read those. She likes Sherlock-themed short story collections."

"He might have been buying a gift for someone. Maybe his mother likes gaslight."

"He wasn't wearing his wedding ring," I said. "He stood at the window, peering inside as though checking who was in the shop before venturing in." I watched Lisa for a few moments. People wore their hearts on the outside of their bodies far more than they knew. "I could be wrong," I admitted at last. "She might have moved on and found another man for herself. She looks happy, and being married to Norman Bloomington isn't a way, in my opinion, to achieve true happiness. I hope she has. Have a nice day. I'll be in the office if you need me." I took my tea and muffin upstairs.

Chapter Four

"This," I said, "is a top-ranked contender for the worst idea I've ever heard."

"Think of it as a pajama party with ghost stories."

"What's a pajama party?"

"A sleepover," Jayne said.

"What's a sleepover?"

"You never went to pajama parties when you were a girl?"

I cocked my head toward my best friend.

"Okay," Jayne said. "I guess not."

"I went to boarding school, like a proper little English girl from South Kensington. Believe me, I wanted nothing to do with any of my schoolmates when I didn't have to."

"In other people's social circles, preteen girls have parties where they sit up all night in their pajamas, listen to music, talk about boys, gossip about the girls who aren't at the party, and eat chips and pizza and drink soda while they watch horror movies."

"I cannot believe," I said, "I missed so much in my childhood."

Andy Whitehall chuckled. "Sounds like fun to me."

The Game Is a Footnote

It was Saturday evening, and here I was, participating in not only a "pajama party" at Scarlet House but a ghost hunt as well.

I tossed the wool throw I'd brought with me onto the spindly-legged sofa in the front parlor while Andy set about arranging newspapers and kindling in the open fireplace. The house didn't have an efficient modern furnace, so we'd be relying on the fire to keep us somewhat comfortable during the night.

I had to admit, if only to myself, that I'd felt a little frisson of pleasure at lifting the red velvet rope that marked off the parlor and stepping beyond it. I might never have gone to pajama parties as a girl, but I'd toured plenty of castles and stately homes with my classmates, and slipping past the velvet rope had been a serious offense indeed.

"Having been a boy, I was never invited to any of these sleepovers," Andy said as he lit a match and held it to crumpled sheets of newspaper, "but I approve of the pizza and soda part. And the girls in pajamas part." He turned to wink at Jayne, and she gave him a radiant smile.

The third wheel, aka me, stifled a groan. Bad enough that I'd been talked into this, but Jayne had invited her fiancé to keep us company.

I, on the other hand, had turned down Ryan's suggestion of dinner out with the excuse of a late meeting with Jayne to discuss her wedding plans. He hadn't even sounded skeptical. When it comes to wedding planning, men don't have a clue. And they want to keep it that way.

We wouldn't be having chips and pizza tonight, but enjoying a picnic catered specifically for us by West London's best restaurant, The Blue Water Café, where Andy was the owner and head chef. Another inducement to get me to agree to this. Andy had also provided sustenance, at the Historical Society's expense, for the two men who'd be spending the night out in the barn—Dave Chase, the retired veterinarian, and Craig Jones, the neighbor. Andy had brought plenty of soft drinks to see us through. No beer or wine, we'd decided, as this wasn't intended to be a party, and we were supposed to be keeping ourselves alert.

"I cannot believe," I said, "I'm actually ghost hunting. Do not ever, under pain of death, tell my sister that."

Jayne chucked. My older, smarter, prettier, thinner sister, Pippa, was some sort of shadowy, powerful force in the British government. Pippa made one phone call and things happened. Instantly. I had my suspicions as to whom she worked for, but those had not been confirmed. The only kink in Pippa's job-focused, logical, organized life had occurred recently when she'd fallen in love with my friend Grant Thompson, and Grant had moved to London to be with her.

Andy popped the tab on a soft drink can. "What's the plan then?" He was a small man, slightly shorter than me, thin and wiry, with a mop of dark blond hair, sharp facial features, and warm brown eyes that filled with joy whenever he caught sight of my friend. I thoroughly approved of their engagement. I won't say I'm entirely responsible for them getting together, but I'd tried my best.

Jayne had earlier told him why we were here. In answer to his question, I said, "The plan, not that there is one, is to stay awake. Listen. Observe. I'll admit that strange things have been happening here. Or rather that people believe strange things have been happening, which isn't always the same thing. Whether it's kids playing pranks, a homeless person trying to find a place to shelter from the cold, or imaginations wildly out of control, no one's going to show themselves tonight. Not with someone in the house. Dave's out in the barn with Craig Jones. They're going to have a worse night than us."

"What are you attempting to accomplish then?" Andy asked.

"I know absolutely nothing about the habits of ghosts, nor do I want to, but I suspect the presence of people in the house overnight won't deter them from doing . . . whatever they like to do of an evening. When no supernatural presences make themselves known to us, I can tell Leslie and the rest that the house is not haunted. They can then look elsewhere for the cause of the disturbances. Essentially, we are eliminating the impossible, so the museum people can then investigate whatever remains, however improbable that might be."

Andy stood up and dusted off his knees. Flames tore through the crumpled newspapers and leapt eagerly from one piece of kindling to another. "Didn't Sherlock Holmes say that?"

"Words to that effect. *The Sign of Four.*"

"I'm rather looking forward to this." He grinned at Jayne and she grinned back.

Yup. Third wheel.

"What did Mrs. Ramsbatten have to say about what happened?" Jayne asked.

"Nothing of significance." Before going to the shop this morning, I'd popped into my neighbor's home to ask her about recent events. "She noticed that Robyn appeared to be upset when she came into the kitchen after leading the class through the house. Robyn's a highly controlled woman, not given to displays of emotion" (unlike that Sharon Musgrave, my neighbor had added). "Robyn asked if another docent had come into the kitchen via the pantry, and Mrs. Ramsbatten said she hadn't seen anyone. She asked Robyn if something was wrong, but Robyn brushed it aside, saying she must have been mistaken. Mrs. Ramsbatten, as you know, is extremely astute, and she could tell that Robyn wasn't as unconcerned as she tried to appear. But nothing else happened that day, so she put it out of her mind."

"Did Mrs. Ramsbatten notice any of these strange occurrences on other days?" Jayne asked.

"I asked her that, but it's hard for her to say. She hasn't been working here for long, so she wouldn't know if items were out of place or not." I smiled. "Although she did wonder why the master bedroom chamber pot was stored on the top shelf of the linen cupboard. Hard to get to in a rush in the night, she said."

Andy laughed.

"As long as we're here, we'll do a proper job of eliminating the impossible. I'm going to do a walk-through of the house. Make sure everything's tucked up for the night."

Neither Andy nor Jayne leapt to their feet to offer to accompany me. It was six o'clock and already dark. The first drops of the expected rain pattered against the windows, and branches scraped the house under the increasing force of the wind. I'd closed the shop at five and gone home to grab the overnight bag I'd earlier prepared and get my dogs. As this whole thing was Leslie's idea, she'd agreed to look after Violet and Peony tonight. I'd debated bringing them with me, thinking their canine senses might come in useful. But Violet's a cocker spaniel and Peony a bichon frise. They're both highly intelligent and fiercely loyal, but neither is exactly guard dog material, and this was a very old house, not to mention a public one. Their strong canine senses were more likely to pick up mice in the walls or traces of the numerous people who passed through here every day.

As I was leaving Leslie's, Uncle Arthur texted me to check in, as he does a couple of times a week when he's away. Formerly the master and commander of one of Her Majesty's great battleships, he spends most of his time in his natural environment, which is at sea. I hardly ever see him. He left shortly after Christmas, off for a month of sailing in the Mediterranean. On the way, he made a quick stop in the U.K. to handle some financial affairs, and a minor mishap resulted in a broken ankle. I believe a visit to a pub might have been involved, but don't hold me to that. He's now resting at my parents' home, grumbling that London in January is no place for a retired gentleman.

I'm sure my mother is grumbling about an unexpected extended visitor.

I'd replied to his text: *Spending the night in a supposedly haunted house. Fear not—Jayne will be there.*

Uncle Arthur: *Good for Jayne. With V and P?*
Me: *Dogs at Leslie's*
He: *All right then. Night love.*

Uncle Arthur regularly checked on the health and safety of the dogs. Not on me or our jointly owned business.

Scarlet House had electricity, but the few modern lights were dim and an attempt had been made to keep their presence discreet. In the parlor, a single electric bulb was mounted in a corner of the ceiling, barely giving enough light to read by. I lifted a solid iron candlestick off a side table. A box of matches lay next to it, and I struck a match to light the candle. The wick caught and the flame leapt.

"If you hear my screams," I said, "come running."

Andy gave me a thumbs-up.

I held the candlestick high and left the parlor. The hallway was dark, and my candle threw a circle of flickering light that failed to reach the corners or the end of the corridor. I touched my pocket, checking I had my phone. Perhaps the gesture was as much to confirm that I was grounded in my own time as to ensure I had it with me.

I took the phone out and switched on the flashlight app, and with it in one hand and the candlestick in the other, I ventured upstairs. Ahead of me, the wide oak staircase ascended into darkness. Painted portraits lined the walls. Gentlemen in tight collars, full beards, or bushy whiskers, and ladies in starched bonnets or flower-covered hats. These were store-bought prints, acquired by the Historical Society to provide atmosphere. The only original portrait hung in the front hall, a small card taped beneath it, saying it was George Scarlet, painted in 1892. George's face was pink and pudgy, his hairline thin, and his eyes almost popped out of the paint. I couldn't see much else under the enormous black beard and the whiskers that flared out at the side of his face as though he were attempting to grow wings. His expression was downright frightening.

An ornately carved wooden table sat at the top of the stairs, bearing a porcelain vase painted in the Chinese style that had been hugely fashionable in Victorian times. The philodendron inside the pot was lush and the leaves well dusted. A switch was barely visible through the foliage, and I flicked it. A forty-watt bulb came on above me. Satisfied it was working, I turned it off, then switched off my flashlight app.

I'm anything but a fanciful woman, but I wanted to take a moment to absorb the atmosphere of the house. The hallway was dark, the flickering light of my single candle serving only to emphasize the darkness. Four doors led off the hallway, with a small, deeply recessed window at the far end. If Robyn had stood where I was now, the thing she'd seen—the thing she'd thought she'd seen—would have been framed by the window. It had been daytime, and the winter sun had shone all day Thursday. A figure standing there would have appeared as nothing but an outline, which could be why Robyn couldn't describe the figure's appearance. She'd described the clothes, but that might have been nothing but her brain filling in what she expected to see.

I went into each of the rooms in turn. A master bedroom, a nursery, a second bedroom decorated with dolls and wooden toys, and another room ready for guests. On my previous visit to Scarlet House, I'd thought they were playing at history, rather than recreating it. In the spotlessly clean barn, in particular, everything was arranged for modern sensibilities. The immaculate wooden planks of the barn floor; the sparkling, rust-free farm utensils on display; the plump happy animals who'd never end up on someone's dinner plate. The well-scrubbed, well-groomed, cheerful farmer, happily going about his chores. Scarlet House had originally been a rough-walled, one-room home. One room for a married couple and their seven children. The family had prospered, and the house had expanded over the centuries into some version of the large, comfortable recreation it was today. It hadn't always looked like this. If ever it had.

The furniture was a mixture of genuine antique and faithful reproduction. Solid wooden cabinets, bed frames, tables, a rocking chair, a baby's crib on runners. Straw-stuffed mattresses, quilted bed coverings, wooden children's toys, including a rocking horse and porcelain dolls with painted faces and handmade dresses.

None of the furniture or objects on the first floor—what Americans confusingly call the second floor—had been destroyed in the fire, although there had been considerable smoke and water damage to the floor and walls, requiring extensive renovations. I stepped over the velvet ropes, feeling quite naughty, and examined the rooms. None of them had closets, but I opened the tall, solidly built wardrobe in the master bedroom and the chest at the bottom of the bed in the guest room. They were empty, used for decoration only. Feeling rather foolish, along with naughty, I put my candle on a table, got down on the floor, and swept the light of my phone under the beds. I found nothing: scarcely any dust bunnies, mouse droppings, or spiderwebs, never mind a person attempting to conceal themselves.

I left the nursery as a flash of lightening lit up the hallway, followed barely a second later by a peal of thunder sounding as though it was directly overhead. Branches scraped the windows, and rain pounded on the roof.

I gripped my candlestick. *Could anything,* I thought, *make this night more of a horror-movie cliché?*

Once I'd checked the windows were all secure and no one (or nothing) was hiding under the beds, I found the door to what was likely the servants' stairs, opened it, and peered in. It was an old door, original to the house, covered in layers of paint, but the hinges moved soundlessly. The staircase was steep, the passage narrow, and the light of my candle barely broke the solid darkness. I decided to go back down via the main staircase.

I paused at the bottom of the steps. Andy and Jayne's low voices drifted out of the open parlor door, and Jayne laughed lightly.

The dining room was set for dinner for six, with fine porcelain dishes and silver cutlery. A row of candlesticks ran down the center of the solid oak table. A matching sideboard, with ornately carved cabinet doors, laden with earthenware serving dishes and a vase overflowing with silk roses, stood against one wall. Above it hung paintings of horses, either done by an artist with no talent or one who'd never seen a real horse. The long red drapes were closed against the night, and the fireplace was cold and dark.

The room directly across the hall from the dining room was the master's study. It was a very masculine room: more dark wallpaper, more horse paintings, leather chairs with hobnails gathered around another fireplace also cold and dark. The desk in front of the window was huge, filling a substantial part of the room. I stepped, once again, over the velvet rope to read the sign on a stand next to the desk. This, it told me, dated from 1846 and was one of the few pieces of furniture original to the house, being the actual desk from which generations of Scarlets had conducted the business of the farm.

I opened the door to the room tucked between the study and the kitchen and immediately popped back into the twenty-first century. A desktop computer had been turned off for the night, but the blue lights of the modem shone. A telephone, a real landline soon to be as out of date as the chamber pots in the bedrooms, sat on the computer table. Aprons hung from pegs on one wall, and high-button boots were lined up beneath. The other wall contained a dozen small lockers, with a variety of locks and name tags taped to the doors, no doubt where the docents put their bags and car keys when they were working in the house.

I next went into the kitchen. The fire had been extinguished for safety when the volunteer staff left, although in earlier days, when one couldn't drive to the store at any time of the day or night to get fire starters, the kitchen fire would never have been allowed to go out in winter. The enormous open fireplace took up most of one wall, a colorful hearthrug in front of it. A rocking chair had been placed close to the fire, alongside a basket containing brightly colored wool and several sets of knitting needles. The contender for New England's longest scarf lay on top of the basket, a riot of orange, green, and blue wool, with a bit of purple thrown in. Massive iron hooks were attached to the bricks above the fireplace, an empty iron pot hanging from one of them. Cabinets displayed dishes and more pots and pans. A well-scrubbed pine table filled the center of the room, covered with various sizes of mixing bowls. Sharon had called to tell me she'd left some of her special period-appropriate home baking out for us. I eyed the offering. Those biscuits looked about as appetizing as rocks, and I knew from past experience they tasted the same. Tomorrow morning, before we left, I'd feed them to the pigs. Let Sharon think we'd enjoyed them.

I tested the door leading to the outside and found it locked. Next, I peeked into the pantry off the kitchen. Shelves contained rows of preserves in glass jars; woven baskets held potatoes, onions, and squash. Despite it being January, none of the vegetables were sprouting. Direct from the supermarket, no doubt. A woven rug, faded with age and use, lay on the stone floor. Another door was on the far side of the pantry. I opened it to see a dark narrow staircase leading up. "Anyone in there?" I called. My voice echoed faintly back to me.

Satisfied the house was secure, I returned to the parlor. I stomped heavily on the floorboards as I walked and coughed before entering. Jayne smiled demurely at me from the couch. I needn't have worried about interrupting anything—Andy was crouched in front of the fire, adding logs to the blaze.

"Storm coming," he said.

"Storm's here," I said as the room lit up and thunder roared, and the foundations of the old building shook.

"I wonder how many storms this house has seen," Jayne said.

"A lot," Andy said. "But not many thunderstorms in January. Not normal for this time of year." Satisfied with his work, he pushed himself to his feet. "Do you want me to check on the guys in the barn?"

"Thanks, but I'll do it," I said. "I want to have a look around outside anyway."

"You're a braver woman than me, Gemma Doyle," Jayne said.

"If this were a horror movie, they'd say I'm too stupid to live. But it's not, and I'm not." I put my candlestick on the table. An open flame wouldn't last long against the force of the wind outside.

Andy handed me a cooler. "I brought supper for the guys in the barn."

I slipped my raincoat on and accepted the cooler. "I have the key." Robyn had stopped at the Emporium, in the afternoon, to give me a key to the house. "I'll lock the door when I leave. No point in being responsible for the night's security and then leaving the front door unlocked."

Outside the house, the property boasted strong electric lights. The one over the front door lit up the porch and part of the parking area and the front lawn. An electric light was mounted high on a pole between the barn and the house, and lights glimmered from inside the barn. Past the barn, the physick garden, where volunteer gardeners grew plants and herbs that would have been used for medicinal purposes, was winter bare. The kitchen garden at the rear of the house would be so as well. The rain was falling hard, and I pulled my hood up before splashing through puddles as I ran across the driveway. The pigs heard me first and started grunting. The chickens and sheep joined in, the donkey brayed softly, and a man called out.

"It's me," I yelled. "Gemma."

The barn, solid and substantial, been built in the mid-nineteenth century and painted a cheerful red. Hay was stored in the loft overhead, and several enclosures, separated by chest-high wooden walls and doors secured with solid metal bolts, kept the animals apart and out of the food sacks and bins.

Dave Chase and Craig Jones had made themselves comfortable in the main area, where museum staff gave talks about life on the farm. When the house itself had been unusable following the fire, Sharon Musgrave and the other docents had moved some of their pots and cooking equipment in here and set up a fire pit to lecture on how families had "made do" when necessary.

Craig and Dave had "made do" with camping chairs, laptop computers, an electric heater, and a six-pack of beer. I handed

Dave the cooler, and he introduced me to Craig without saying why I was here or what I was, apparently, supposed to accomplish. Craig was a slightly overweight man in his late forties, clean shaven even at this time of the evening, with plump lips, prominent eyes, a wide smile full of good teeth, and a limp handshake. Both men were ready for their night in the barn in padded vests worn over thick sweaters, and jeans and heavy boots.

I pointed to the door from behind which came the squealing of pigs. "Can I have a peek at them?"

"Go ahead," Dave said.

The old wooden door was secured by a metal latch. I lifted it, the door swung back, and I stepped into a small, dark, dusty room, crammed with feed sacks and assorted equipment. I peered over the half wall into the pigs' enclosure: two males and two females, one a solid black, the others mottled shades of brown, all of them mighty substantial animals. The farm was hoping, I'd been told, for piglets in early spring. Children love piglets, and they, plus lambs and chicks, would be popular draws for school trips.

Back in the main area, I lowered my hood and shook rain off my jacket. "It's nice of you to keep Dave company," I said to Craig.

"In exchange for grub from the café? No-brainer, that one," Craig said. "You're the bookstore lady, right?"

"I am."

"I'm not much of a Sherlock man myself, but my wife likes those books."

"She should pop in one day," I said.

"Craig and Cassie recently moved to the Cape," Dave said. "Craig's a financial advisor and Cassie's an author."

"Is she? I'm sorry, but I don't recognize the name. Does she write under Cassie Jones?"

"Yup."

"Anything I'd be interested in stocking?"

"Not up your alley," Craig said. "She writes nonfiction historical books for young adults. Right now Caribbean pirates are her thing."

"She'd still be welcome to have a signing at my shop," I said. "I like to help local authors when I can."

"I'll mention that to her. You're English, right?"

"Direct from London."

"Cassie helped in the house over the Christmas season," Dave said. "Craig's volunteered to give me a hand with the animals and put in some work in the gardens come spring."

"You have my number, Dave? In case anything happens."

"I do. And a key to the house if I have to get in and you aren't answering. I have to say, Gemma, this is all rather odd. What do Robyn and Leslie expect is going to happen tonight, and if something does, what are we supposed to do about it?"

"I'm here as a favor to Leslie Wilson, that's all. Maybe nothing happening is what they need to hear, and then everything can go back to normal."

While we talked, Craig opened the cooler and peered in. "This looks great."

A pig grunted in agreement.

Chapter Five

We enjoyed a delicious picnic supper of cold potato and leek soup, salad, and a crab and shrimp quiche, followed by chocolate cupcakes provided by Jayne, and tea out of a thermos, and then we played a few hands of cards. I wandered through the house every hour or so, peeking around corners and sheepishly checking under beds and behind furniture, convinced I was wasting my time. I received no phone calls from the barn.

Jayne had told her staff she'd be in late tomorrow, what passes as late for Jayne anyway, but she'd curled up on one of the hugely uncomfortable, stiff-backed, spindly-legged sofas, covered herself with a blanket, and fallen instantly asleep.

It had gone past midnight. The fire smoldered in the grate, the candles in the ornate candelabra on the side table dripped wax as they burned down, and the storm raged outside. Andy and I played gin to the sound of Jayne's gentle breathing. "Do you have any idea what you'd like to have in terms of your wedding reception?" I asked, although I suspected I already knew the answer.

"Whatever Jayne wants," he said.

"Gin." I laid down my cards. So far I'd won every round. Andy hadn't yet realized that the expressions on his face when he picked up a new card or studied his own hand were as clear as the print in a Sherlock Holmes novel.

"What Jayne and my mom want," he added.

"Is your mother likely to have strong opinions?"

He counted his cards. "Nah. I have three sisters. They all had big splashy affairs. Mom's gotten the wedding planning bug out of her system. I—"

"Shh!" I lifted my hand. Andy raised one eyebrow in a question.

"Did you hear something?"

"I heard thunder."

"That wasn't thunder." I'd heard a low rumble, but it hadn't come from outside. I got to my feet.

Andy reached for his flashlight. I grabbed the iron candlestick off the table. "Wake Jayne. Tell her to stay here and keep her phone close."

I headed for the door as Andy bent over Jayne and shook her gently. "Something's happening, honey. Probably nothing, but Gemma and I are going to check."

She threw the blanket off and leapt to her feet. "No way am I staying here alone. Unlike Gemma, I'm not too stupid to live." Her long blonde hair was tousled, and the marks of the sofa cushion were imprinted on her left cheek. She picked up her small flashlight, gripped it tightly, and gave me a determined look. "Lead on, Gemma."

I did so. I'd heard a thump—I was sure of it. A thump followed by a rustling sound. As if a mouse were sprinting across the floorboards. Although it would have been a heck of a big mouse.

Outside the parlor, the house was dark. Our weak flashlights and the flickering candle lit up only a small stretch of the hallway in front of us. Thunder crashed, and Jayne let out a small squeal. She and Andy, I noticed, were gripping hands.

I wasn't sure where the sound had come from. I didn't think it had been overhead, so I cautiously started to lead the way down the hallway.

Another peal of thunder, sounding far too close. Jayne yelped; Andy sucked in a breath.

Not thunder, someone pounding on the front door. The three of us ran to open it. I twisted the lock, pulled the door open, and a man fell in. His woolen sweater was soaked, and water dripped off his nose.

"What—?" I began

"The barn," Craig gasped. "Something . . . in the barn!"

With the door open, even over the pounding of the rain, I could hear the uproar of the animals. The old wooden barn shook and groaned as something heavy, probably the combined weight of the four pigs, crashed against it in an attempt to escape. The chickens clucked in fright, and the sheep cried out. The donkey contributed its part to the effort by attempting to kick down the old building.

"Where's Dave?"

"I left him trying to calm the animals."

It wasn't working. They were getting more and more frantic. By the way they were behaving, I momentarily feared the barn was on fire, but no flames glowed behind the windows or shot out of the roof, and no smoke drifted on the wet air.

"He sent me to see if you're okay here," Craig said.

"We are. Andy, could you go and see if Dave needs any help." Andy threw a look at Jayne.

"I'm fine here," she said. "With Gemma."

Andy ran into the night, not bothering to go back for his coat. He put his hands over the top of his head in a useless attempt to provide some shelter from the driving rain. Craig followed, and they splashed through the rapidly forming puddles in the barnyard. A flash of lightening combined with the strong electric lights overhead to illuminate their path.

A second later thunder roared. I was expecting that, but not expecting the cry that followed.

A woman screamed. A second woman screamed, and I realized that one had been Jayne.

I whirled around. Jayne's hands were to her mouth. All the blood had drained from her face, and her eyes were wide with fear. I didn't know where the first scream had come from, and as I hesitated, wondering where to go, a steady stream of clattering erupted in the kitchen, as though the solid wooden cabinets had tipped over and every pot and pan had fallen onto the floor.

"Gemma! What's happening?" Jayne cried.

"Call 911. Then go into the parlor and lock the door behind you." I sprinted down the hallway.

"I'm not going in there by myself!" She ran after me. I heard her yelling into her phone, "Police. We're at Scarlet House

Museum. Someone's in the house. And in the barn. Hurry, hurry!" And then to me: "Gemma, she says we have to get out of the house."

I ran into the kitchen.

I stopped so abruptly Jayne crashed into me.

The huge open fireplace was dark and cold, the pot hanging from its hook. The rocking chair sat in place, unmoving, the basket of wool and knitting needles next to it, waiting to be picked up to resume work on the scarf. The dishes stood in neat lines on the open shelves of the antique cabinet, heavy pots stacked below.

The only sound was our deep breathing, the branches rubbing against the walls, the rain spattering the windows, and the 911 operator calmly saying, "Police have been dispatched."

"I . . . uh . . . might have been too hasty," Jayne said. "Everything seems . . . okay here."

My phone rang, and I checked it quickly. Andy. "We're fine," he said. "What's happening in the house?"

"Nothing, it would appear."

"The animals are calming down. We've been checking their pens, but I don't see anything amiss."

"We called the police, but I don't think we need them."

"Okay. I'm coming back to the house now."

I hung up. I took a long look around the kitchen. I was about to tell Jayne to meet the police at the door while I searched the rest of the house when I noticed something out of place. I crossed the room in three quick strides and bent down. A wooden rolling pin was on the floor, rolling between the legs of the cabinet and the wall.

Chapter Six

"Perhaps don't mention this to Ryan."

"Gemma," Officer Stella Johnson said, "I am not going to not make a report. Jayne called 911. That's on the record."

"I'm not asking you not to report it. Just, maybe, slip it somewhere in the bottom of the pile, electronically speaking."

She simultaneously rolled her eyes and shook her head.

Andy had started a fire in the kitchen fireplace, and Jayne worked the pump over the sink to get water to fill the iron kettle. Then she found a collection of thoroughly modern tea bags shoved to the back of a shelf.

We were gathered around the big table, gripping mugs of strong, sweet tea. Sweaters were laid on chairs pulled in front of the fire, shoes lined up before the grate, and raincoats dripped from door frames. The kitchen smelled of wet wool and damp socks.

The storm had moved on at almost the exact moment the police arrived, sirens screaming and blue and red lights breaking the night. Stella Johnston and her partner had burst into Scarlet House, weapons drawn, senses on high alert, to find the same thing we had—nothing.

I'd gone upstairs with Stella to search the house while her partner remained with Jayne in the kitchen, and the officers in the next car to arrive checked the barn. This time we came down via the back staircase, nothing but a dark, damp, cramped, ill-lit space that led into the pantry and the kitchen beyond. We checked all the doors and windows and found them secure.

Not a single thing appeared to have been disturbed. Except for the rolling pin. I pointed that out to Officer Johnson, and she touched it lightly with her foot. It rolled into the wall and bounced back again. "Might have fallen off the shelf," she said.

"I was last in here about an hour ago, and it wasn't there then."

"Maybe you missed it."

I didn't reply.

The police eventually left, telling me to contact them if anything else occurred tonight.

"Wouldn't have thought of doing that," Andy mumbled as they splashed their way across the driveway to their cars and drove away.

"What do you think happened, Gemma?" Jayne asked.

"Let's go into the kitchen. I need a cuppa and time to think."

I heard a shout and looked down the driveway to see a woman running toward us.

"That's my wife, Cassie," Craig said. He and Dave had joined us to report that all was quiet in the barn; the animals had curled up and gone back to sleep.

"What's going on?" Cassie asked. She was in her mid-forties, tall and softly rounded, dark hair loosely tied into a long braid down her back. She wore a calf-length winter coat over yoga pants and a T-shirt, and rubber boots.

I left Craig to explain and led the way down the hallway. The others trotted along behind. I noticed everyone peeking into dark corners while trying not to look too nervous. Jayne made another pot of tea, and we settled around the kitchen table.

"Strangest thing," Dave said.

"Would you say this was the same pattern of behavior the farm animals showed on Thursday night?" I asked.

"Can't say. I wasn't here when it happened. Craig? Cassie?"

"We were in bed and were woken by the noise coming from the barn," Craig said. "We called Dave and the police, and ran over to see what was happening."

"What we found was nothing happening." Cassie and her husband exchanged glances. She had her hands wrapped tightly around her teacup, as though needing the warmth. The fire had caught, and the strong flames had taken hold. If anything, the kitchen was too warm.

"Like tonight." Jayne said. "You don't suppose we imagined that scream and all that noise, do you, Gemma?"

"I do not. The two of us, at the same time?"

"What then?" Dave said.

"Is it . . . possible?" Cassie said. "I mean, this is an old house, and . . ." Her voice trailed off.

I said nothing. I leaned back in my chair, closed my eyes, steepled my fingers, and thought.

I heard the pushing back of chairs, the draining of teacups, and the sound of people creeping away, but I ignored all that. When I opened my eyes, the kitchen was empty. I had come to no conclusions, and I had no theories. I had not imagined things, and I did not believe in ghosts or hauntings.

Someone all too human had been in this house tonight, for their own purposes. As to whom that might have been, what those purposes might have been, and how they had managed to get in and out again without being seen, I had absolutely no idea.

*　*　*

After a sleepless night spent sitting in a stiff-backed chair, phone in hand, candle burning next to me, eyes fixed on the door, I arrived at the Emporium at noon on Sunday in time to open up. As I passed the window, I glanced into the tearoom to see that the place was almost full. Jayne didn't regularly serve a proper afternoon tea Sunday to Thursday in the slow season, but plenty of locals came in to enjoy a late, leisurely Sunday breakfast.

Last night's storm had left an aftermath of wet streets, full puddles, downed branches, and fallen trees, but the pale winter sun had risen over the ocean, and everything was drying nicely. City crews had been out first thing, clearing away broken branches and checking power lines.

I unlocked the door of the Sherlock Holmes Bookshop and Emporium and flipped the sign on the door to "Open." Moriarty emerged from his bed under the center table to greet me. Not to greet me, exactly, but to demand the filling of his food bowl. I ran up the seventeen steps to the upper level,. After hanging my coat and scarf on the hook behind the door to my office and stuffing my bag into the bottom drawer of my desk, I did as I'd been ordered and refreshed his water supply, put out food for the day, and cleaned the litter box.

By the time I got back downstairs, Ashleigh was coming through the sliding door adjoining the Emporium to Mrs. Hudson's, take-out cup of coffee in hand. Ashleigh doesn't usually work on Sundays, but I'd phoned her this morning and asked her if she could fill in. Dave had called Robyn as the first of the sun's rays touched the rim of the sea, and Robyn summoned members of the museum board to an emergency meeting to be held this very afternoon. My presence had been requested. More than requested: demanded. I don't normally attend board meetings of organizations I don't belong to, particularly if I'm ordered to appear, but I felt an obligation this time. My presence at Scarlet House last night had been an attempt to "eliminate the impossible." At that, I had failed. Rather than eliminating anything, all that had been achieved was the opening up of a heck of a lot more questions.

Ashleigh looked very punk rock this morning. Her hair was colored a lurid pink and tied in bunches, or pigtails, with bright yellow ribbons. Two red circles were painted on her cheeks, and her eyelids were a deep blue. Her skirt came to well above her knees, and pink and blue striped socks were pulled up to those knees. Ashleigh was short and slight, with expressive green eyes; a round, lightly freckled face; and a small cleft chin. Dressed like that, she looked a great deal like Bunny Leigh, the former pop star, must have in her youth.

"Thanks for this," I said.

"Happy to do it," she replied. "Not a lot else to do on a day like today."

"Nice outfit."

"A couple of the customers yesterday were telling me about this old-time singer who's in town. They showed me pictures of her they're carrying around in case they can get an autograph. I liked the look."

"She was here yesterday. In the store."

"Was she? I guess she didn't buy anything, unless Gale served her."

"You probably wouldn't have recognized her. She wasn't dressed as she might have been in her glory days. How's Gale working out?"

"Great. I like her and she seems to love the store. That's important in an employee, isn't it? When we had some down-time, I told her about my ideas for expanding the franchise."

"Did you now?" Ashleigh has plenty of ideas as to how I should run my business. They don't always coincide with mine.

"She gave me her phone number in case I need her to come in in an emergency someday and you're not around. I hope that's okay?"

"Emergency backup? Absolutely. I have to leave for this meeting at two. I should be back before closing time, but if I'm not—"

"I know the routine," she said as the bell over the door tinkled cheerfully, and the day's first batch of customers came in. Two women headed directly for the gaslight fiction shelf.

"I'm going to get myself tea and something to eat, and then go upstairs and start unpacking those boxes that came in yesterday." A new batch of Holmes- and London-themed jigsaw puzzles. Puzzles had proved to be popular items over the long winter months. The Sherlock Holmes Bookshop and Emporium is primarily a bookshop specializing in Sherlock Holmes books, original and pastiche, as well as novels set in his era, called gaslight, and nonfiction to do to with the life and times of Sir Arthur Conan Doyle, his creator, but we also sell anything and everything to do with the Great Detective. You might be surprised at how much there is of that stuff.

I went through the sliding door as Ashleigh approached the customers. "Can I help you ladies?"

"Oh yes. We can't get enough of that TV program *Bridgerton*, and we hope you have something similar."

"Not the same time frame," Ashleigh explained, "as *Bridgerton* is Regency, but we have plenty of novels set in the Victorian era. Have you read Victoria Thompson?" She pointed to a book on the display rack.

"I love the mood of that cover," another woman said. "I'll buy it just so I can look at it!"

When she saw me coming, Fiona reached for the tea canister without asking what I wanted. I gave her a grin and said, "and a blueberry muffin, please."

She bagged the muffin and handed it to me along with the tea. She dropped her voice and said, "What happened last night, Gemma? Jayne doesn't want to talk about it, but she's noticeably jumpy this morning. I heard the police were called to Scarlet House."

"False alarm," I said. "The police found nothing of interest." That was no lie. Fiona's face fell in disappointment, but she said, "Some people are saying Scarlet House is haunted. Do you think that's true?"

"Rumor travels fast in this town."

She grinned. "A tourist town in the middle of winter, and a damp winter at that. What else are we going to talk about?"

"What else indeed."

I returned to the Emporium to take my tea upstairs. Movement in the reading nook caught my eye, and I glanced across the room. A small woman had taken a seat in the comfortable wingback chair. She wore a dark coat, scarf wrapped several times around her neck, hat pulled down to her eyebrows, and large sunglasses. The chair faced the window, but she was twisted in her seat. It was Bunny Leigh, and she was watching Ashleigh, now searching the shelves. I considered going over and asking Bunny if she needed assistance, but decided not to. If she wanted privacy, I was happy to give it to her. Besides, those puzzles wouldn't unpack themselves.

Chapter Seven

The Scarlet House Museum is closed to the public on Sundays in winter, so the board met around the dining room table. Sharon Musgrave had been in earlier, whipping up another batch of her dreadful period-appropriate biscuits. Before I left in the early hours of this morning, my mind had been full of the events of the night, but I'd remembered to take the earlier batch and toss them over the fence into the pig enclosure. They, at least, seemed to appreciate them.

Several cars were parked in front of the house when Jayne and I drove up. An ageing Toyota Corolla, held together more by rust than metal, followed us up the drive, and a man got out. He was in his forties, tall and thin, with stooped shoulders, a high forehead, a prominent nose, not a lot of hair, and small watchful eyes that peered at the world from behind thick lenses. He wore a sports coat with elbow patches, brown trousers, and trainers that had seen better days. A laptop was tucked under his arm.

I waited for him to reach us and held out my hand. "Gemma Doyle. You're Ethan, the chap from Yale."

He grinned at me. "A genuine Englishwoman. London accent, very posh. I did some graduate work at Cambridge. A couple of the best years of my life. Ethan Evanston. I'm doing my PhD on eighteenth- and nineteenth-century New England social history. Family and farm life is my focus. Families exactly like the Scarlets. I enjoy working here, at the house. The atmosphere's perfect for me."

The front door was unlocked, and we walked in. I gave the stern painted visage of George Scarlet a nod of greeting, and then Jayne and I hung our coats on the pegs by the door before going to the dining room to join the meeting. Jayne looped her bag over the back of her chair, and I put mine on the floor as we settled around the table. Sharon bustled in and out, serving tea and coffee, refilling the cups, proudly producing her baking. She'd dressed in her costume, a long brown dress, white apron, lacy linen cap, although everyone else wore their regular clothes. She'd thrown a shawl over her shoulders as protection from the winter chill that permeated the house outside the kitchen.

Representing the board were Robyn, Leslie, Dave Chase, and Ben Alderson. Robyn sat at the head of the table, nervously, or perhaps impatiently, tapping the wood with a fingernail. The scarlet badge that indicated a supporter of Scarlet House was pinned to her jacket. Craig and Cassie Jones had come as witnesses to the events of last night, as had Jayne and I. Andy couldn't make it because he needed to be at his restaurant.

Robyn's face had tightened when she saw who came in with us, and she cleared her throat. "Ethan, this is a meeting of the board. You won't find it at all interesting."

"You never know," he said, taking a seat at the table, "what I might find interesting. Sometimes *I* never know."

"The meeting is not open to the public."

"I don't mind. Just pretend I'm not here." He opened his laptop.

"Drop it, Robyn," Dave said. "I told Ethan what happened last night and that we were meeting this afternoon to discuss it."

"Why would you do that?"

"Because he's interested in the house, of course."

"Not that talk of hauntings is going to do my thesis any good. Or my reputation." Ethan threw a smirk at Robyn. Her lips tightened, but she didn't answer. Prominent historians didn't usually care for ghostly interpretations of historical events. Haunted or not, what happened at Scarlet House in the twenty-first century shouldn't be of any use to him. Based on that smirk, I decided he simply liked getting under her skin. And based on the look on her face, it was working.

Once that was settled and everyone was served, Sharon sat down. Robyn tapped her teacup with a silver teaspoon to get our attention. "This is an informal meeting. I don't want any minutes, Sharon."

Sharon looked up in surprise. She'd placed a notebook and a pen at her place and was preparing to start recording the conversation. "We can't have a meeting without writing down what's been said."

"If I say we can, we can."

"I don't agree," Ben said.

"I don't care if you agree or not," Robyn said. "This is not a formal meeting. So no notes."

He looked like he might argue, but then he sighed, leaned back in his chair, and let it go. Not for the first time, I got the feeling that the board members of the Scarlet House Museum had learned to pick their battles with the strong-willed Robyn.

Ethan bent his head over his laptop and typed away.

"Dave gave me an overview of the events of last night on the phone, but I'd like to hear again what happened," Robyn said. "Dave, you go first, and then Gemma, please."

When we'd finished, both of us keeping it brief and including a minimal amount of drama, Craig said, "Scared the life out of me. One minute everything's calm and peaceful, and the next it sounded like the end times had arrived."

"Hardly calm and peaceful," Jayne said. "There was a storm going on."

"Yes, but that was outside. I mean in the barn. In the house."

"Could the storm have been what upset the animals?" Robyn asked.

"I wouldn't have thought so," Dave said. "They're used to coastal weather. But you never know. If one of them got a fright, and scared another . . . it all builds from there. Since helping out here, I've learned to expect the unexpected when working with farm animals." He turned to me. "Except for the time I volunteered in Africa, I spent my career as a dog and cat vet. Totally different kettle of fish, those."

"Were you and Craig together when the animals woke up?" I asked him.

The men exchanged vacant glances and half shrugs. Dave spoke first. "It's difficult to be sure. It was dark and late, the storm building, and I might have been snoozing on and off.

Hard to get comfortable in those camp chairs. Craig got up and—"

"That was earlier, remember?" Craig gave an embarrassed shrug. "We might as well be honest here. We shouldn't have, but we brought a couple of beers. Thought it would help to pass the time."

"Really, Dave," Robyn said.

"In my defense, Craig brought them. Although honesty forces me to admit, I didn't need my arm twisted to have one. Or two."

"Or three." Craig spoke to Dave but glanced at Cassie, sitting across the table from me. She gave him an almost imperceptible nod, and he continued. "I'd gone out earlier to . . . uh . . . answer nature's call, but that was some time before. Dave, you were sleeping when the animals cried out. Sleeping deeply, judging by the snoring. Don't you remember me yelling at you and you waking up with a start?"

"Yeah that sounds about right," Dave said. "Three beers shouldn't have knocked me out like that, but it had been a long day. We ran into the pens to see what was going on. The pigs were squealing to beat the band, the chickens flapping about so much I was afraid they'd hurt themselves. The donkey was braying and trying to kick down the door. We didn't see anything, not a single thing, that might have woken them. I told Craig to run to the house to get help, but I didn't need it. The animals calmed themselves down, and soon enough it was as though nothing had happened."

Ethan snorted.

Everyone, Robyn most of all, ignored him.

"Was there any trace of smoke?" I asked. "Any indication there'd been threat of a fire?"

Dave shook his head. "By the way they were going on, that's the first thing I thought. But no. Not a whiff."

"Animals," Cassie said hesitantly, "are known to be sensitive to supernatural forces."

"You're talking about pigs and sheep here," Ethan said. "They're not known to be sensitive to anything but who's coming to feed them."

She ducked her head. "Just a comment. I didn't hear them this time. I missed it all. I woke up and went to the kitchen for a glass of water and saw the police cars leaving."

"It could have a natural explanation," Jayne said, "but what happened in the house didn't. If I'd been alone, I might have thought I mistook thunder or the sound of the wind howling around the house for a scream. But Gemma heard it too."

I nodded. I had.

"You're sure it was a scream?" Ben asked.

"Positive," Jayne said. "I think. It—"

I interrupted her. "It sounded like the voice of a woman, at any rate."

"She—or whatever it was—gave one piercing scream and then stopped. To be followed by . . ." Jayne swallowed.

I said nothing.

"Followed by what?" Robyn asked.

"It sounded as though the animals had escaped from the barn and were rampaging through the kitchen. Dishes fell, crockery broke. As if the cabinets had all fallen over at the same time and spilled their contents."

As one, the board of Scarlet House and their guests glanced nervously around the room. Even Ethan couldn't keep his air of disinterest at bay and surreptitiously checked the shadows in the corners. Jayne held her arms out. "When Gemma and I got to the kitchen, we found everything in its place. All quiet once again. Peaceful. Even the thunder had stopped."

Dave and Craig nodded in confirmation of what we were saying. Sharon's color was high, and her eyes shone with excitement as she pulled her shawl tighter around her shoulders. Ben looked dubious, and Cassie shook her head. Leslie shifted in her chair. Ethan was staring at his screen, but his fingers had stopped moving. Robyn's face was tight with what might be anger. An interesting reaction, I thought.

"You called the police," Robyn said at last. "You shouldn't have done that without my permission."

"I don't need your permission," I said. "But to be fair, if I must, I had reason to believe a woman was in distress, and thus we contacted the authorities immediately—"

"As the good citizens we are," Jayne said.

"Quite," I added. "That it turned out to be a false alarm is of no consequence. The police answer plenty of false alarms in their time."

"Of course, of course." Robyn waved her hand.

"You were brave to stay in the house for the rest of the night." Cassie glanced at her husband again. "I would have run as fast as I could."

"Cookie anyone?" Sharon offered the plate.

Ben absentmindedly reached for one. "Okay, we have mysterious noises in the night. We had things moving around. All that's sure to have a logical explanation." He bit into the biscuit. His mouth puckered and he coughed. Not wanting to give offense, he finished the "treat" and swallowed heavily. A long drink of water followed.

"No, thank you," I said as Sharon attempted to pass the plate my way. "Late lunch."

Cassie and Craig accepted one. Craig ate his in one bite, with no adverse reaction, but his wife bit a corner off, and her face scrunched up. "These are . . . different."

"Made as they would have been over an open fire with whatever the farm wife had on hand. I try whenever possible—"

"Not now!" Robyn snapped. "We aren't here for a lecture on prehistoric cooking."

Sharon's lower lip quivered, but she tried to pull herself together as she sniffed. "Pardon me for doing my job."

"Do it another time," Robyn said. "Ben's right. All this has a logical explanation."

"For once," Ethan said, "I agree with Robyn."

"Not only noises in the house, remember," Dave said, "but something upset my animals. Again."

"What about the woman you saw upstairs, Robyn?" Leslie asked. "The woman who shouldn't have been there. Do you think she . . . uh . . . might have been in the house last night?"

"I explained that," Robyn replied. "I've written a memo that I intend to circulate tomorrow, reminding all volunteers they are to sign in and out for their shift. Things have been getting lax around here of late. Particularly in light of Gemma's recommendation that we control access to the keys to the house, I thought it pertinent to remind people of their duties."

"Who did you distribute the new keys to?" I asked.

Robyn had the grace to flush. "We . . . uh . . . didn't get around to that yet."

"You didn't get around to—you mean you didn't have the locks changed yesterday, as we'd discussed?"

"Yesterday was a Saturday. The locksmith charges extra on weekends. I thought it could wait until Monday."

I groaned. Here I'd been spending the night in a house I assumed was secure, only to discover that everyone and their goat still had keys. "You are telling me now that all our late-night visitor had to do was unlock the door with an old key they might have had on hand, and walk in? Ethan, do you have a key to the house?"

"Nope. Never been given one. Now that you mention it, that might be a good idea."

Robyn stood up. "If we're finished here."

"Finished?" Dave said. "We've barely begun."

"I want to know what you're going to do next," Cassie said. "We live next door, remember, and I don't want to have to keep worrying about strange things happening."

"Perhaps Gemma could—" Leslie said.

"No." Robyn put her palms firmly onto the tabletop and leaned over it. "It was your idea to invite a couple of outsiders to poke their noses into my business—I mean our business." She turned to me. "I'm sorry, Gemma, but you should never have been involved."

I said nothing. I never mind poking my nose into other people's business. Not if the situation interests me. And this one did.

"No more," Robyn continued. "I'll have no talk of ghostly presences. The locks will be changed tomorrow, as I have arranged. I'll instruct the volunteers to sharpen up. This is an old house, and strange things happen in old houses. Noises, I mean. Particularly in a storm as intense as the one we had last night. You people"—she glanced at Dave as well as me—"were expecting to find ghosts coming out of the woodwork. And you found exactly what you hoped to find."

I didn't bother to point out that I hadn't hoped to find a ghost coming out of the woodwork or anywhere else. Dave said, "That's unfair, Robyn. More than one of us—"

"You were asleep, by your own admission. A residue of a dream, forced to the forefront when you were woken so abruptly."

"What woke me so abruptly is the issue."

She ignored him. "I'm going to recommend to the full board that we call McDonald Restoration to do a complete analysis of their earlier work. Clearly they created a structural flaw in the house during their repairs, or at best they overlooked one, and it needs to be addressed immediately."

"McDonald isn't going to admit they made a mistake," Ben said.

"If necessary, we'll hire another firm to go over it as well."

"We can't afford that," Leslie said. "We're barely operating within our budget as it is, with all the expenses after the fire and then being closed down for months because of the pandemic."

"I don't intend to pay McDonald to fix their errors," Robyn said. "If I find they did shoddy work, I'll be expecting to be recompensed."

Cassie got to her feet, and Craig scrambled to join her. "This has nothing to do with us," she said. "Sort it out among your-selves." They left.

"It's obviously entirely up to you, as a board, to decide what you want to do," I said. "But I'd strongly advise against attempt-ing to shove these incidents under the rug."

"I am not shoving anything under the rug," Robyn said. "I'm suggesting a logical course of action in light of recent events."

"Sit down, Robyn," Ben said, "and let's talk this over. In one way, I'm inclined to agree with you. We don't need word get-ting out that Scarlet House is haunted. Respectable school and church youth groups will stop coming, but every ghost hunter in a one-hundred-mile radius will descend on the place."

"They'll come from a lot farther than a hundred miles." Dave got to his feet. "I'm off too. I'll check the barn before I go."

"No one's saying we need to broadcast our business to all and sundry," Leslie said, "but we can't pretend nothing's hap-pening here."

"Nothing is," Robyn said. "I'm going home. My husband and I have dinner plans. If anyone has any brilliant ideas, you can call me in the morning. Ethan, I'm locking up. Time for you to go."

I caught Jayne's eye and gave her a jerk of the head, suggest-ing we leave. We'd accomplished nothing by coming here, and we'd accomplish nothing more by staying. I'd walked to work, as I usually do, and had accepted a lift with Jayne to the meeting.

We stood up. "I gave you some advice the other night, and I'll repeat it now," I said. "You need security here, twenty-four seven, at least for a while. Goodbye."

"Why don't you take some cookies with you?" Sharon said. "There seem to be plenty left."

I scooped up my bag and bolted for the door, but I wasn't fast enough. Sharon followed, cookie plate in hand. "I know you have a bakery, and I wouldn't want you to think I'm competing with you."

"Not a chance of that," I said.

"Do you ever outsource your cooking? I'm thinking I'd like to start up a business. Small at first, of course." She thrust the plate at Jayne. "Why don't you take these and see what your customers think?"

Jayne threw a panicked look at me. I took the plate and put it on the piecrust table beneath George Scarlet's portrait. "Jayne can't serve food if she doesn't know it's been prepared under strict health department guidelines. Sorry. You understand, I'm sure."

It was warm in the hallway as heat from the fireplace flowed out of the kitchen. Sharon shrugged the shawl off her shoulders, revealing a brooch pinned to her bodice. It was large and ugly, a red stone about the size of a golf ball in the center, surrounded by small chunks of glass. The piece was dull under a layer of grime, dirt caught in the claws holding the glass in place. Yet another example, I thought, of how Scarlet House revised history. A farm wife like Mrs. Scarlet wouldn't have a piece like that, and even if she did, she wouldn't wear it with her day dress.

"Are you sure you want to take on more work?" I asked. "You're busy here. Don't you keep the books for the house as well?"

"Yes, and I have a few other bookkeeping clients. It's just that . . ." She threw a nervous glance toward the dining room.

"Robyn's under a lot of strain. She and her husband are having money problems, and now these strange things are happening. You understand what it's like. Sometimes she makes things . . . difficult."

*   *   *

"What do you think's happening at Scarlet House?" Jayne asked as she drove south on Harbor Road in the direction of Baker Street. It wasn't long past four thirty, but the sun was already lowering over the tall trees to the west. The commercial fishing pier was quiet on a Sunday, and not many people were strolling on the boardwalk despite the nice day. The ice cream stand was closed; the colorful umbrellas and outdoor chairs, put away; the awning, rolled up. At the Blue Water Café, the spacious dining area jutting over the water was stark and empty. A handful of cars were in the parking lot: Andy and his staff, getting ready for Sunday dinner.

"What do I think? I think someone's going to a lot of trouble to play a prank on Scarlet House."

"Who? Why would anyone do that?"

"That's the question, isn't it? Robyn Kirkpatrick's heavy-handed management style hasn't made her popular among the board members and other interested parties, to the point that even Sharon is thinking of leaving. Everyone involved in the museum is a volunteer. As a whole, volunteers don't care to be bossed around. It's likely she hasn't been voted off because she's effective at what she does, and no one else wants her job. None of them want any more trouble, not after the disruption and infighting when Kathy Lamb had to be replaced in that position."

"A practical joke?"

"One that's been taken to extremes. If this keeps up, someone might get hurt."

"Do you have any idea who's behind it, Gemma?"

"Not in the slightest. Sharon, as we discovered the other time, drinks more than she probably should, but I've seen no sign of her drinking at the house or being under the influence when she's there. Clearly, she likes the idea that the house is haunted."

"You think so?"

"Oh yes. Her delight at the mention of ghostly possibilities was written all over her face. She's not smart enough, or organized enough, to pull all these separate incidents off. Not by herself, and I don't think she has many friends—if any—at the museum. Dave would never do anything to upset the animals—my take on him anyway, for whatever that's worth."

"It's worth a lot, Gemma. What about Robyn herself?" Jayne pulled the car into an empty spot outside Mrs. Hudson's Tea Room. The restaurant was closed, most of the lights off, and we could see Jocelyn and Fiona going about their end-of-the-day tasks.

"Robyn? I can't see it. She's clearly unsettled by what's happening, no matter how calm and collected she tries to appear. She is, however, smart enough and organized enough to be behind it. I suppose it's possible she could have some idea of doing something dramatic to solve the problem she's created, and thus cementing her position on the board. If I was interested enough in the personal dynamics of the board of Scarlet House, I might look into it."

"You're not interested?"

"I am not."

"You're not going to investigate?"

"I am not. This has nothing to do with me. With us. I advised Robyn to change the locks, and she chose to wait until the rates were cheaper. I suggested they hire a security agency to keep an eye on the place, and that's as far as I'm going to go. Up to them, if they take my advice or not, and I'm guessing not. Your mother's welcome to talk things over with me if it's bothering her, but really, Jayne, I'm not wasting my time investigating childish pranks. As it happens, I have a date with Ryan tonight, and I'm looking forward to it. He's been away on a short vacation with his dad, and yesterday I had to brush him off so I could sit up all night in a creepy old house. You have a wedding to organize and your own love life to carry on with."

Jayne laughed lightly. "Andy and I did have fun last night, though. Until that stuff started happening anyway."

I opened the car door and Jayne twisted in her seat. She peered into the back. "Drat! Do you see my purse anywhere, Gemma?"

I looked. "No."

"I put it on the back of my chair for the meeting. I don't remember bringing it with me when we left—you were in such a rush to get out of there all of a sudden."

"Trying to escape from Sharon and her baking. I sincerely hope, for her sake, she doesn't pursue that idea of setting up a homemade biscuit business." I climbed into the car and crawled around the back seat, sweeping my arm across the floor. "Not here."

"I'll have to go back for it. Do you think they'll still be there?"

"They were making noises about leaving, but it's worth a try. I returned the key to Robyn." I jumped back into the car. "I'll come with you. We need to set a date to get together with Andy's mother to make wedding plans."

Jayne steered the car into the light traffic. As she passed the Emporium, I glanced in. A handful of shoppers were browsing. Ashleigh was standing next to the life-size cardboard cutout of Benedict Cumberbatch and Martin Freeman, talking to a diminutive figure in a black coat and scarf, hat and sunglasses.

Jayne did a U-turn in the empty library parking lot and went east on Baker Street to Harbor Road. Across the street from the Emporium, Maureen McGregor stood in the doorway of number 221, outside her shop, Beach Fine Arts. Her arms were crossed over her chest, her habitual scowl firmly planted on her face. If anyone had been in mind to be shopping for postcards of Cape Cod or local handicrafts, one look at Maureen would have them scurrying away.

"She looks like a secret service agent standing guard outside while the president's shopping with his grandchildren," Jayne said. "Do you think she does that on purpose?"

"To frighten potential customers away? Nothing would surprise me, Jayne. Over the winter, we have customers. I sell books and puzzles, and West Londoners still want coffee and good baking from you, but not a lot of us are in the market for seashell art or wooden boards that say 'Life's better at the beach.'"

"Because we *know* life's better at the beach."

"We do. Which gives me an idea. Things are slow everywhere. I can try to talk Ryan into taking another round of vacation time. Why don't the four of us rent a beach house for a few days? We might not want to go swimming, but we can enjoy walks during the day and nights around a fire."

Jayne turned her radiant smile in my direction. "I'd love that. I'll ask Andy. No, I'll *tell* Andy."

She turned left onto Harbor Road, drove past the street where I live, Blue Water Place, and soon came to the entrance to Scarlet House Museum. Only one car remained in the parking lot.

"Looks like the meeting's over," Jayne said. "Do you know whose car that is?"

"It must be Dave's. It was here last night. It's possible Sharon's still in the house, if she walked or got a lift. She might have stayed behind to tidy up. If she offers us any more biscuits, run. I'm convinced her recipe is the same as was used for the Royal Navy's hardtack. Perfect for lasting the entirety of a six-month voyage to Australia."

We got out of the car and approached the house. The outside lights were on, but nothing shone from inside. Jayne tried the door and found it locked. While she knocked, I glanced around. All was quiet. A couple of crows settled into the bare branch of an ancient oak tree looming over the barn. The doors to the hayloft were open. One crow cawed to another, and a third arrived to settle next to them. Then a fourth.

"I'll go around to the back," Jayne said. "If Sharon's in the kitchen, she might not hear us."

The Game Is a Footnote

"Hold on a sec." I started walking toward the barn. The door to the pig enclosure was open, and the four pigs were rooting at the ground. The donkey brayed softly, but otherwise no undue noises came from within.

Jayne fell into step next to me. "What's that?"

"I don't know." One of the pigs moved, and I could see what they were interested in. I broke into a run. The mud of the barnyard was thick after last night's rain, and my fashionable winter ankle boots sunk into the muck, making it hard going. I recognized the yellow tags warning of an electric wire running through the rough wooden frame of the fence, and took care to keep myself away from the wire as I climbed over the fence.

"Call 911," I said to Jayne. I yelled at the pigs and shoved them to one side. I dropped to my knees, heedless of the mud and goodness knows what else dragging me further down.

The blank, unseeing eyes of Dave Chase stared up at me.

Chapter Eight

"Do you know any farmers?" I asked Jayne.

"There's Martha, who owns the berry farm near Sandwich, where I get my berries in season."

"Maybe not the sort of farmer I'm thinking of." I watched police officers trying to drag enraged pigs away from the body in the barnyard and stuff them back into the barn. No sooner would they get one struggling swine in than another would escape, and the chase would start all over again. This crime scene was going to be a mess. More than it already was. Someone had to be able to take control of the animals, thus my question about farmers.

"Incoming." Jayne pointed up the driveway as Ryan Ashburton's car pulled in. The lean six-foot-three frame of the man I loved climbed out. His blue eyes settled on mine, his handsome face twisted in disapproval, and then his gaze moved away, checking out his surroundings. He wore jeans and a black leather jacket over a dark blue shirt. The badge clipped to his belt glistened in the last rays of the setting sun. A uniformed officer spoke to him. She then turned and pointed in our direction. He grimaced, thanked her, and headed our way.

The Game Is a Footnote

Jayne and I were leaning against the barnyard fence, watching the activity. We were not far from the center of town, and police cars had arrived quickly following Jayne's call. I checked Dave for signs of life, although it was obvious by the angle of his head that Dave Chase's neck had been broken, almost certainly from a fall. I'd looked up to see the open doors of the hayloft directly overhead before hustling a shocked Jayne out of the barnyard. The pigs had edged closer, eager to see what was going on.

"I should be surprised to see you two here," Ryan said. "But I'm not."

"Hi," Jayne said.

I gave him a rueful grin. What can I say? Trouble seems to follow me whether I want to lead the way or not. I checked his eyes for signs of anger but saw none. Only resignation. He rubbed one hand over his strong jaw. He'd shaved recently, probably in preparation for our dinner date tonight, and his cheekbones were sharp in the shadows cast by the dying light. The date, I assumed, was off.

We all turned at a shout, in time to see the generously proportioned, weak-of-heart Officer Richter, who'd apparently lost his footing in the mud, flailing about, trying to keep himself on his feet. He failed and he slipped and fell, hard, into the muck, landing flat on his back. A giant black pig broke for freedom and charged the fallen man. Richter screamed, sounding much like the pig, and stumbled to his feet. Another cop laughed before catching sight of Ryan's face, and he hurried to ensure his fellow officer was unharmed.

"Officer Johnson," Ryan bellowed, "get a vet out here, and get these animals under control."

Stella Johnson raised one hand in acknowledgment and spoke into the radio at her shoulder. Past her, I saw another car arrive and park next to Ryan's. A forensic van pulled in after it.

"You called this in?" Ryan said to Jayne.

She nodded.

He raised one eyebrow at me and ran his eyes over my body. I suspected he wasn't admiring my feminine charms, but checking out my condition. My lovely fashionable ankle boots (new this season, I might add) were so thick with mud, inside and out, I could hardly lift my feet. My trousers were filthy up to the knees, and specks of mud (and I didn't want to think what else) spattered the front of my jacket. I wiped at my face, and my fingers came away dirty. "I checked the man for signs of life while Jayne made the call. It was obvious he'd broken his neck, so I tried to keep the pigs away until help could arrive. In that, I fear, I was unsuccessful."

A pig squealed as an officer grabbed its thin curly tail. An officer squealed as he slipped and fell against the electrified wire.

"Johnson," Ryan yelled, "get the power to that thing cut."

She yelled back, and he said, "No, I don't know where the power source is. Cut it all."

"It was obvious was it?" Detective Louise Estrada said to me. It was her, my nemesis, who'd driven in ahead of the forensic officers.

"I happen to know the desirable position of a human head relative to the shoulders," I said. "And I can tell when it is not in that position."

The Game Is a Footnote

Jayne touched my arm lightly, warning me not to antagonize Estrada. The detective didn't like me and didn't fully trust me, but I thought she was starting to accept that I did know what I was talking about. Most of the time anyway.

The lights illuminating the barnyard flickered once and then went off, but the ones above the door of the house and in the area between, did not. The final traces of daylight were fast disappearing, and cops began switching on their flashlights.

Finally, the last pig was shoved into the barn, and the door slammed shut. We could hear excited squeals and solid bodies striking the old wood, trying to knock the building down. It didn't look that sturdy to me, but I reminded myself the barn had stood for many decades, if not centuries. The donkey brayed, sounding more as though he was asking what was going on than panicking, and the sheep and chickens added their comments. I know nothing about the behavior of farm animals, but I found it interesting that tonight, when genuine excitement was going on in the barnyard, the other animals were not in what I'd call an uproar.

"If you can find food to throw over the wall," I said, "it might calm the pigs down for a while."

"You have vast experience in handling farm animals, do you?" Louise Estrada said.

"No, but I have had boyfriends." I glanced at Ryan. "Present company included." He did not reply, but instead called once again to Officer Johnson. "Get some pig food into that pen. If you can't find pig food, use Richter."

"This crime scene, if it is a crime scene," Estrada said, "is going to be nightmare to process."

We watched as two forensic officers cautiously tested the electric wire, found it safe, and then climbed over the fence to land ankle deep in mud.

"Gemma, is that you? What's going on?" We turned to see Craig and Cassie Jones crossing the lawn between their house and the museum. A uniformed officer intercepted them before they could reach us.

"Those are the immediate neighbors," I said. Traffic on Harbor Road was slowing as people strained to get a look at the activity, and in some of the houses lining the street, people were standing on porches and decks, watching.

"I'll speak to them later. Is the house unlocked, do you know?" Ryan asked as he pointed to the museum.

"No," Jayne said. "We knocked when we got here, but no one answered. That car next to mine belongs to . . ." She swallowed and dipped her head.

"Determining why you two arrived in such a timely fashion will be our first order of business," Louise Estrada muttered.

"As to that," I said. "We were here for a meeting earlier. We left when the meeting broke up, and Jayne didn't realize she'd forgotten her bag until we got to the store. We came back, hoping someone would still be here to let us in. And we found—" I indicated the barnyard.

"The Historical Society owns this property—is that right?" Ryan asked.

"Yes."

"We'll need to get whoever's in charge down here."

"Are you two on the museum board?" Estrada asked. "I wouldn't have thought this place would be of any interest to you, Gemma. Haven't you been known to say that what we in America call history, you English call yesterday's news?"

"I might not have put it quite in those terms," I said. "The earliest part of this house was built in 1648, and even in England that's considered to be an old house."

"Irrelevant," Ryan said. "What were you doing here? What was this meeting about?"

"We were here last night in . . . a private capacity, and we needed to discuss the . . . events of that night with the board members." A drop of cold rain fell on my shoulders. I glanced up to see the first of the night's stars disappearing as fast-moving clouds swept in from the ocean.

"We have to get a tarp over that scene ASAP," Ryan said. "From what I can see, the deceased looks to be directly beneath that door up there, which indicates a possible fall."

"Such," I said, "would appear to be the case, judging by the angle of the neck and the lack of other obvious signs of trauma."

"I need to check it out. Louise, get that scene secured as best you can."

The skies opened, and in a few seconds those unfortunate enough not to be wearing a raincoat—which included me—were soaked to the skin.

"I'll do what I can." Estrada pulled up the hood of her jacket. "Which isn't going to be much. What a mess."

"The museum board chair is Robyn Kirkpatrick," I said.

Ryan nodded. "I remember her from the earlier case."

"I have her number—do you want me to call her?"

"No. Give it to me, and I'll do it." He pulled out his phone.

Officer Johnson trotted up. "I contacted the vet we use, Detective. She's on her way."

Raindrops splashed on his phone, and Ryan tried to cover it with his sleeve. "Let's get on that porch."

He ran for the house, and Jayne and I followed while Estrada went to help set up shelter from the rain. Ryan tried the door to the house and found it locked.

"Improved security," I said.

"Gemma's idea," Jayne said.

One eyebrow rose. "You're acting as security consultants now?"

"About that—"

He lifted a hand. "Save it. I need to examine the scene before it gets any more disturbed. Give me Kirkpatrick's number, and I'll call her after I've done that."

I pulled out my own phone and read off Robyn's number.

"But first," he said, entering the number in his phone, "is there any reason you know of that would indicate this wasn't an accident?" He pointed to the open door of the hayloft.

Jayne and I exchanged glances. "On the surface, no. Dave's primary responsibility here was to take care of the animals, and being in the barn was part of that. Otherwise I know nothing about him or his personal life other than that he was a retired vet. Strange things have been happening here, which is why Jayne and I were at the meeting earlier."

His eyes narrowed. "What sort of strange things?"

"Of a haunting nature."

"You are kidding me."

I gave him a "what can I say?" smile.

"Detective!" Officer Richter yelled. "Over here!"

"I have to check out the scene before it gets any worse. I want to hear about this 'haunting nature,' but it can wait. You two can leave. I know where to find you."

"Thanks," Jayne said.

"I don't mind staying," I said.

"I'm sure you don't," Ryan said, "but you did find the body, and that makes you and Jayne witnesses, if not suspects, if it turns out to be other than an accident."

"You can't possibly think—" Jayne protested.

He lifted one hand. "No, I don't. But I will conduct this investigation according to the book. In the meantime, there's no point in you two hanging around getting wet. Wetter. I'll talk to you after I've examined the scene. Which is going to be a challenge all in itself."

We looked across the yard, to the sodden officers struggling to erect a tent over Dave Chase's body, the forensic people slipping and sliding in the muck, their white crime-scene overalls no longer resembling anything white. Louise Estrada was leaning so far out of the hayloft door, she was in danger of falling herself. The pigs had gone quiet for a few minutes while they happily gobbled up the extra food they'd been given, but they were once again trying to force their way out of their enclosure to the sounds of encouragement from the chickens, the donkey, and the sheep.

I glanced toward the road. At least the sudden rain had driven most of the curious indoors.

"Are you going to the store, Gemma?" Ryan asked.

"No. Ashleigh will have closed at five. I'll go straight home."

"I'll call on you there. Jayne, you can go home. Louise or I will get your statement in the morning. Obviously there's no point in telling you not to discuss the situation, as you will no matter what I say." He ran down the steps and sprinted across the yard.

"Let's go," I said to Jayne. She put her hands over her head, and we broke out of the shelter. The rain was bucketing down now, and we splashed our way to her car. By the time we got inside, we were both wet right through. My wool jacket and scarf had soaked up enough water to fill a small lake.

Jayne pulled a damp tissue out of her coat pocket and tried, without much success, to dry her hands. "I still don't have my purse. Do you suppose the museum will be open tomorrow?"

"They might be ordered not to. Ask Robyn to drop it off for you, if she's allowed in the house. She owes us a favor. Although she won't see it that way."

Jayne abandoned the attempt at drying off and turned the key. The engine roared to life, and she turned the heat up high. "Good thing Sunday's early closing. You couldn't go to the store looking like that."

"Looking like what?"

"Like a mud wrestler."

"There's such a thing as a person who wrestles with mud? Why would anyone do that?"

"Not wrestling with mud, wrestling with—never mind. You're filthy, and I can only assume I'm not much better."

"You look fine. As always." I studied the knees of my trousers. "Although I get your point. Home it is."

She threw the car into gear and drove slowly down the driveway, weaving between police cars and forensic vans. "What do you intend to do now?"

"Now? Make a substantial mug of tea, have a hot shower, put on clothes that are warm but also suitable for being interviewed by the police. And then I might make some phone calls and do some internet searches."

"I thought that might be the case. Why?"

"I have questions, Jayne. I intend to try to find answers."

"You think Dave didn't fall?"

"He fell. That's obvious. Whether or not he was aided in that fall is the main question. Speaking of questions, pull over."

"Why?"

"So I can ask questions."

Jayne parked at the edge of the driveway about ten feet before it met Harbor Road. All the lights were on at the Joneses' house, and Craig and Cassie stood on the deck, watching the police activity. I wrapped my scarf tighter around my neck, not expecting it to do much good, and got out of the car.

Their house was more modern than Scarlet House, built in the middle of the twentieth century. It was small and nondescript, made of red brick typical of its era, with a large lot and single garage. The only recent additions to the exterior were a black steel roof and a wide deck wrapped around one side and the back, facing the Scarlet House property. An awning had been erected over the door, and it provided shelter to Craig and Cassie while they sipped wine and watched the activity. Craig had changed into jeans and a striped jersey, but Cassie wore the clothes she'd had on at the meeting.

Craig gave me a wave when he saw me, followed by Jayne, climbing the deck steps.

"Gemma, Jayne. You look like a couple of drowned rats," Cassie called. "Get over here."

I needed no further invitation to seek shelter. Tonight's rain was not only wet but cold, on the verge of turning to ice.

"What's going on over there?" Craig said. "We tried to get close, but the cops told us to leave."

"Never mind that," Cassie said. "Can I get you a hot drink? Hot chocolate maybe, or something stronger?" She held up her wineglass in invitation.

"No. Thank you," I said. "I have to get home and dried off. The police will be around to talk to you shortly. I can't say too much about what happened, you understand?"

The drapes were open and lights were on inside. Through the sliding door I could see a comfortable living room of paintings of ocean scenes, plush sofa and chairs, a bookcase full of paperbacks and boardgames, and a large coffee table.

"I recognize Dave's car," Cassie said. "It's still there, surrounded by police cars. Has he had . . . an accident?"

"I'm sorry, but yes," I said. No point in denying it.

"Is he going to be okay?" Craig asked.

"Unlikely," his wife replied. "An ambulance came, but it was in no hurry when it left. And the cops are still there." She gave Craig a sharp look before turning back to me. "How terrible. We didn't know him well, but I liked him."

Craig avoided his wife's eyes and took a long drink of his wine. I suspected they'd been arguing earlier.

"Did you leave immediately after the meeting?" I asked.

"You know we did," Cassie replied. "We were the first to go."

"We're not interested in the bickering of a bunch of volunteer board members," Craig said. "I'd said my piece about what happened last night."

"Did you come straight home?"

"Why are you asking this, Gemma?" Cassie said.

"As you can see, the police are interested." I turned and pointed to the house and barn. The lawn and parking lot were full of vehicles. Flashing red and blue lights of police cars reflected off the driving rain, and men and women called to each other as they splashed through puddles. Night had fallen, but powerful lights had been brought in to illuminate the barnyard, creating a circle of bright white light inside the wider darkness. Rain pounded against the steel roof, and I could no longer hear the sound of the pigs. Perhaps the vet had arrived to calm them down. "I'm interested," I added.

"Surely the police don't suspect foul play?" Craig said. "Dave wasn't young, and he could have stood to lose a few pounds."

I didn't answer that. I hadn't said Dave was dead. Cassie had come to that conclusion, but I had no intention of confirming it.

"As I recall, you two left not long after we did," Cassie said. "I saw you drive away. So I can ask the same question of you. Why did you come back?"

"Fair enough. Jayne forgot her bag, and we were hoping someone would still be here who could let us in. Instead we found a disturbance. Jayne still doesn't have her bag."

"I can only hope," Jayne said, "the police are too busy tonight to be running random checks of drivers' licenses."

"I suspect you're in luck on that front," I said.

"We came straight home," Craig said. "It's only a minute at most, cutting across the lawns. Cassie went into the kitchen to start dinner, and I went to my study to check my email. I opened a bottle of wine, poured us each a glass." He lifted the one in his hand in evidence. It was almost empty. "I'd brought a glass to Cassie, slaving away over a hot stove, when we heard the cops arriving and stepped out to see what was going on. We tried to go over there, but a cop intercepted us and ordered us go to home. He said someone will be around to talk to us later."

"Did you see what time the others left the board meeting?"

Craig shook his head, and Cassie shrugged.

I studied their faces but saw nothing there but curiosity mixed with a touch of sadness. As Cassie had said, they didn't know Dave well.

"I wonder if this will frighten off the buyer," Cassie said.

My ears pricked up. "Buyer? You're selling your house?"

"Not this house. We don't own it anyway—we rent. I meant Scarlet House."

"Scarlet House is for sale?" That was news to me.

"Not as far as most of the board knows." Craig laughed.

"Came as a surprise to us too," Cassie said. "A man knocked on our door, said he was interested in buying it and was speaking to people about the neighborhood. Asked if the schools are good ones, about the crime rate, whether tourist traffic is a problem in the summer—that sort of thing. I asked Dave about it, and he said first he'd heard of it."

"When was this?"

"Couple of days ago maybe," Craig said.

"It was Thursday," Cassie said. "I remember because I'd just come in from my yoga class, and that was the night of the disturbance in the barn."

"Did you get this person's name?" I asked.

"No," Craig said. "I don't think he said."

"What did he look like?"

Craig shrugged. "Middle age. Average height. Average weight. Brown hair. He wore a gray coat over a suit and tie. I didn't ask him in. We talked in the doorway."

"Did you see his car?"

"Nope. If he was canvassing the neighbors, he might have left it further down the street."

"American accent?"

"Why are you asking?" Cassie's eyes narrowed and she studied my face. "I don't see what any of this has to do with you."

"Maybe I'm just the curious sort."

"You know what they say about curiously and the cat?"

I assumed the question was rhetorical, so I said nothing.

Craig finished his wine. "Sure I can't get you one?"

"Incoming," Jayne whispered to me.

I turned to see the tall slim figure of Detective Louise Estrada picking her way through puddles in the Scarlet House driveway, heading our way. Officer Johnson was with her.

"No thanks," I said. "We have to be going." I tried not to break into a run as I descended the steps. Estrada and Johnson had stopped beside Jayne's car, and the detective was peering in the windows.

"I'm here," Jayne called.

Estrada straightened. "You didn't get far."

"We're acquainted with Mr. and Mrs. Jones," I said. "We popped in to say hi as long as we were passing."

For some reason Estrada didn't look as though she believed me. "If Detective Ashburton didn't mention it, don't leave town until we've taken your statements."

I jumped into the car. "No place to go other than home and work. Come along Jayne, don't dawdle."

While we were waiting at the end of the driveway for a break in the line of cars, a Lexus SUV took the corner on two wheels, spraying water everywhere. Robyn Kirkpatrick was driving, her eyes fixed on the road in front of her, her hands tight on the wheel.

"That didn't take long," Jayne said.

"Ryan probably didn't even need to call her. The West London grapevine will be in full force. Wait a minute, will you."

I turned in my seat to watch. Robyn came to a screeching halt in front of a uniformed officer who'd lifted one hand to order her to stop. He bent over and spoke into her window. The bright crime-scene lights illuminated the interior of the car, and I could see her waving her hands in the air. The cop straightened up and spoke into the radio at his shoulder.

A minute later, Ryan came out of the barn and headed her way. He'd found a rain slicker somewhere.

I was interested in hearing what Robyn had to say, but Ryan had told me to leave, and it wouldn't be wise to ignore that request. Or was it an order? Dating a cop had its disadvantages.

"Let's go," I said to Jayne.

*   *   *

Jayne dropped me at the end of my driveway. "Do you need any help?" she asked.

"Help?"

"Asking questions."

I grinned at her. "The best you can do is keep your ears open. Judging by the speed with which Robyn arrived, the news is spreading and fast. Let me know what you hear. You can do one specific thing for me, though. Ask your mother if she knows anything about the house being for sale. The man Craig and Cassie mentioned might be wanting to buy it, but that doesn't necessarily mean it's on the market. The Historical Society owns it, and I can't see them selling it, but you never know."

"I'll ask her."

"Thanks."

I opened the door and swung my legs around, but stopped when Jayne said, "It might be nothing but an unfortunate accident, you know. Just a coincidence it happened after all that . . . ghostly stuff."

"Coincidences happen. But the universe is rarely so lazy."

"You've said that before. I forget the quote."

"From the *Sherlock* TV show. Sherlock talking to his brother Mycroft. The point being, I will assume it is not a coincidence until proven otherwise."

"You don't think . . ." Her voice trailed off.

"Think what?"

"Never mind."

"Do I think Dave Chase was either shoved out of the hayloft door by an angry ghost or so frightened by such that he panicked and fell to his doom in an attempt to escape? No, I do not."

"What do you think happened then?"

"I genuinely have no idea, Jayne. Not yet."

"Ryan won't be pleased if you get yourself involved."

"That's no longer up to me. I am involved. I didn't want anything to do with this supposed ghost hunting, but despite that I was in the house last night. I was with Dave earlier today, only minutes before he died. As were you. Having said that, I promise I will confine myself to satisfying my curiosity by conducting internet searches and asking general questions of involved parties. Nothing more."

"Why do I not believe you?"

I gave her a smile and touched her shoulder. Her long blonde ponytail continued to drip rainwater. "First things first. You need to get home and get yourself warm and dry. As do I. I also haven't forgotten we have a wedding to plan. I can do two things at once."

"You have a business to run."

"Three things. Good night, Jayne."

"'Night Gemma."

Chapter Nine

Peony and Violet greeted me with their usual over-the-top enthusiasm. They weren't so enthusiastic about going outside when they checked the weather conditions, but I managed to shove them out and slam the mudroom door behind them. I kicked off my ruined boots, hung my useless jacket and scarf on a hook to drip onto the tiled floor, and went into the kitchen. I filled the kettle and set it on the stove. By the time I'd done that, the dogs were whining to get back in. I toweled them off as best I could while the kettle came to a boil. When the kettle screamed to announce it was ready, I left the dogs rubbing the last of the rainwater off themselves and onto the carpet and prepared a giant pot of tea. I took a cup with me and hopped into the shower. I stood under the steaming water for a long time, letting it dispel my chill. When I was finally warm, I sipped my tea, toweled off and dried my hair, and dressed in sweatpants, a thick wool jumper, and cuddly reading socks.

I poured a fresh cup of tea and settled on the couch in the den with my iPad.

At first glance, Dave's death appeared to be nothing but an unfortunate accident. He'd been up in the loft, probably getting hay for the donkey and whatever else eats hay. He'd slipped on something—maybe he'd felt unwell and suffered a dizzy spell—and he'd fallen through the open door to the ground below. It wasn't far, and he might have escaped with little more than a broken arm or twisted ankle, but he was unlucky enough to fall at a bad angle, and had broken his neck.

I would have left it at that—and considered the incident to be none of my business—if not for the mysterious events at Scarlet House over the past week. I hadn't imagined the woman's scream, the distressed animals, or the sound of pandemonium breaking loose in the kitchen. Because of these events, which I'd witnessed myself, I couldn't discount the museum workers' stories of misplaced objects and sightings of vaguely shaped people where there should be none.

I don't believe in ghosts, and I'd concluded that someone was playing a prank on the museum for unknown reasons. But Dave's death had upped the stakes considerably. It's possible that he, spooked by all the talk of ghosts, had been frightened by something that wasn't there, tried to run or even jump out of the door, and fell to his death.

Ryan would have full forensic details and autopsy results shortly. If the police concluded it was an accidental death, so be it. Until then . . .

First, I checked the publicly available real estate listings and found no mention of Scarlet House.

I know many of the people involved with the museum from the previous incident , so I started with Cassie and Craig

Jones, whom I had not met previously. He was, as someone had told me, a financial advisor. He'd been with a big firm in New York City for a number of years before striking out on his own and starting his own company, C&C Investment Services. From what I could tell, the business wasn't doing all that well, although that might have more to do with bad timing than bad management. He'd started the venture a few months before the pandemic hit. Searches of online booksellers confirmed that Cassie Jones was the author of a number of moderately successful children's and YA nonfiction books. I went to her web page and saw pictures of the woman I'd met posing on sandy beaches under palm trees or at book signings. From what I know about publishing, which is a good deal, I estimated that Cassie's income from her writing was enough to maintain the couple in a middle-class lifestyle, as long as they had no unnaturally large expenses I didn't know about, while Craig's investment firm fought to find its footing.

I'd barely begun my investigation (aka snooping) when headlights washed the windows, a car stopped outside, and the engine died. I got to my feet and pulled aside the drapes. Ryan had brought Louise Estrada with him. Meaning they had not decided the case had no merit or the killer had confessed; Ryan wasn't here for our date.

Curses.

Violet and Peony, who'd been napping on the carpet at my feet, beat me to the front hall. I opened the door as the police made their way up the path and climbed the steps. The dogs were overjoyed to have company, particularly Ryan because they know him well. Ryan gave them both enthusiastic pats while

Estrada tried to appear as though she wasn't pleased at the attention they lavished on her.

They both wore yellow rain slickers, their mud-encrusted shoes made sloshing noises as they walked, and their hair was sopping wet. Ryan was in need of a haircut, and tonight he'd tried to towel it off without much success. He hadn't combed it back down, and the hair stuck up in all directions. I decided I liked it like that: quite cute. Estrada had tied hers into a messy black ponytail, without looking in a mirror, leaving the hair lopsided and lumpy.

"Miserable night," Ryan said. "The temperature's dropping fast, and that water's going to freeze solid overnight."

I'd had the foresight to throw two fresh towels over the chair in the front hall. I handed them each one. Even Louise Estrada smiled her thanks at me before she rubbed at her face.

"Tea's made," I said. "Or would you like something colder or stronger? I can probably even rustle up a mug of coffee, if you'd prefer that."

"Not for me." Estrada shuddered. "I've had your coffee before."

"Richter made a coffee run for everyone earlier," Ryan said. "We're good, thanks."

"I was surprised to see him at the scene," I said. "I thought he decided to put in for early retirement after his second heart attack."

"Changed his mind when he realized he had nothing to do to fill his time if he left the job. Much to the dismay of all of us on the force," Estrada said. "That last remark is not for public consumption."

I led the way into the living room. The police followed me after kicking off their muddy shoes, and Peony and Violet eagerly followed them. I motioned to my guests to take seats, hoping they wouldn't notice the layer of dust on the furniture. We don't use this room unless we have formal company, and that hadn't happened for some time. I prefer to sit in the den when I'm on my own, particularly in the winter, with real logs burning in the fireplace. Uncle Arthur has his own suite on the first (what Americans call the second) floor.

Uncle Arthur and I jointly own this house, as well as our businesses. It's a saltbox house, a traditional Cape Cod design of one and a half stories, the half being at the front, built in 1756. It's far too large for two people, but Uncle Arthur and I love it for its closeness to town and its historical charm, artfully renovated with thoroughly modern upgrades.

Ryan and I sat down, but Estrada went to the window and looked out into the night.

I wouldn't have expected Ryan to beat about the bush, and he didn't. "Robyn Kirkpatrick arrived shortly after you and Jayne left. Someone had called her, she said, to tell her the police were at the house."

"I suspected as much."

"She informed us that the board held an emergency meeting in the house earlier. That meeting ended around four thirty, and everyone went their separate ways. She gave me the name of those present and said Sharon Musgrave had been left to lock up. I remember Kirkpatrick and Musgrave from the Lamb investigation."

I nodded.

"You and Jayne were at the meeting," Estrada said to the window. "Although you're not only not on their board; you're not even members of the Historical Society."

"Did she tell you why we were there?"

"Briefly," Ryan said. "But at the time I was more interested in what she could tell me about Dave Chase's activities and apparent state of mind."

"State of mind? You don't think he killed himself by jumping out of a first-floor window to a reasonably soft landing? The desired result would be less than guaranteed."

"By state of mind, I meant preoccupied, disturbed. She said not that she'd noticed. Other than them all being concerned by recent events at the museum."

"Robyn Kirkpatrick is totally self-obsessed; she wouldn't have noticed if Dave had been curled up weeping in a corner. Although in fairness, I didn't think he seemed particularly disturbed. No more than the rest of them."

"By which you're alluding to why you'd been called in." Estrada turned and faced me. She shook her head. "I shouldn't have been surprised, but I was. Is there anything you won't stick your proper English nose in?"

"I was invited to, as you call it, 'stick my nose in.' Believe me I didn't do so voluntarily."

"Irrelevant," Ryan said. "Kirkpatrick says Dave went to the barn to check on the animals when the meeting broke up. His car was still in the lot when she left. The others were also leaving, but it was getting dark, and she can't be sure who left when."

"Same for me, I'm afraid," I said. "Jayne and I had no reason to linger, so we did not. Traffic was heavy for January, so it took us about five minutes to drive to the shop, a couple of minutes to discover Jayne's handbag had been left behind and to decide whether to return for it. Six minutes to return to the house, as we had to go west on Baker Street before turning around. We were gone for fifteen minutes, maximum. Did Craig and Cassie Jones have anything to add?" I asked Estrada.

"Only that they were first to leave the meeting and—hey! We're asking the questions here."

"Fill us in on why you were there, Gemma," Ryan said. "If Sharon Musgrave was the last to leave, other than Dave Chase, I should be talking to her first, but considering it's you, I'd like the background before I do that."

I leaned back in my chair, steepled my fingers, and closed my eyes. I heard Violet snuffle and the soft click of Ryan's fingers as he beckoned to her. Peony's nails tapped on the hardwood floor as he hurried across the room to get in on the action. Estrada shifted her feet and sighed. She was as interested in hearing what I had to say as Ryan, but pretending not to be. Outside, a car drove by, splashing rainwater. The rain had taken on a harsher sound as it turned to ice pellets. Not a pleasant night to be out.

I related the story, beginning with what I'd been told had happened earlier in the week, and ending with Jayne, Andy, and me spending Saturday night in the house. I kept my narrative plain and direct, unembellished with speculation or unnecessary drama.

I opened my eyes. Ryan and Estrada were both staring at me.

Estrada spoke first. "This . . . commotion you heard. You don't really think . . ."

"That the house is haunted? No, I do not. Sounds—a woman screaming, crockery breaking—can be reproduced by anyone with a smartphone or digital recorder. Farm animals are not my area of expertise, but I assume they can be frightened." I eyed Violet and Peony. They didn't react badly to thunderstorms, but I knew of dogs who would panic to the point of hurting themselves. "Objects can be moved, and once suspicion is planted in people's minds, it becomes even easier to convince them they're seeing what shouldn't be there. No, the house is not haunted. The important question, therefore, must be, why is someone pretending it is?"

The room fell silent. Eventually Estrada said, "Do you have a theory as to that?"

"I do not. After our night's adventure, I informed the board I wasn't going to do any more. Someone, I thought, was playing a practical joke on them. The death of Dave Chase makes this no longer a practical joke. If he was murdered, that is. Do you have any thoughts regarding that yet?"

Estrada and Ryan exchanged glances. Obviously that information would be confidential, but there was no denying I'd been of help to the police in the past. Whether they wanted my help or not.

I was pleased Estrada was the one who answered. Ryan had no doubt of my abilities. She was less convinced. "Not as yet. That hayloft is, as could be expected, full of hay and dust, not to mention spiders' webs and mouse droppings. And dead mice. We found traces of different footprints, but as the farm is run as a volunteer endeavor several people help with it. We're having the place fingerprinted, but that's going to be a nightmare: old wood, some rot, hay, dust, rusty farm implements. Not to mention that, considering the weather, it's natural for people to be wearing gloves, whether they attempted to disguise their prints or not. Still, we'll be talking to anyone who had reason to be in the hayloft recently."

"There wasn't any hay in the donkey's stable," Ryan said. "We can assume, for now, that Chase went to get some before leaving for the night. Louise and I had a good look around up there, and we can see nothing the man might have tripped over. As Louise mentioned, the barn's old, but it's tidy and well maintained, for a working barn, at any rate. Chase had been helping out at the farm for a couple of years, meaning he should have known his way around up there and how to handle the hay."

"The idea that he might have jumped in some sort of attempt to end it all is ridiculous," Estrada said. "It was only luck—bad luck—that he broke his neck."

"Bad luck for him," Ryan said, "As for whoever caused him to fall, that's still to be determined."

"You believe he was murdered," I said.

"Manslaughter, possibly," Estrada said.

"We're acting on that assumption," Ryan said. "The autopsy's scheduled for tomorrow morning, and that might tell us more. It's entirely possible he had a heart attack or, say, stumbled and lost his footing when he was unfortunately standing close to the open door."

"Do you know anything about Chase's personal life, Gemma?" Estrada asked.

"Nothing. He's a retired vet. I understand he's a widower. I don't know if he has children."

"Robyn Kirkpatrick went into the business office in the house," Ryan said. "She gave us the emergency contact information on Chase's volunteer agreement. A son in California, by the name of Kyle."

I shook my head, indicating I'd never heard of Kyle Chase.

"I called him, and he'll be arriving tomorrow."

"The son says he hasn't seen his dad for a couple of years," Estrada added.

"Were they estranged?" I asked.

"It doesn't appear so. Kyle Chase and his wife are both doctors, and they have teenage kids. Hard for them to get away for a visit, and a lot of older people weren't wanting to travel during the pandemic. We'll be checking his whereabouts over the last couple of days, to confirm."

Ryan stood up, and Louise Estrada stepped away from the window.

"Thank you for your time," he said very formally. "If you can think of anything—"

"I know where to find you. There is one thing you might want to know. I have no idea if it's relevant but . . ."

"Go ahead."

"Thursday afternoon a man was knocking on doors along that section of Harbor Road. He told people he was interested in buying Scarlet House and wanted to know more about the neighborhood."

"How do you know this?" Estrada said.

"Craig Jones told me. I assume he didn't mention it to you?"

She shook her head.

Which, I thought to myself but didn't say, is why I can find out things the police cannot. I ask questions and I observe, but I have no authority behind me. No one has any reason— or they think they don't—to be wary of me. Even people who have nothing to hide can be so intimidated by police attention they become tongue-tied or don't want to "bother" the detectives with trivialities. Trivialities that later prove to be vitally important.

"I didn't know the house was for sale," Ryan said.

"Apparently it's not. It's not listed on any realtor's site anyway. Which begs the question, if the house is not for sale, and someone wants to buy it, what might they do in order to get it onto the market?" I showed my guests out.

I stood at the front window for a long time. The police got into their car, the lights came on, and they drove away. All was quiet on Blue Water Place. I checked my watch—past ten. Late to pay a social call. Not too late for me, but I understand that people don't react well to knocks on their door once they've gone to bed. Not too late, however, for a phone call.

I used my phone to search for the number I needed on 411. com. Sharon Musgrave wasn't exactly an enthusiast of the latest in technology, so I hoped she'd still have a landline. As people increasingly relied on their mobile phones, it was getting harder and harder to find a number if you hadn't been given it. On the other hand, mobile phones make it a great deal easier to track a person's movements and get a record of who they'd called. Unfortunately, the downside of having no proper authority in police matters is that I don't have access to that sort of information. Legally anyway.

"Hello?"

"Hi, Sharon," I said cheerfully, "Gemma Doyle here. I hope I didn't wake you?"

"Gosh, no, Gemma. I've been on the phone. Did you hear what happened? I can't get over it. Dave died. It must have been not long after the meeting. Just goes to show, doesn't it?"

I didn't ask what it went to show. Now was not the time for a metaphysical discussion of the meaning of life and death. "How did you hear?"

"Robyn called me the moment she found out. She would, wouldn't she? She knows how important Scarlet House is to me. I went over there right away. I wanted to check that everything was okay, but the police posted someone on the driveway and I couldn't get close. I told them who I was," she said, sniffing in disapproval, "but they said no admittance. I suggested to Robyn we meet at her house for a planning meeting, but she said she was too upset, and tomorrow would do."

"Plan for what?"

"Damage control, of course. I know you tried to help us identify the reason for the haunting, Gemma, but this is now far beyond your abilities."

"My abilities?"

"We need an exorcism."

"You do?"

"Robyn said the police are regarding Dave's death as an accident. What they call misadventure." That wasn't what they'd told me, but I assumed they wanted to downplay it until they knew more. "We know better, don't we?"

"It might have been an accident, Sharon."

She snorted. "That's what the board will want to put out. I say we have to deal with this and deal with it now before there's another death."

Sharon's mood had shifted quickly. Earlier today she'd been musing about leaving Scarlet House and taking up the life of a baker. Now she was leaping eagerly into full damage control mode. Sharon wanted to be seen as someone important, to have a valuable role to play—that was obvious. How far, I had to ask myself, would she go to get that role?

"I can't say how long it will be before the police let you back onto the property."

"Robyn can be very convincing. Which is why I, in turn, need to convince her to see things my way. No one's going to want their child going to a place where the former residents are actually killing people, now are they?"

"I guess not."

"What will happen to Scarlet House if visitors stop coming? We might get a few ghost hunters, people like you—"

"I'm not—"

She paid me no attention. Sharon was in full flight, and nothing would stop her now. "We rely on school and church youth groups touring the house and farm, families on vacation in summer, gardeners wanting to see our historic gardens. Not ghost hunters. As it is we're struggling to recover from the loss of revenue over the pandemic, which was bad enough, but then there was the fire before that. I won't say the situation is dire—not yet—but if we lose any more income, we'll be in tough straits indeed. I don't suppose you know how much an exorcist charges?"

"Uh, no. Not something I've ever had to consider. What do you mean, 'tough straits'?"

"I don't suppose they're cheap. It must be a very specialized field. Maybe we can find a priest or someone like that who'll do it for free. We're a nonprofit organization— right?—important to the larger community."

"Sharon, what—?"

"I'm making a quick note to ask Robyn if she knows such a person. Someone who'll do it with the utmost secrecy, so to speak. We wouldn't want word getting out. That would do our reputation no good at all. I wonder if I can find any records in the history books of how they did exorcisms in the seventeenth and eighteenth centuries. That would have more effect on our ghost, wouldn't you think?"

Maybe not a good idea. I thought of *The Scarlet Letter* and mass hysteria. This was Massachusetts, after all, and not so far from Salem. Violet jumped onto the couch beside me and I rubbed at her ears. "Sharon, what—?"

"Thanks for calling Gemma. That was a good idea. I'll get right onto it."

"Sharon. Wait! Don't hang up."

"Oh, sorry. Isn't that why you called?"

To suggest an exorcism? "I'm wondering if you've spoken to the police yet."

"What about?"

"What about? About the death of Dave Chase, of course."

"Oh, that. Yes, a detective called me. She wants to come around first thing tomorrow to get my full statement. I told her

The Game Is a Footnote

I don't have the time. I need to meet with Robyn, and it's important we waste no time. But she was quite insistent."

I had no trouble believing that. I was only surprised Estrada hadn't hauled Sharon down to the station to teach her the meaning of *important*. "I've been told you locked up after the meeting was over. Is that right?"

"Yes, I did."

"Did you see Dave when you left?"

"No. He said he was going to check on the animals. I had no need to go into the barn. We don't lock it at night."

"How many cars were in the parking lot when you left?"

"I don't know."

"You didn't notice?"

"I didn't go that way. I walked over, like I usually do, so I left via the kitchen door."

When I'd found Sharon's phone number, it had given me her address as well. I called up a quick mental map of West London and located Sharon's street. North of Scarlet House, running inland. Sharon lived close enough that it wouldn't be a long walk between her place and the museum. Twenty or thirty minutes, maybe.

"I cut through the kitchen garden and out the gate into Westland Road."

"There's a back gate?"

"Oh yes. I use it all the time."

"I don't suppose this gate has a lock."

"Why would it?"

I rolled my eyes to the ceiling. "What did you mean a moment ago when you said the museum was facing a dire situation?"

Sharon sighed. "As you know, we're owned by the West London Historical Society, not by the town or the state. We get a small stipend from them for operating expenses, but it hasn't been enough, and every historical group's competing for the same money. Even more so since the pandemic, of course. We got unofficial word that the state will be slashing the amount it gives us for the next fiscal year. At the same time, everything has gotten so expensive lately. Property taxes are going up, and the cost of animal feed is way up. Plus we had all that work needed after the fire and furniture to replace, and revenue dropped when visitors stopped coming. One of our biggest donors has informed us they won't be making a contribution this year. I didn't mean what I said earlier about leaving the house, Gemma. I don't know what I'll do if we can't keep the museum going and we have to sell Scarlet House. It's"—her voice broke—"my life."

Chapter Ten

I'm not the only one who doesn't hesitate to make late-night phone calls. While I was talking to Sharon, my phone buzzed to tell me I had an incoming call. Serval incoming calls, all from Irene Talbot, crack reporter at the *West London Star*. Irene was a good friend of Jayne and mine, but I knew she wasn't calling for a friendly chat. I sent her a text: *not talkin'*

Irene: *Death at Scarlet House. Sources say you were there.*
Me: *Don't believe everything you hear.*
Irene: *Pleeeeeeze*
Me: *Come to shop tomorrow. Noon.*
Irene: *Shall I wear trench coat sunglasses and fedora?*

I didn't reply.

I sat up for a long time, looking into the financial affairs of Scarlet House. From what I could see from information publicly available (and some not intended to be publicly available) the museum was indeed in "dire straits." They'd raised a substantial amount of money after the fire to repair the house and replace what had been lost, and it had all been spent. Then the pandemic struck, and the number of visitors dropped dramatically. Every nonprofit organization in Massachusetts was in the same situation, and they all had their begging cups out asking for government help. Last year's page on the society's website, thanking "generous donors," showed a substantial donation from "Anonymous," but this year no "Anonymous" was listed. Robyn and Eric Kirkpatrick had given ten thousand dollars last year and another five thousand this year. A generous amount, but not as much as "Anonymous." I tried to access the details of the financial records, but I hit a firewall. Given some time, I could get in, but I decided to leave it, for now. According to Sharon, the museum was in danger of closing. If it did, the donors would want their money back, and that would mean selling the house and property.

Fortuitously, there seemed to be a buyer ready at hand. What a coincidence. Had that buyer decided to edge the museum closer to bankruptcy to sweep in and get the property at fire sale prices? It had to be considered.

I called Ryan.

"What? What?" said a sleep-filled voice.

"Hi. It's Gemma."

"What's happened? Are you all right? I'm on my way."

"Nothing's happened. I had an idea I wanted to share with you."

He groaned. "Okay, I should be used to this by now, but I'm not. Gemma, it's three AM."

"It is? I glanced at the time display in the corner of my iPad. All was quiet outside, and the dogs had gone off to bed. The rain had stopped. "Oh. Sorry. It can wait."

"I've been out in an icy rain all night. I just got in and collapsed into bed. I have a meeting with the team to go over preliminary forensic results and witness statements at six thirty. Never mind. I'm awake now. What's up?"

"If you insist. The financial situation at Scarlet House is not good. It's a nonprofit organization, and expenses are up, way up, and income is down, way down. It looks as though income for the forthcoming year will be down further as the state's cutting back its contribution. And also, a major donor, one who goes by the name of "Anonymous," has dropped out."

"How do you know this?"

"Donors, individual, corporate, and government, are thanked publicly on the web page."

"And revenue figures?"

"Not so public, but let's not worry about that for now."

He groaned, and I carried on quickly. "Mainly I know this because Sharon Musgrave told me. She's the bookkeeper, so she would know exactly what the situation is, and she is seriously worried that the house will have to be sold."

"Okay. And you think . . ."

"I think it's entirely possible a buyer might try to nudge the Historical Society further in the direction of bankruptcy by ruining their reputation, driving visitors away, and upsetting the volunteers."

"If that's the case, it might explain the supposed hauntings, but not the death of Dave Chase. Far too drastic a step."

"Agreed. If this mysterious buyer is not on the museum board, and considering he was canvassing the neighbors without identifying himself, that's almost certainly the case, he would have needed the help of someone inside the museum to get access, to set up the sound devices and so on."

"Dave Chase."

"Entirely possible. Although, it doesn't provide us with any reason why Dave had to die. If he was murdered, that is."

"Okay Gemma, you've given me something to work with. First thing tomorrow, I intend to have a look at Chase's finances. If he'd been paid off to help with this, I might find a record. Is that all?"

"For now."

He chuckled. "So I can go back to sleep?"

"For now."

"Do you know that I love you?"

I was about to say, *for now*, but I bit my tongue. This wasn't a joking matter. I had no doubt about Ryan's feelings for me, and I had absolutely no doubt about my feelings for him. But we'd traveled a rocky road to be together, and our relationship was important to me. He'd accepted my help (aka interference) with other cases, but his partner and his bosses didn't entirely trust me. I feared that one day I'd cross a line I didn't even know was there, and he'd have to decide between his job and me.

"I love you too," I said before I hung up.

Chapter Eleven

Mondays are always slow at the store, particularly in January, so I got up late and enjoyed a leisurely breakfast. Ashleigh was scheduled to open the shop today, and I decided to take advantage of being the boss and going in when I felt like it. I checked the online news from the *West London Star*. The death of Dave Chase was prominent, along with a statement from the chief of the West London police to the effect that an arrest was expected shortly. I read nothing into that: *expected shortly* is standard police political code for "don't have the faintest clue."

The story, bylined Irene Talbot, was brief. She laid out the facts of what had happened, with little speculation. A photo accompanied the article: steady driving rain, hooded figures staring at something at their feet, the old barn looming in the background, traces of red and blue lights breaking the gloom of the night. I peered closely, and thought I saw myself. Jayne and I were standing by the fence, watching people gathering in the barnyard. The photo was grainy, probably taken from a distance. One of the neighbors or a passerby must have taken this picture and sold it to the newspaper. The museum board would not be pleased. They wanted to keep rumors of the supposed haunting of Scarlet House quiet, but this photo could be used on a poster advertising a horror movie.

I'd let the dogs out when I first got up, but once I finished my breakfast, I put the news aside and prepared to take them for a walk. They danced around the mud room while I put on my coat and boots and got down the leashes. I'd peeked outside earlier to see trees sparkling with a layer of ice. The walking would be treacherous, but the sun was shining, and the weather report said the temperatures were above freezing, so the ice shouldn't last long. I decided to take the dogs to the beach today. It was lovely walking there in the winter when no one was around and the sea was deep blue with cold, the shore rimmed with ice as delicately formed as lace. I grabbed my car keys and opened the door. Violet headed straight for the Miata, but Peony wandered off to sniff at a patch of grass. I called to him to come.

A curly white head popped over the hedge at the side of the driveway. "Good morning, Gemma."

Violet raced around the hedge. Peony tried to stuff himself through.

"Good morning, Mrs. Ramsbatten," I said. "Looks like it's going to be a nice day."

"A reward for us putting up with the storms of the last couple of days. Are you off to work? Don't let me keep you."

"Not yet. We're going to the beach for a walk."

My neighbor smiled at me. The hedge between us shook as Peony encountered a tangle of branches. Violet whined at Mrs. Ramsbatten, demanding attention.

"I heard the news on the radio. Dave Chase died yesterday. I'm so sorry. Do you know what happened, dear?"

"No."

"But you were there. You and Jayne. I saw your picture in the paper."

Mrs. Ramsbatten was in her eighties. She'd recently lost her driver's license when she failed the eye test. I assumed that was a distance problem only. Obviously nothing was wrong with her ability to see things close up. "Tea, dear?"

"Whyever not," I said. "But first . . ." I bent over and grabbed Peony by his wiggling hips. He was quite thoroughly stuck. I pulled, and he barked and wiggled and eventually he backed out of the tangle. He rounded the hedge as though his dignity wasn't disturbed in the least. I followed.

We climbed the steps to the house and went inside. Mrs. Ramsbatten helps care for the dogs when Uncle Arthur's away and I'm at the shop all day. She and her friends from the West London Garden Club maintain our garden, as I have a black thumb, and Uncle Arthur, who spent almost all of his adult life at sea, has no interest.

"Have a seat, dear," she said. "I'll put the kettle on and be right back."

She bustled off to the kitchen, and I settled myself on a pink damask-covered chair while the dogs rushed about the room, sniffing at everything.

There was a lot to sniff at. Mrs. Ramsbatten called herself a collector. She collected everything. And I mean everything. Every tabletop (and there were a lot of tiny tables) was covered with ornaments: porcelain dolls of various sizes with colorful dresses and painted cheeks, animal figures ranging from a dog much like Peony to a tusked elephant, Wedgewood and Royal Doulton teacups, souvenir plates from the Florida panhandle or Michigan, lighthouse models from the Outer Banks. On the walls, paintings hung so close together they almost overlapped: everything from good Cape Cod scenes by well-known artists, to velvet images of tropical sunsets, to a poor reproduction of the Mona Lisa. The collection of clocks alone could fill a shop. I ran my finger across the foot-high statue of the Bodie Island Lighthouse on the table beside me and checked for dust. Not a speck.

I put the statue down as Mrs. Ramsbatten bustled in with the tea tray. A proper tea tray too, with a tea pot covered by a knitted cozy, two china cups in matching saucers, a small jug of milk, and a bowl of sugar. She'd added a plate of chocolate biscuits as well as two dog treats.

"This is new." I held up the lighthouse statue.

"A gift." She found a place for the tray on the least crowded of the tables. "From the daughter of a good friend who works in a library in that lighthouse. Isn't that charming?" She tucked her skirts underneath herself and sat down. "Shall I pour, dear?"

"Please do."

"Have you seen Lauren lately?" she asked me as she served the tea. She added a splash of milk and a few grains of sugar without asking and put a chocolate biscuit on the saucer. Also without asking.

Lauren Tierney was twelve years old, and she knew Mrs. Ramsbatten from when she'd stayed with me for a few days last year. "She came into the shop last week, needing a book for a gift to take to a birthday party. She seems to be doing well at her new school. She's made friends and has joined some of the social clubs."

"I'm glad. Now, to matters at hand. Dave Chase. What happened?" The sharp blue eyes studied my face.

"He fell out of the hay loft. Broke his neck on the ground below, in the pig enclosure."

"An accident?"

"Still to be determined. Some of the board members were at the house for an emergency meeting earlier, and Dave went to tend to the animals before he left." I shrugged. "No one knows what happened after that."

"Why were you there?"

I explained about returning for Jayne's bag. "Do you know anything about the financial affairs of the Historical Society? Particularly as regards Scarlet House?"

"The West London Historical Society is Scarlet House," she said. "They have no other interests. What do you mean by financial affairs? Do you suspect skullduggery is afoot?"

"Not necessarily." I sipped my tea. Earl Grey and properly made. Violet and Peony had swallowed their treats in one gulp and were once again following their noses around the room. "Times are tough for nonprofits everywhere. I'm only wondering."

"I'm not on the board. Just a volunteer, and a recent volunteer at that, so I'm not party to their financial affairs. Would you like me to join the board? Perhaps the budget committee?" Her blue eyes twinkled. "I can be a spy."

I smiled at her. "A woman after my own heart. No need. Those things take time. You know a lot of people in the community. Have you heard anything about the house possibly being sold?"

"Sold! Good heavens, no. Where did you get that idea?"

"A vague rumor."

"No reason I'd know about it, I suppose. I can ask around. I can't imagine Sharon Musgrave being okay with that, Gemma. Her enthusiasm for the house is beyond what I'd call reasonable."

"What about Robyn?"

"Robyn? My impression is that being the chair of the board of an important historical site is more important to Robyn than the house itself. She values her position in the community, Robyn does. If there wasn't a Scarlet House, she'd be the chair of the symphony or the art gallery or something similar."

"That's my feeling also. Did you know Dave Chase well?"

"Hardly at all. He spent most of his time out in the barn. He came into the kitchen now and again to warm up and have a cup of coffee, but that's about all. I don't know that we ever exchanged one word other than hello and goodbye. He was a retired veterinary surgeon, I believe. He liked animals."

It wasn't easy, but I made room on the side table and put my empty cup down and started to stand. "I won't keep you any longer."

"One more minute, please dear. About the things that were supposedly moving around in the house. The original reason for you being brought in. Has anything else happened on that front?"

I dropped back down and told her about the events of Saturday night. Her eyes opened wider and wider as I spoke. "Surely you don't think—"

"That the house is haunted? No, I don't. I believe someone wants to make it *appear* the house is haunted, and they're doing a good job of it. I find it hard to believe Dave's death is unrelated."

"What happens next?"

"Nothing. It's over. The mysterious events at the house, I mean. Things went too far, and a man died. By accident or misadventure or malice aforethought, I don't know. The police will get to the bottom of what happened to Dave, eventually. In the meantime, the person or persons responsible for the strange events will be so spooked, no pun intended, they'll keep their heads down."

"You're sure of that, dear?"

"Absolutely."

* * *

I arrived at Mrs. Hudson's Tearoom shortly after twelve. The restaurant was about half full with the regular lunch crowd from shops and businesses along Baker Street, and the lineup for take-out service was short. "Is Jayne in the back?" I asked Fiona when it was my turn to be served.

"Where else would she be?"

"Fair enough. Never mind the tea today. I'll have a roast beef sandwich please."

"No tea! Alert the press." She handed me a prewrapped sandwich, and I ducked around the counter to stick my head in the kitchen. "Hey there. Goodness, are you on strike?"

Jayne was leaning against the counter, munching on a scone, a fresh cup of coffee resting next to her. Her apron was streaked with melted chocolate and her right cheek dotted with flour. "Most amusing. I'm not allowed a refreshment break?"

"No."

"Are you just getting here? You're late today."

"I'm expecting it to be a slow day, so Ashleigh can handle it. I had tea with Mrs. Ramsbatten, and then the dogs and I went for a lovely long walk along the beach. There's nothing like the morning after a storm. Did you see our picture in the online paper?"

"I did not. And I do not want to."

"Just as well. Did you give your statement to the police?"

"Yeah. Louise came in earlier. I didn't have a lot to say. They knew why we'd been at the house, and I don't know anything about what might have happened to Dave." She popped the last piece of scone into her mouth, picked up her coffee mug, and said, "Did you solve the case overnight?"

"Sadly no. If you hear anything more about Scarlet House being for sale, can you let me know?"

"You think that's significant?"

"Until I learn otherwise, yes. Invite your mum to come for tea at four o'clock. I have a few questions about the Historical Society."

The timer next to the stove dinged, and Jayne put down the coffee and reached for her mitts. "Will do." A wave of heat hit me as she opened the oven door and took out a tray of golden shortbread.

"Maybe save some of those for your mum," I said.

"You mean save them for you."

"That too. Cheerio. Have a nice day." I waved my sandwich bag at her and left Jayne to her cinnamon-and-sugar-scented domain.

The sliding door between our businesses was open and I went into the Sherlock Holmes Bookshop and Emporium.

A handful of customers browsed the shelves. Irene Talbot was standing at the sales counter, chatting to Donald Morris. Moriarty was stretched out on the counter between them, allowing Irene to stroke his belly. Donald wore a Harris-tweed sports jacket, blue tie, and ironed trousers. He'd tossed his favorite Inverness cape onto the stool behind the counter.

Oops. I'd forgotten that I'd arranged to meet Irene here at noon. "Good morning, all," I said.

"Good afternoon," Irene replied, pointedly checking her watch.

"Is it that late already? Sorry."

A gorgeous arrangement of fresh flowers, white lilies and pale peach roses in a clear glass vase, stood on the shelf against the wall, beneath a framed print of the cover of Beeton's Christmas Annual, December 1887, and the glass statue that had been awarded to Uncle Arthur for his enthusiastic promotion of the exploits of the Great Detective. "Those flowers are lovely. Did you bring them?"

"My gift to you, dear," Donald said with a small bow. "I haven't been in for a while and when I passed the florist, I hoped they might liven up the shop on a dreary winter's day."

"That was very thoughtful. Thank you." I was touched by the gesture and thus didn't tell Donald that lilies are most commonly used in sympathy bouquets.

"I've come for that new biography of Sir Arthur you called to tell me was in," he said.

"It's upstairs. I'll run up and get it."

A couple of people were studying the volumes on the non-fiction shelf, and I suddenly realized something wasn't quite right. "Donald, why are you behind the counter, and where's Ashleigh?"

"I don't know."

"You don't know?"

"I know why I'm behind the counter—I'm working for you in the absence of anyone else. I arrived about an hour ago, Gemma. The door was open. I called, but no one answered. Some customers came in, so I helped them. You remember I did that the time you had to rush Jayne to the hospital."

"Yes, but—"

"I sold two copies of the complete set of the originals, copies of *Observations by Gaslight* by Lyndsey Faye, *Castle Shade* by Laurie R. King, *The Disappearance of Inspector Lestrade* by Bob Madia, and several of the "I-am-Sherlocked" mugs. The others paid cash when I asked, but one lady didn't have any on her, so she said she'd return later and pay because I still haven't quite worked out how to accept credit. I hope that's all right?"

"Yeah, fine. Did you check the loo?"

"Why would I do that?"

"For Ashleigh?"

"Not specifically, but I did call out."

"Wait here." I ran up the seventeen steps to the first floor, Moriarty hot on my heels. If I ever again open a bookshop, I will not get one with the offices and storage rooms on an upper level and no lift. The door to the small washroom was open, and one glance told me no one was inside. Overseen by Moriarty, I checked the storage rooms and my office. Nothing.

I ran back down, barely avoiding plunging to my doom as the cat wound himself between my legs.

Donald had gone to assist the shoppers. He was piling books into their arms, chatting about the merits of joining a Sherlockian society, while they blinked in confusion.

"Not there?" Irene asked.

"No."

"Sir Arthur was, of course, deeply interested in spirituality," Donald said. "There should be a copy of *Through a Glass, Darkly* here somewhere. Let me see—"

"We're only browsing," the woman said.

"Not a problem," Donald replied. "Won't be a moment."

She staggered to the counter under the weight of the books and dropped them with a distinct thud. Moriarty, fresh from having attempted to kill me, leapt up next to her. She smiled and gave him a pat. "What a lovely cat. Yes, you are so lovely aren't you, big boy? Or girl. Are you a girl?"

"Boy," Irene said. I'd taken out my phone and was calling Ashleigh.

"Will you look at the time, Betty," the man called, as Donald located the volume he was looking for and shoved it into the man's hands. "We have that boat to catch."

Betty didn't stop admiring Moriarty. "Boat?"

"Yes. You know. The boat cruise."

"Oh, right. The boat cruise. I suppose I should buy one book. It can be a Christmas gift for your father."

"Christmas is eleven and a half months away," he said.

"If you're interested in the spiritual life of the Victorians in general," Donald turned back to the shelves, "you'll enjoy—"

The man shoved the book onto the shelf and made a break for the door while Donald's back was turned. His female companion tore her attention away from Moriarty, much to the cat's displeasure, lifted the topmost volume off the pile, put it aside, and said, "I'll take that one please."

"Gemma?" Irene said.

I looked up from my phone. "What?"

"Lady wants to buy a book?"

"She does?"

"Yes, she does. You run a bookstore, right?"

"Oh yeah. Sorry." I went behind the counter, rang up the purchase, accepted her credit card and ran it through the computer, stuffed the book in a bag, and handed it to her. "Have a nice day. Do come back another time."

She gave me a long look, said goodbye to Moriarty, and left at a rapid pace. Moriarty smirked.

I followed the customers, flipped the sign to "Closed," and locked the door.

"What are you doing?" Donald said. "Those people will discuss what books they want to buy and come back."

"You don't have a key to the building," I said. "Therefore the shop was open when you arrived."

"Yes, but—"

"The tearoom opens before the Emporium, so they don't unlock the joining door, we do. All of which means Ashleigh was here this morning. She is not here now, and she did not lock the shop when she left. She's not answering her phone."

"Is her purse here?"

"It's not in the upstairs storage room, where she usually leaves it, but she doesn't always carry a bag. Not if today's outfit has baggy enough pockets to keep her keys and some cash. She walks to work."

"What do you think happened?" Irene asked.

"I don't know. And I do not like not knowing." I went to the rear of the shop to check that door. Locked, as it should be. I opened it and peered outside. The alley was quiet. I made another call. "Gale, hi. Gemma here."

"Good afternoon Gemma. How are—?"

"Have you heard from Ashleigh today?"

"Ashleigh? No. Should I have? Was I supposed to work today? I'm sorry, but—"

"I wasn't expecting you. It's just that I'm not entirely sure where Ashleigh is at the moment."

"What does that mean?"

"Can you come in? I'll pay time and a half for the short notice."

"Happy to. I've nothing on today. When do you want me?"

"Now."

"Uh. Okay."

I hung up and turned to see Irene, Donald, and Moriarty staring at me.

"You think something's happened to Ashleigh?" Irene said.

"She's a responsible employee. If she'd taken ill or had a family emergency and had to leave, she would have called me. She would have locked the door when she left."

"Maybe she tried, and you didn't answer," Donald said.

"I've had no missed calls today. Wait here." I ran into the tearoom. This time I didn't bother to take my place in the line and wait my turn. "Fiona, did you see Ashleigh today?"

"She gave me a wave when she opened the door."

"What time was this?"

"I didn't look, but I assume it was nine thirty, when the store opens. Isn't she there?"

I next went into the kitchen. Jayne was scooping batter into cupcake tins, and Jocelyn was unloading the dishwasher. I asked them if they'd seen Ashleigh, and they both replied in the negative.

If Ashleigh had taken ill so suddenly she needed assistance, she would have come to the tearoom. If she'd called for an ambulance, surely someone would have seen it and all the kerfuffle the arrival of medics involves. If she'd staggered out into the street, people would have helped her, and it would have been noticed in the tearoom, even if the Emporium had no customers at the time.

I ran across the street, too preoccupied to wave a thank-you to the cars screeching to a halt in front of me.

By the time I got to the far sidewalk, Maureen was standing in her doorway. "That was dangerous," she said. "Don't they teach children in England to look both ways before crossing the street?"

"Have you seen Ashleigh today?" I was of the opinion that the only reason Maureen owned a shop on Baker Street was so she could keep a disapproving eye on everything. She certainly didn't spend much time actually working. The front windows were still full of tacky Christmas decorations and seasonal merchandise such as bad drawings of Father Christmas relaxing on a snow-covered beach. "Ashleigh? You mean the girl who works for you? The one with the weird clothes? She opened up, spot on time. I was pleased to see that. You have a haphazard approach to the running of your business, Gemma. More than once I've had to mention your irregular hours to the Baker Street BIA, not that I wanted to complain, of course, but we have standards to maintain on the street."

"Did you see her again? After nine thirty?"

"I don't spend all day standing at my windows watching your store, Gemma."

"Sure you do, Maureen."

Her lips tightened, and I realized that if I was going to get anything out of her, I'd have to be nice. I smiled. It wasn't easy.

She huffed. "No."

"No? You didn't see her again?"

"Why are you asking? Can't you keep track of your own employees?"

It would appear that I couldn't keep track of my own employees. Not today anyway. I said nothing, simply continued smiling inanely.

Maureen relented. "I might have observed some movement in the store after opening, but it's hard to tell in the daylight. A few customers arrived." She sniffed in disapproval, and I took that to mean that the Emporium had more customers today than did Beach Fine Arts. "Around eleven, I had a delivery at the back door. An important collection of original Cape Cod art. I had to receive the goods, ensure the clumsy deliveryman didn't break anything, and then decide exactly where to best display the new pieces. The next time I looked outside, to check the weather conditions, of course, I saw that silly man arriving."

"Silly man?"

"The one who thinks he's Sherlock Holmes. Unmistakable in that ridiculous coat with the little cape stuck on the top."

"Donald Morris." Donald didn't think he was Sherlock Holmes. He simply wanted to imitate his idol.

"He didn't come out again, and not long after Irene from the newspaper went into your store. Maybe ten minutes later, you walked up the street and went into the tearoom."

Sherlock Holmes had the Baker Street Irregulars. I had Maureen McGregor. Just as good.

"Thank you." I turned to go.

Maureen fell into step beside me. "As long as she's here, Irene I mean, I'll pop into your store and speak to her about my new art display. I want to get a feature in the paper, but she's not returning my calls."

"I'll send her over, why don't I? Looks like you have a customer."

A woman had slowed as she approached us. She hadn't actually stopped, and she wasn't actually looking into the window of Beach Fine Arts. But, just in case she was interested, I didn't want Maureen to miss out on a sale.

Maureen half turned to look behind her, and I bolted across the street. Fortunately, this time no cars were coming.

While I'd been out, Gale had arrived and the shop had reopened. Jayne, still wearing her hairnet and apron, had joined Donald.

"Where's Irene?" I asked.

"She saw you talking to Maureen and fled before Maureen could march over here and waylay her. I gather she's been dodging Maureen all week," Jayne said. "I told Jocelyn to watch the cupcakes and came in to find out what's going on. What is going on? Donald says you can't find Ashleigh."

"Ashleigh was here at nine thirty for opening. She left sometime between eleven and eleven thirty," I said. "She walked out, leaving the door unlocked and the sign saying 'Open.' She's not answering her phone." I tried again. It immediately went to voicemail. "Ashleigh," I said, "Gemma again. I am getting worried. Please call me."

The chimes over the door tinkled cheerfully, and three nicely dressed, silver-haired women came in. They were laden with bags from shops up and down Baker Street, giving them the appearance of serious buyers. "Gale," I said, "can you mind the shop, please. Ashleigh might have taken ill. I'm going to her place to check on her."

"Sure," Gale said to me, and then she called to the women, "Let me know if you need any help, ladies." She grabbed the pile of nonfiction books the earlier customer had abandoned and took them to where they belonged.

"Allow me to accompany you, Gemma," Donald said. "If something unfortunate has occurred, you might need manly assistance."

Neither Jayne nor I laughed. Donald did mean well, and his quick thinking had saved my life when we were in England. "Do you know where she lives, Gemma?"

"I've never been there, but I know her address. We can walk."

"I'm coming with you." Jayne pulled off her hairnet, and her long blonde ponytail sprang free. She stuffed the net into her pocket. "Safety in numbers, and all that."

"Okay. Gale, call me if you hear from Ashleigh."

"Will do."

Ashleigh had an apartment above a shop a couple of blocks further up Baker Street, away from the ocean. We walked quickly. I hadn't taken my coat off, and Donald had swept up his Inverness cape before heading for the door. Jayne was wearing a short-sleeved T-shirt, but the sun shone brightly in a clear sky, and the wind was light, and we didn't have far to go. The sunshine had done it's work, and the residue of ice deposited last night dripped from the overhead wires and tree branches. An icy drop landed on the top of my head.

"What do you think's happened, Gemma?" Donald asked.

"You, of all people, should know it is a capital mistake to theorize without data. And I, at this time, have absolutely not one iota of data."

"Can't you take a guess?" Jayne said.

I didn't reply. Ashleigh's address was in my employee files as 508 Baker Street, apartment two. A shoe shop occupied the ground level at that number. I stood on the sidewalk, looking up. The building was two stories tall. Curtains were drawn across the apartment windows. A small door—wood warped, paint flaking—was inset between the shoe shop and a computer repair establishment. I turned the handle, and it opened easily. I stepped into the dark hallway, and Jayne and Donald squeezed in behind me. A steep staircase wrapped in deep gloom led directly up. There were no windows. Jayne found the light switch and flicked it. A forty-watt bulb came to life, giving barely enough illumination for us to see by. I went first. The stairs ended at a small landing, with doors leading off either side. I knocked on the door to the left, the one with a number two hanging crookedly from a rusty nail. I put my ear to the door but heard nothing. I knocked again and called, "Ashleigh, are you in there? It's Gemma."

I could hear Donald and Jayne's breathing and cars driving past on the street. Otherwise, all was quiet. I rapped on the door, louder this time. I phoned Ashleigh's number and held my ear to the door once again, trying to detect the sound of ringing from inside. Nothing.

Donald began patting his pockets. "Why don't we leave a note under the door? I have paper here somewhere."

This was an old building, as most of the ones on Baker Street are, and the lock appeared to have not been updated since the first tenant moved in. I found a straight pin in a side pocket of my handbag and crouched in front of the door. I slipped the end of the pin into the lock.

"Do you think that's a good idea, Gemma?" Jayne said. "She's been missing not much more than an hour."

"In situations such as this," I said, "time may be of the essence." A couple of deft twists, and I heard the tumblers click. I haven't had to pick a lock in several years, and I was rather pleased that my skills had not deserted me. I pulled leather gloves out of my coat pocket, put them on, and gently opened the door. "I'm coming in, Ashleigh," I called as I stepped over the threshold. "Don't touch anything," I said to my companions.

A row of hooks, hung with layers of coats and scarves, was next to the door on both sides, boots and shoes of all types lined beneath. Beyond that lay the living room. The room was comfortably and casually furnished with a cheap secondhand sofa set, a scarred coffee table, a plywood build-it-yourself bookcase, and a large-screen TV, turned off. Everything was clean and organized. The curtains were pulled across one wall, a hallway led in the other direction, and a small kitchen opened directly onto the main room. The appliances were dated but clean. A few dirty dishes and glasses were stacked on the counter next to the sink. Other than that, the kitchen was tidy, but not excessively so.

Light flooded into the room, and I turned to see Donald pulling back the drapes. "Best not to touch anything," I said. He pulled his hands away with a gasp.

Three doors led off the dark hallway. I opened the first. A bathroom. Towels draped over the towel rack, makeup spread across the counter, toothbrush and toothpaste in a stand, shower curtain open. I touched the towels with my elbow, and then did the same to the inside of the shower curtain. Both were dry. The next door opened onto a bedroom. The bed was roughly made, covered by a flower-patterned duvet. A dresser held jewelry boxes, a box of tissues, and more makeup. A copy of *An Unexpected Peril* by Deanna Raybourn lay on the night table, an Emporium bookmark about a quarter of the way in.

I opened the closet door. It was, as I would have expected, stuffed full of clothes and accessories. Two pink suitcases and a well-used backpack were on the floor next to a tumble of shoes.

I left Ashleigh's bedroom and peeked in the final room. It might have been the wardrobe room of a repertoire theater. I recognized Ashleigh's safari outfit, her ladies-who-lunch dresses and suits, her gardening attire, the tailored blue or gray business suits, frilly dresses in shades of pink and lilac. One wall was lined with still more shoes and hats. I did not see my employee.

"She does have a lot of things," Jayne said.

"She's not here," I said. "Let's go."

"What now?" Donald asked when we were again gathered on the small landing.

I thought. As Jayne had said, Ashleigh could hardly be called missing. She'd been seen not much more than a couple of hours ago. Her behavior, however, was uncharacteristic enough to have me seriously worried. As I said, I don't put much stock into coincidences: less than twenty-four hours previously, I had discovered a dead body, quite possibly the result of murder most foul.

I led the way down the stairs and onto the street. When we were standing in the winter sunshine, I took out my phone once again and placed a call.

"Gemma?" Ryan said. I heard the muffled sound of a car engine.

"Are you busy?"

"Am I busy? What kind of a question is that? I have a fresh murder case on my desk. Of course I'm busy."

"If it's convenient, can you come at once? Never mind that: even if it's inconvenient, can you come at once? Something's happened that might relate to the Dave Chase situation."

"Louise and I have just left the bank, and we haven't gone far. We've passed the Emporium and are currently heading west on Baker Street."

"What do you know? Coincidences do happen. I think I see you." I stepped off the sidewalk and lifted my free hand.

Louise Estrada's car came to a screeching halt inches from my toes. The driver of the car behind her leaned on the horn. Ryan leapt out, grabbed my arm, and pulled me to the sidewalk. Louise drove slowly away, presumably searching for a place to park.

"Are you nuts!" Ryan yelled at me. "Jayne, Donald, can't you keep this woman under some sort of control?"

Jayne and Donald wisely said nothing.

I shook my arm free. "No harm done. I got your attention."

The anger disappeared in a flash, to be replaced by a soft gentle smile. "Okay, sorry I yelled. You gave me a fright, that's all. You certainly know how to keep life interesting, Gemma. What's up?"

Car safely parked, Louise Estrada joined us. I explained the situation as briefly and succinctly as I could. Jayne nodded enthusiastically, and Donald added to the narrative. Donald was not clear and succinct, and eventually Louise cut him off.

"You are kidding me," she said when I'd finished. "This woman was seen at nine thirty this morning calmly going about her business, and you lot are racing around town trying to make it into a kidnapping? Let's go, Detective."

"Kidnapping?" Jayne said. "Oh my gosh, I never considered that. Who would kidnap Ashleigh?"

"Hold on a sec," Ryan said. "I understand why you're concerned, Gemma. You know Ashleigh well enough to trust her with your business, but she's an adult woman, and she's not answering her phone. I can't start an investigation based on that."

"It's uncharacteristic of her," I said.

"I understand, Gemma," Estrada said.

I stared at her. "You do?"

"She's your employee, and you might even consider her to be a friend. You're worried. But Detective Ashburton's right. We can't do anything about it. Not without a heck of a lot more. I suggest you call the hospitals. She might have felt unwell and grabbed a cab."

"Not without locking the door," I said firmly. "And letting me know what was going on."

"You don't know that," Ryan said. "Maybe she's not as dedicated to your store as you think she is. Maybe, for reasons of her own, she decided to quit and didn't think she owed you an explanation. Did you check the cash register?"

"No," I admitted.

"I did," Donald said. "When I processed a sale in the absence of a store employee to do it. There was some cash, but I didn't count it."

"We don't do much business in cash these days," I said.

"No one does," Jayne added.

"Was anything out of place in the shop? Any signs she might have left not entirely of her own free will?" Ryan asked.

I had to admit I'd seen nothing amiss. "Donald, you arrived before me. Did you tidy anything up?"

"No," he said. "Everything was as expected."

"Too bad we can't ask Moriarty," Jayne said.

"Moriarty was his normal self when I arrived," Donald said. "If that means anything."

"It does," I said. "If there had been a recent disturbance, he would have been agitated."

"Why don't you go around to her house and see if she went home sick? She might have simply forgotten to call you," Estrada said. "Do you know where she lives?"

"Here," I said.

"Here?"

I pointed up. "There. I knocked on her apartment door but got no answer."

"That's right," Donald added quickly. "Gemma knocked. Quite forcefully. She didn't break in. That wouldn't be right."

Ryan shook his head.

"What are you saying, Mr. Morris?" Estrada asked.

"Donald's saying nothing," I said. "He's telling you what happened."

"We have to be going," Ryan said. "If you haven't heard from Ashleigh by this time tomorrow, call me again, and I'll see what I can do. But until then . . ." He shrugged.

"I understand," I said. "Speaking of work, any developments on the Chase case?"

Ryan lowered his voice. Donald and Jayne instinctively stepped closer. People swerved around, most paying us no attention, although one or two threw curious glances our way. "We've been to his bank. Nothing out of the ordinary there, far as they can tell. No excessive or unusual withdrawals or deposits. The investigation is ongoing. We did a canvass of houses near the museum this morning. A neighbor reported that someone had been asking about the area, probably with an eye to buying, but that person didn't say which house he was interested in."

"Did you get a description?"

"Averaged-sized, middle-aged white male in a winter coat."

"Any forensic evidence from the deceased's body or the hayloft?"

"As I said, the investigation is ongoing."

"Which means," Estrada added, "as the people who were first on the scene, we're expecting you and Jayne here to contact us if you remember anything. Anything. And to do so immediately."

"Naturally," I said. "One more thing . . ."

"Only one?" she asked.

"For now. What do you know about a woman who calls herself Bunny Leigh?"

Ryan and his partner exchanged glances. Ryan's face was blank, but Estrada said, "Old-time pop star. Before my time, but some people remember her, and they're excited about her being seen around the area. I heard she's taken a house near here for the winter, but that's only as a matter of common gossip. She hasn't come to police attention. Why are you asking?"

"No reason."

"Like I believe that," Estrada said. "Keep it to yourself. We're done here, and you'd better get Jayne inside before she turns into an ice sculpture."

I looked at my friend. Jayne had wrapped her arms tightly around herself, and she was bouncing on her toes. She was shaking and her lips had turned blue. "I'm f-f-fine." Her teeth clattered.

"She's fine," I said.

Donald swept off his Inverness cape and gallantly tossed it over Jayne's shoulders.

Estrada walked away. Ryan gave me a half wink, and the edges of his mouth turned up in the smallest of private smiles before he followed her.

The clerk in the shoe shop was watching us through the windows. I went in to ask if he'd seen Ashleigh today and got a negative reply. I then asked if he'd heard any excessive noise coming from the flat above this morning, and he gave me a blank stare. I got the same results at the computer store.

Chapter Twelve

I walked back to the Emporium with Donald and Jayne.

"Can you call her friends?" Jayne suggested.

"I know next to nothing about Ashleigh's private life. She's only been in West London for a couple of years, and the Emporium's the only job she's had here. I've never seen her outside the shop or the tearoom except once in the grocery store. She's friendly to everyone who comes in, but not excessively so, as though she's greeting a personal friend. She's never mentioned a boyfriend."

"Doesn't mean she doesn't have one," Jayne said.

"She did tell me she went out with a friend on Friday." I looked up the number for the fish market and asked for Wendy. I heard noses in the background, and then a woman came to the phone.

"Sorry to bother you at work. My name's Gemma Doyle—"

"The woman from the bookstore."

"Yes. Ashleigh Saunderson works for me, and I understand you're a friend of hers."

"I am, yeah. What's happened?"

"Nothing to worry about. I seem to have misplaced her, and I was wondering if you've spoken to her today."

"Nope. No reason I should have."

"When you saw her on Friday, did she say anything about plans she might have been making, maybe to go away?"

"No. Why?"

"Thank you." I hung up.

"Nothing?" Jayne said.

"Nothing. I know I keep saying it, but Ashleigh's a reliable employee. She wouldn't have decided to run away with some random man—or woman—on the spur of the moment, leaving the door open and me unnotified."

"Maybe she didn't have any choice?" Jayne said.

"Possible," I admitted. "But for the moment, I'll consider that unlikely. In the middle of the day, leaving through the front door into a busy street?"

Was it possible? Anything was possible, including that someone had kidnapped Ashleigh as a warning or threat to me. In that case, I would expect to have received a message by now.

We parted at the doorway to the Emporium. Jayne gave Donald his coat and went back to work in Mrs. Hudson's, and Donald said if I didn't need him any longer, he'd be off home.

The police weren't going to look for Ashleigh, and I accepted that they had procedures to follow. I, however, could do exactly what I wanted, and I intended to. My question to Ryan and Estrada about Bunny Leigh hadn't come completely out of the blue. She'd been in the Emporium at least three times. A substantial number of people come into the Emporium, and I wasn't going to try to hunt them all down. But the former pop star hadn't been browsing; she hadn't been admiring my merchandise, looking for a good book, or shopping for gifts. She'd been watching Ashleigh.

I needed to know why.

I opened the door. The chimes tinkled overhead, and three faces turned to me. Gale's held a question, and I shook my head. The two women with her were Robyn Kirkpatrick and Sharon Musgrave.

"Oh good," Robyn said. "You're back. We've been waiting."

"I'm sorry, but this isn't a good time."

"We realize you're working," Robyn said, "but we only want a few minutes of your time." She glanced around the Emporium. A handful of people browsed, and a young couple came in from the tearoom, take-out cups in hand. "Do you have somewhere we can talk? In private."

I sighed. "My office. Upstairs. Gale, if you hear from Ashleigh, let me know immediately."

Moriarty broke away from sniffing Donald's flowers and bounded up the stairs ahead of us. I showed my visitors into my office and asked them to take a seat. They glanced around. I only have one visitor's chair, and it was piled high with books waiting to be shelved. "You can move those books and take a seat." I dropped into the chair behind my desk.

Robyn picked up the books and looked around, searching for someplace to put them. Finding nothing suitable, she handed them to Sharon and sat. She was well dressed, as she usually was. A calf-length, navy-blue cashmere and wool coat with a wide collar and double rows of gold buttons. A blue scarf, black leather boots, black slacks. Her hair was perfectly arranged and her makeup immaculate. But all that careful grooming couldn't hide the purple circles beneath her eyes or the worry lines radiating from the corners of her mouth.

Sharon dumped the books onto the floor. Never as perfectly put together as Robyn, the signs of worry were even more prominent on her face. Her coat was missing a button, the edges of her scarf were unravelling, and her boots were scarred with signs of age and use. One bootlace dragged on the floor.

Moriarty perched on a high shelf and watched us through narrowed eyes. His tail twitched.

"I assume you're here about what happened at the museum last night," I said. "If someone told you I'm the one who found Dave's body, they were right. I didn't see what happened, and I can't tell you anything more, even if I knew anything more, which I don't. You showed up mighty fast last night, Robyn. How did you hear?"

"Cassie Jones called me. She said the police were at the house. A lot of police. With all that's been happening—" She sighed. "I wanted to find out for myself."

"Poor Dave," Sharon said. "I can't believe it."

"Did you know him well?" I asked.

"Only from the museum," Robyn said. "He joined us about two years ago. He was an invaluable member of our little group. So dedicated to the animals and the Scarlet House Farm."

I glanced at Sharon. She nodded enthusiastically as Robyn spoke.

"You didn't socialize outside the museum?"

Two heads shook. "Dave was a private person," Robyn said. "If he did come to social functions, he kept largely to himself and left early. His wife died some years ago, and he doesn't see his only son much, if at all."

I said nothing. Robyn shifted in her chair. Sharon shuffled her feet. Moriarty's tail twitched. The screen saver on my computer featured the stately homes of England. At the moment it was showing Highclere Castle, familiar to fans of Downton Abbey. I don't quite remember why I have a screen saver of the stately homes of England. I installed it in a rare moment of homesickness perhaps.

The silence dragged out. I'm quite good at sitting patiently, and I've learned that not everyone is. Finally, Robyn took a breath, looked directly at me, and said, "We're asking if you have any ideas, Gemma."

"Ideas? What sort of ideas?"

"About what happened. To Dave."

"The police are investigating."

"Yes, but . . ."

"What Robyn means," Sharon said, "is that we thought . . . you found out who killed Kathy Lamb, so maybe you can do the same this time."

"I am not a consulting detective. I'm a shop owner. A shop owner who should be working in her shop. Leave it to the police. The West London police are very good at their jobs."

"But you're better, Gemma," Sharon said. "Everyone says so."

"I might have been of some minor assistance to the police in the past. I might have arrived at the logical conclusion shortly before they did. They would have arrived there eventually." *Maybe.*

Robyn shifted again. She dipped her head and engaged in an intense study of the rings on her fingers. The diamond in her engagement ring was a good two carats, although it needed cleaning, and the row of rubies on the third finger of her right hand would likely have cost in the thousands. I waited. "The thing is, Gemma, I tried to talk to Detective Estrada about my suspicions but she dismissed me. I . . . I mean Sharon and I thought you might have . . . noticed something."

Despite my better instincts, I asked, "What suspicions?"

"About Ethan."

"Ethan? You mean the chap who's doing research at Scarlet House?"

Robyn nodded enthusiastically. "Yes, yes. I said from the beginning something was not quite right about this supposed research he's doing. Didn't I, Sharon?"

"You did? I mean, yes, Robyn, you did. Absolutely. Right from the beginning." Sharon's cheeks bulged when she smiled at me. She twisted her hands together.

"Not quite right in what way?" I asked.

"I do not think," Robyn declared, "he's interested in presenting the Scarlet family in the best light."

"Surely it's not his job as a historian to present anyone in a good light or a bad light, but to tell the facts."

"The facts! You mean the facts as he presents them to suit his thesis. He's out to destroy the reputation of the Scarlet family, and thus of us. Of Scarlet House."

I glanced at Sharon. She was watching Robyn, a confused look on her face.

Moriarty watched the two women through narrow eyes.

"I'd think learning that the original builders of the house and members of the family were a bunch of scoundrels and scallywags would bring more visitors your way," I said. "Not fewer."

Robyn's lips tightened. "We are the inheritors of the Scarlet family's legacy as much as the conservators of their property. It's up to me—up to us at the Historical Society, I mean, to ensure that legacy is kept intact."

"Whatever," I said. "It's a heck of a leap from thinking the man's picking and choosing historical facts to accusing him of murdering someone."

"We're not accusing—" Sharon began.

"Yes, we are," Robyn snapped. "The man's in his forties for heaven's sake. He still doesn't have his PhD thesis finished. Any chance of getting a full-time teaching post at a university is slipping out of his reach and quickly. Never mind securing a tenure-track position. He cannot afford any more delays. I suspect Dave discovered something that will completely destroy Ethan's theories. And thus, Dave had to be silenced before he could tell me—tell us, I mean."

"If you have proof of this, Robyn, take it to the police."

"I told you I spoke to them, They aren't interested."

"They don't always tell concerned parties what they're thinking or in what direction their investigation is going. If there's some reason to question Ethan in particular, they will do so. Were either of you here in my shop earlier today? Before noon?"

"What does that have to do with anything?" Robyn asked.

"It's just a simple question."

"No," Sharon said. "I wasn't, anyway."

Robyn shook her head.

"Do you know my shop clerk, Ashleigh?"

Their faces were blank. "I'm sorry to say I don't shop here," Robyn said. "Your stock is not entirely to my taste. I might have seen her once or twice when I've been in the tearoom, but otherwise, no. Sorry."

"Me neither," Sharon said.

"Did you get the locks to Scarlet House changed at long last?" I asked.

"Yes," Robyn said. "The locksmith was around first thing this morning. I'll take steps to ensure the distribution of keys is strictly controlled."

That, I suspected, wouldn't last long. Someone would need a key for some nebulous reason, and they'd be given it with strict instructions to return it, but they never would get around to giving it back, so a new one would be cut and maybe a second spare, just to be sure, and it would be put under a plant pot for the use of the absentminded. And the number of keys available would expand exponentially.

I stood up. "Don't let me keep you."

Sharon stepped away from the wall with a relieved sigh, but Robyn wasn't finished. "Word is starting to spread about the so-called haunting. One of our docents called me this morning to say her granddaughter heard at school that Dave was killed by the ghost of Josephine Scarlet, who's angry because Dave brought in sheep and the farm had always had goats."

I didn't laugh. But I wanted to. "You shouldn't be listening to schoolyard gossip."

"The reputation of the house is on the line! We had an email this morning from a ghost hunting society in Boston asking when they could tour the house. At night, preferably!"

By the reputation of the house, I assumed Robyn meant her reputation as the chair of the board. Her status in the community was important to Robyn, and regardless of the reputation of the long-ago Scarlet family, she didn't want any hints of mockery attached to her name.

I spread out my arms. "All this has nothing to do with me."

"We hired you to disprove the ghost theory. And look what happened instead."

"I don't recall being hired to do anything. As I remember, I agreed to do a favor for Leslie Wilson and spend the night at the house. I did so."

"Something happened that night," Sharon said. "The night you were there. Something unexplainable."

"Nothing is unexplainable. The explanation has simply not been found yet."

"Who did you tell what happened?" Robyn asked me. "Did you and Jayne Wilson tell people the house is haunted?"

I was getting more than slightly annoyed. First, Robyn wanted to engage me to find a killer, and then she turned around and accused me of being a rumormonger. "I did not, considering I don't believe the house is haunted. I believe someone is playing tricks, for unknown ends, and that those tricks got out of hand and ended in a man's death. Now, if you'll excuse me. I have to get back to work."

Moriarty leapt off the shelf and landed on my desk.

Sharon put her hand on Robyn's arm. Robyn yanked it away as though the other woman had stuck her with a pin and stalked out.

Sharon gave me an apologetic shrug. "Sorry, Gemma. I didn't know she was going to accuse Ethan of the murder. Or you of spreading rumors. She told me she wanted to ask if you'd noticed anything last night. She doesn't handle pressure well."

"Were she and Dave close?" I asked.

"Not particularly. Not so I noticed anyway. I sometimes thought he found Robyn a bit overbearing, bossy. I once overheard traces of an argument between them. He accused her of interfering in things she didn't know anything about."

"Do you know what he meant by that?"

"The farm and the animals, I assumed. The care and feeding of pigs isn't exactly part of Robyn's skillset. I'd better go. We came in her car, and she's likely to drive off without me rather than wait." Sharon scuttled out the door and down the steps. From my desk, Moriarty looked at me.

"None of my business," I said to him. "But, because I'm a curious sort . . ." I followed the two women. Moriarty streaked past me and flew down the stairs.

Sharon needn't have hurried. By the time I got downstairs, Robyn was on her phone. She'd taken herself to the reading nook by the windows and was pacing back and forth. She might have tried to keep her voice down, but the anger in it came through loud and clear. The stack of puzzles on the games table had been disturbed, and I hurried over to put them into order. Robyn had her back to me and was speaking to the window. The acoustics in this part of the shop are quite good. The big bay window throws the sound back, directly toward the center table.

"This is not a good time, Eric. I'm well aware of your priorities. But they are not mine. I have to deal with this. You can go without me. Your mother will hardly care if I don't put in an appearance, eightieth birthday party or not."

I could see her face reflected in the window. Narrow eyes, tight lips, color rising in her cheeks. The sound of the voice on the other end didn't leak out of the phone, but I knew her husband was named Eric.

"How dare you!" she said. "This is not a waste of my time, and my money is mine to do with as I choose." Robyn shoved her phone into her jacket pocket. She turned quickly as I bent over the table, giving a Baker Street Irregulars board game a final placement.

"Thank you for your time," Robyn snarled at me. "Sharon, I'm leaving." Robyn threw the door open and marched out. Sharon scurried after her.

"What got her so upset?" Gale said from behind the sales counter.

The customer she was serving was a regular in the shop. Iris Cunningham had a vast network of grandchildren and grand-nieces and -nephews, and always bought them books for birthdays and Christmases. She chuckled. "Robyn Kirkpatrick is trying so hard to squelch word that Scarlet House is haunted, she's fanning the flames even more. Some people never do learn when to stop talking. Hello there, Moriarty. I was wondering where you got to." The cat leapt onto the counter and rubbed his head against Iris's sleeve.

"Why does she care so much?" I asked. "Obviously the museum's important to her, nothing wrong with that, but it is just a volunteer position, isn't it?"

"Rumor has it, Robyn's marriage is on the skids. Money problems, people say. Eric's an airline executive, and I've heard that their retirement funds are wrapped up in hotels and airlines, and we all know what a bad time those industries have had over the past couple of years. It's been a difficult time for lots of marriages. Some couples come together under adversity. Some do not. Thank you, dear. Have a nice day. You too, Moriarty." She gave the cat a final pat and accepted her bag of books from Gale.

"Do you know who Bunny Leigh is?" I asked her.

"The singer? She was my daughter's idol back in the day. For about a year, all I heard was Bunny this, and Bunny that. Rachel chopped almost all her hair off and dyed what little remained bright pink to imitate Bunny at one point." She chuckled. "Her father was fit to be tied."

"Did you know she's been seen in West London?"

"Oh yes. Everyone's talking about it."

"Do you know where she's staying?"

"No. Why are you asking?"

"No reason."

"I'll be off then. Have a nice day." The chimes over the door tinkled behind her.

Moriarty stretched languidly and then launched himself across the gap to land on the shelf behind the counter. He sniffed at Donald's flowers.

"You didn't find anything at Ashleigh's place?" Gale asked me.

"No. She wasn't there. Do you know anything about Bunny Leigh?"

"I'd never even heard of her until this week."

"I'd like to have a chat with her. Keep your ears open, will you? Maybe, under the pretext of gossiping, ask the customers if anyone knows where she's staying."

Gale's eyes shone with interest. "I can do that. Ashleigh told me it would be exciting working here."

"Excitement," I said, "I would happily do without. It does, however, seem to be unable to do without me."

Chapter Thirteen

R obyn and Sharon's visit had planted additional questions in my mind, but the death of Dave Chase would have to wait, as I had something more important to do.

I'd seen Bunny Leigh, former teenage pop sensation, in my shop. She had not been showing any interest in our books or merchandise or even the props used to decorate the space, but rather paying an unusual amount of attention to Ashleigh. Ashleigh was now missing. Chances were good those two things were related.

I returned to my office, settled myself behind the computer, and opened the ever-reliable Google. I didn't have to resort to anything sketchy or possibly verging on illegal to find out much of what I needed to know.

Bunny Leigh, as everyone had told me, had been a singing star in the late 1990s and early 2000s. A simple search of her name brought up hundreds of pictures. Her trademark look had been snug-fitting T-shirts sparkling with glitter and cute sayings, and short, brightly colored skirts worn with knee-high socks and sparkly trainers, what Americans call sneakers. Her hair was often colored to match the clothes and tied into tight bunches with bouncing bright ribbons. I played a couple of short tracks of her music. She had a not-bad voice, but it was pitched too high and too giggly for my taste, and the music behind it was mindless pop, each song sounding much the same, with lyrics the like of "ooh, ooh" and "baby, baby" and, for a change, "ooh, baby." Her star had streaked brilliantly across the sky, but it had soon burned out, as is so often the case. Too much partying, too much alcohol, too many drugs, bad choices in boyfriends, all contributed to her decline. All that plus the simple fact that teenage tastes change rapidly, and new stars appear on the scene to flame out in their own turn. Bunny's real name was Leigh Saunderson, and she was from Lincoln, Nebraska, and was still the pride of the local high school. She'd sung with a band in school, but she'd soon departed for the bright lights of L.A., leaving the bandmates and her school and family behind. When her singing star began to dim, she tried her hand at acting, but that hadn't amounted to much, and according to IMDb, she hadn't appeared in anything since 2012. I didn't find much news about her after 2015. A few sightings at popular restaurants or at a party thrown by another of the rapidly aging people who'd also been a bright young thing around the time she had. A couple of "whatever happened to" articles. Her name had been linked with plenty of men over the years, but she'd only been married once, in 2017. The marriage hadn't lasted more than a year. I studied a picture of the couple together, but nothing about him was familiar. There hadn't been a single word about Bunny in the press in almost two years, until a small piece in the *West London Star* reported that she'd come to West London to spend the winter and had been spotted chatting to "fans" at Mrs. Hudson's Tearoom.

At least we got a mention. I hoped people in search of a Bunny Leigh sighting would be following that up.

I leaned back in my chair, steepled my fingers, and studied the picture I'd enlarged to fill the screen. It showed Bunny when she was in her glory days, all smiles, colorful hair, colorful clothes, bright green eyes, a scattering of freckles on her nose, cute little cleft chin. Happy. Her face was flushed as she signed autographs after a sold-out concert.

I had learned something about Bunny Leigh that wasn't part of her biographies, nor could it be found in the gossip press.

She had a daughter who looked exactly as she had at the same age. That daughter was named Ashleigh Saunderson, and she worked at the Sherlock Holmes Bookshop and Emporium.

I'd noticed the resemblance between the two but had dismissed it as one of Ashleigh's regular changes of identity, attempting to imitate the young Bunny.

I gave myself a firm mental kick.

Chapter Fourteen

I had Ashleigh's emergency contact information in my employee files. I decided her disappearance could be considered an emergency. I dug through the file and made a phone call.

"Hello?" said a tentative voice.

"Good afternoon. This is Gemma Doyle from West London, Massachusetts. Is this Mrs. Saunderson?"

"Yes, it is. Can I help you?"

"Ashleigh Saunderson works for me at the Sherlock Holmes Bookshop and Emporium. Are you her grandmother?" Ashleigh was from Lincoln. When she'd come to work for me, she'd told me she longed to get away from that small, deadly dull (her words) town surrounded by nothing but corn fields, and see the sea. I knew she'd been raised by her grandparents, and she'd put them down as next of kin on her employment form. I'd followed up her references and spoken to the owners of the shops where she'd worked when she was at school and following graduation. I knew nothing else about Ashleigh's life because she'd chosen not to share it with me. Which, of course, is her right.

I suspected she had problems with her sense of self-identity, manifested by the constant changing of not only clothes but her entire persona, but again that was none of my business as long as she was a good, honest, reliable employee.

"I am," Mrs. Saunderson said. "Is something the matter?"

"I've had some trouble contacting her and am wondering if you've heard from her in the last day or so?"

"She calls her grandfather and me every Sunday. What day is today?"

"Monday. Did she ring you yesterday?"

"Yes. Nine o'clock in the evening. On the dot. She knows we worry. Her being off in your big city and all."

I wondered how large Lincoln was if West London was considered a big city.

"While I have you, Miss Doyle, let me tell you that Ashleigh simply loves working at your store."

"That's nice to hear."

"She says you're such a scatterbrain you're always haring off in one direction or another and almost never there, and she's left in charge."

"Oh," I said.

"It's giving her good experience for when she eventually opens her own chain of bookstores. She particularly enjoyed it last winter when you were away and your grandfather helped out. Such a wonderful old man, she said, with so many great stories. They closed the store early several times to go to the pub. Like a real Englishman. I can tell you're English. I love your accent."

"That would be my great-uncle, not my grandfather, but I'm glad they get on. Anyway—"

"Perhaps you could give her some extra vacation time before things get busy in the summer. We'd love to have her home for a few weeks."

"I'll consider it. You haven't heard from her today?"

"No reason I should. Unless something's wrong?"

"What about your daughter, Leigh?"

"Leigh? Why are you asking about Leigh?" The kindly old lady, wanting her granddaughter to visit more, disappeared in a flash, and ice poured down the line.

"Has she called you in the last week or so?"

"I haven't spoken to that girl in twenty-two years, and I have no intention of doing so now." Ashleigh was twenty-two years old. "Why are you asking about that? What's happened?"

I was at a loss for words. And that doesn't happen very often. A man's voice sounded in the background, followed by Mrs. Saunderson's muffled reply: "She's asking if we want our ducts cleaned."

"Hang up!" the man yelled.

"Goodbye," Mrs. Saunderson said.

I was left staring at the phone in my hand. When I'd realized Ashleigh was almost certainly Bunny Leigh's daughter, I'd felt relieved. She'd gone away with her mother and was therefore safe. Why she hadn't told me she was leaving might have a simple explanation. But now . . . if Bunny hadn't seen her parents since Ashleigh was born, did that mean Ashleigh had never met her mother? If so, what could be Bunny's motivation for coming to West London? To see the daughter she'd given to her parents to raise? Or to get revenge on them for exiling her?

I checked the clock on the computer screen. Three thirty, almost time for my daily partners' meeting at Mrs. Hudson's with Jayne. I pushed myself away from the computer and went downstairs.

Gale was ringing up sales, and Moriarty was once again sniffing at Donald's flowers. Who knew the cat was such a plant lover?

"I'm going next door for a meeting with Jayne," I said. "Back in about half an hour and then you can go home."

Gale waved at me.

The tearoom closes at four and the day was winding down. Only two tables were taken, groups of middle-aged women relaxing over the remains of their afternoon tea. These days a full afternoon tea, even in England, isn't a regular occurrence, but a special occasion. An event saved for celebrations or a treat when on vacation. Jayne doesn't regularly serve the full, formal tea on Mondays in the off-season, but she will handle special requests.

Speaking of special requests, Fiona put the contents of her tray on the table in the window alcove where Jayne and I like to have our afternoon meetings. Leslie Wilson had already taken a seat, and she greeted me with a smile. Her gloves and hat lay on the table next to her, and her winter coat hung on the hook by the door.

"Lovely," I said, pleased that Jayne had saved us some shortbread. No scones or tea sandwiches today. The shortbread was accompanied by almond croissants with jam and butter and a pot of tea. Darjeeling, judging by the heady scent. "Fiona, I need you to keep your ears open for any mention of Bunny Leigh. I want to talk to her, but I don't know where she's staying. Can you ask Jocelyn as well?"

"Sure."

"What's that about?" Leslie asked me.

"I need to find Bunny, and with some urgency."

Jayne slid onto the bench seat, and I wiggled over to give her room. "Nothing from Ashleigh?"

"No."

"What's going on?" Leslie asked. "What's happened to Ashleigh, and why are you looking for Bunny Leigh?"

I filled Leslie in about Ashleigh. I didn't say what I'd discovered about their relationship, but I told them I'd seen Bunny watching Ashleigh. "It may be nothing, but I need to talk to her. She's done nothing wrong, so I can't ask Ryan to try to find out where she's staying or to put out some sort of all-points bulletin on her. Not this early anyway."

"Instead, you're calling on the West London grapevine." Jayne poured the tea. "Just as efficient."

"More so," Leslie said.

I added a splash of milk to my tea. "And the grapevine comes with none of that pesky legality stuff. As much as I hate to, I'm going to have to go across the street to Maureen's and ask her the same. If anyone's tuned into town gossip, it's her."

"I'll do that when we're done here," Leslie said. "I can put the word out. If I happen to run into Bunny at the grocery store, why should I say you're wanting to talk to her?"

"Tell her I'd like to have her into the shop for an autograph session."

Jayne cocked her head. "She wrote a Sherlock pastiche novel?"

"Not as far as I know. I have nothing for her to sign, but I'm hoping she won't realize that, and she'll think I'm going to organize some sort of fan event. It's worth a try. I have no other way of finding her."

"Have you called Irene? The paper might know where Bunny's staying."

"I did. She'll see what she can find out, but she told me not to get my hopes up. The only reason anyone knows she's in town is that she was seen on the street, and word started to spread. She's happy to sign autographs and chat briefly if she's asked, but she hasn't sought publicity, and she hasn't arranged any sort of public appearances. It might not even be true that she's planning to be here all winter. Without a guarantee of a story, the paper doesn't have the resources to try to track her down."

"In the old days," Leslie said, "at the slightest whisper she was in town, *The Star* would have had a team of reporters and photographers checking under every bush."

"That's when they had a team, Mom," Jayne said. "Now they have Irene and a summer intern. In the winter they don't even have the intern."

"You can tell Maureen Bunny's come to the Cape to paint," I said. "If she plays her cards right, that is, if she tells me if she hears anything, I'll suggest Bunny exhibit her work at Beach Fine Arts."

"That would be a lie," Leslie said.

"Not coming from you. You're simply repeating what I told you."

Leslie grinned at me, and then she and Jayne helped themselves to croissants and liberally applied butter and jam.

"I assumed when Jayne invited me to this meeting, it's because you're wanting to ask about Scarlet House," Leslie said.

"That was my idea at the time, yes," I said. "Since then I did inadvertently learn a few things of interest."

"Inadvertently?" Jayne said. "You mean you didn't probe and pry and ask insightful questions?"

"In this case the answers came to me without me even having to ask the questions. Leslie, do you have any idea exactly how invested Robyn is in the museum? I mean emotionally as well as financially?"

Leslie cradled her teacup and thought. "Emotionally—more than I might have expected. I love the museum too, and I truly believe it's a vitally important part of Cape Cod history and needs to be treated as such. If it were to close, I'd be sad, but my life will go on. and I'll turn to other things. Sharon cares about it because she loves playing dress-up and making her ridiculous baked goods, not to mention that she has a paid job as the bookkeeper and she needs that income. As for Robyn, if I was to be honest, I'd say the end of the museum would affect her more than the closing of the museum itself."

"Meaning?" Jayne asked.

"Meaning, she'd regard it as a personal failure because she's the chair of the board, but more to the point, she's afraid other people would call her a failure."

"Why are we talking about the museum closing, anyway?" Jayne asked. "I didn't know that was even on the table."

"Nonprofits are always on the verge of closing," Leslie said. "As is any organization reliant on government charity and public donations."

"An anonymous donor made a substantial contribution last year. This person has indicated they won't be doing so this year. Do you happen to know who this anonymous donor is?"

"I do."

"And?"

"And if they want to be anonymous, I have to respect that." She broke off a piece of croissant.

"Okay, don't tell me. If it was Robyn, eat that croissant."

Leslie popped a piece into her mouth.

It was only a guess on my part, although I always insist that I never guess. I'd been told Robyn and her husband were having money problems. I'd overheard them arguing myself, and she'd told him she could spend her money as she wanted. By which I assumed she meant on Scarlet House, but if their retirement savings were in danger, I thought it unlikely she'd be able to donate the substantial amounts she had in the past.

"Dave wasn't any threat to the museum. Was he?" Jayne asked.

"Not as far as we know," I said. "Leslie, how did Dave get on with the other board members?"

"Well enough. His interest was the farm, not the house. He wanted to be allowed to run the farm his way, and that was generally okay with the rest of us. None of us know anything about farming."

"I know nothing about farming either," I said. "But I'd assume there are expenses involved in operating a farm above those of the house. Animal feed, vet's bills."

Leslie dusted crumbs off her fingers. "Yes, but if you're suggesting the farm might have to go in order to keep the house, remember that the barn wasn't damaged in the fire, and none of the animals were harmed. Over the past couple of years, the farm hasn't had nearly as many excess expenses as the main house."

I helped myself to a piece of shortbread. "Was Robyn okay with letting Dave run the farm his way?"

"I believe so. I've not heard anything to the contrary."

"You're not suggesting Robyn killed Dave to keep his costs down?" Jayne said.

"I'm not suggesting anything. I am merely gathering data. Robyn's concerned that Ethan is uncovering unpleasant facts about the Scarlet family in his research. Do you know anything about that?"

"No," Leslie said, "but I can't say it would be a surprise. If you go back far enough, every family probably has its share of black sheep, and there were plenty of things acceptable in the past that are considered bad today."

"Do we have black sheep, Mom?" Jayne asked.

Leslie chuckled. "We're not important enough, dear. Or rich enough."

"Darn," Jayne said.

"I'd have thought that if something scandalous is uncovered about the family," I said, "it would help the house in terms of attracting visitors. Not hurt it. People love shame and scandal. Robyn doesn't appear to agree."

"Robyn has her own concept of propriety."

I popped the last of the biscuit into my mouth and pushed my empty teacup to one side. "I have to get back. Gale's filling in with absolutely no notice, so I promised her she could leave at four thirty. If I want to keep an employee who doesn't have ambitions to be in command of a bookstore empire, I need to not be too scatterbrained."

* * *

"Moriarty sure loves those flowers," Gale said. "He's been munching on them." She pointed to the arrangement behind the counter, and I could see what she meant. The lilies in particular had tiny bite marks taken out of them. "Does he often do that?"

"I don't normally have real flowers in the shop. Those were a gift from Donald. Should a cat be eating flowers?"

"I don't know. Not a cat person myself. When my children were young, we had dogs, but now that I'm living in an apartment, a goldfish is about all I can handle. Will you call me if you hear from Ashleigh? I'd like to know she's okay."

"Sure."

Gale went upstairs for her handbag and then left with a backward wave, passing a group of customers coming in. I put on my best smile and welcomed them.

The stop was satisfyingly busy for the rest of the day. I would have preferred to be out pounding the streets searching for Ashleigh, but that would be nothing but a waste of time. She was unlikely to be found relaxing on a park bench or having dinner at nice restaurant. Every time I could take my attention away from the customers, I checked my phone in case I'd missed a call or a text.

Nothing. Not from Ashleigh and not from anyone reporting a Bunny Leigh sighting. Not even Ryan with an update on the

Chase case or another demand from Robyn Kirkpatrick that I "do something."

I did, however, have an unexpected visitor. Ethan Evanston came in as I was assisting customers. He didn't glance around the shop; he didn't pretend to be interested in anything on display. He leaned up against the counter and watched me. His look, I thought, wasn't friendly.

"Hi," I said, after the latest group of shoppers had left, weighted down, I'm happy to say, by their purchases. "What brings you here?"

"I've been wanting to talk to you."

"Sure. What about?"

"You're not serious about this ghost hunting nonsense, are you?"

I threw up my hands. "Not this again. I never said I was hunting ghosts, no matter that everyone insists I am. I agreed to do Leslie Wilson and the board of Scarlet House a favor because I thought someone was playing a practical joke on them, and it needed to be stopped before it escalated. It did escalate. A man died."

His face relaxed fractionally, and he glanced to one side. "Ok. It's just that it won't do my thesis any good if my dissertation committee gets wind that I'm digging up ghosts. Which I am not, but muck spreads."

Ethan was in his mid-forties. His Boston accent indicated he was from an upper-middle-class family and had received a good education. I noticed he wasn't wearing a wedding ring and that the car he drove was old. His clothes verged on shabby: the coat was pilling, his scarf had holes in it, and his right boot was almost worn through on one side. His lined face and red-tinged eyes made him look older than his years, and he'd missed a spot on the side of his jaw when shaving. I could also see he'd chewed his fingernails down to the quick.

Ethan Evanston was out of money and rapidly running out of time. He needed to get his paper finished if he had any hope of landing a decent job, with benefits, before he turned fifty.

"Do you know a woman by the name of Bunny Leigh?"

He stared at me. "What kind of a name is Bunny? And no, I've never heard of her."

"Just asking. How well did you know Dave Chase?"

He bristled. "I hope you're not trying to pin that on me."

"Pin what on you? His death? I'm not pinning anything on anyone, in the same way as I'm not looking for ghosts. It's just a question."

He visibly tried to calm himself. "Okay. I spoke to the cops, and I told them what I'll tell you. I never met the guy until the other day. Okay? Robyn says it was an accident. He fell out of the hayloft. Isn't that right?"

"I don't know what happened. The police are investigating."

"They can do their investigating without me. I have enough troubles of my own, trying to get my blasted thesis finished. Do you have any idea how time-consuming it is doing original historical research? I finally have an angle on the Scarlet family, and everyone's throwing up nothing but obstacles in my way. You and your ghosts, Robyn and her precious Scarlet family."

"I didn't realize Robyn cared that much about the Scarlets."

"She doesn't. All she cares about is the reputation of the museum. Meaning her loss of reputation if the place is in trouble."

"Is it? In trouble?"

"I don't know. I just know that she's worried. Maybe she worries all the time."

"What do you mean you have an angle on the Scarlets?"

"Dig deep enough and every family has their secrets. That's the job of a historian, isn't it? To dig up the dirt. That bunch at the museum think history should be painted in bright colors and tied with a nice red bow." He gave his head a shake. "Scholarly reputations are not built on red bows. They're also not built on talk of ghosts and other things that go bump in the night." His mouth tightened, and he took a step toward me. I held my ground. "Stop interfering in things that don't concern you."

The chimes over the door tinkled merrily, and Ethan broke his stare. He left the shop.

*　*　*

At five to seven I was ringing up a two-volume set of the original Holmes stories for an elderly man who confessed that he'd seen every representation of The Great Detective on movies or TV but had not read a word of the originals. "You'll find a new appreciation when you hear Sir Arthur's own voice," I said. "Some interpretations are more faithful than others."

He was the last customer of the day, and I followed him to the door to flip the sign and twist the lock. Some inconsiderate person had seriously disturbed the display on the center table, and I went to straighten it before beginning my closing up tasks. This week the display featured the newest books from our gaslight fiction selection. I love the covers of many of these books—dark, wet cobblestone streets; the glimmer of gaslight; women in brilliantly colored, elaborate dresses and enormous hats, or men in dark suits and tall hats. In many, a hansom cab or horse-drawn carriage is seen disappearing into the swirling mist or pulling up in front of a white-pillared Kensington rowhouse, much like the one I'd been raised in and in which my parents still live. Which made me think that perhaps it was time to start planning their intended visit in the spring. I haven't seen them since I'd been in London for a Sherlock Holmes convention. My father, Henry, is retired from his job as an officer with the Metropolitan Police, so taking vacation is no problem for him, but Anne, my mother, still works as a barrister—that is, a trial lawyer—for one of the City's top chambers—aka law office. She needs to plan her vacation time well ahead.

As I was mentally putting together an email to send them, I heard a groan from beneath the center table. I leaned over and peered under the table. I hadn't seen Moriarty since getting back from tea, which was unusual. He's normally most active in the shop in the late afternoon and early evenings. He lay on his side, breathing rapidly, eyes wide open. A thin line of drool dripped out of the corner of his mouth. I crouched next to his bed. "Are you okay, Moriarty?" I asked.

He struggled to his feet, extended his neck, gagged, and threw up.

I scurried backward out of the way. He backed away from the mess and dropped onto his bed.

"Goodness." I wasn't sure if I should do something, and if something, what? He was Uncle Arthur's cat, not mine. The tiny starving kitten had been found in the back alley in a rainstorm one night, brought in to get warm and dry, and he'd never left. I'd never had a pet before coming to West London. I've grown very fond of our two dogs, but Moriarty and I weren't exactly on good terms.

As I debated tucking a blanket around him and leaving him to sleep it off, my phone rang. I grabbed it, hoping it was Ashleigh, but it was Jayne.

"I'm finishing up here," she said. "And heading off. It's turned cold, so I was wondering if you'd like to go to the Harbor Inn for a drink around the fireplace."

"Do you know anything about the health of cats?"

"Nothing."

"Moriarty seems to be sick." He rolled his head to one side and retched up a thin gruel containing what looked like chewed plant leaves.

"I'll come and see."

No more than a minute later, I heard the sliding door unlocking and opening, and Jayne came into the Emporium, dressed to head outdoors in her winter gear. She crouched beside me. Moriarty fixed his amber eyes on her face. "Poor kitty," she said. "If he's been sick, maybe it was something he ate."

"All he's had today is his usual food, unless some fool of a customer slipped him something without us noticing. Come to think of it, he was munching on Donald's flowers earlier. Do you think that might be it?"

While Jayne stroked the cat's heaving sides, I did a quick search on "cats and flowers."

What I found had me snatching up Moriarty and leaping to my feet. "Call the emergency vet. Tell them we're coming in and why. Grab that vase and bring it."

"Why? What'd it say?"

"Lilies are extremely poisonous to cats."

Chapter Fifteen

I let myself into the house with a tired sigh. As the lights of the taxi backed out of the driveway, Violet and Peony danced around my legs, happy to have me home. I dropped next to them and gave them both heartfelt hugs. "He's going to be okay," I said.

I let the dogs into the yard and went into the kitchen, where I filled the kettle and put it on the stove. We'd made it to the vet in time. If I'd left it overnight, the doctor told me, Moriarty would have suffered irreversible kidney damage, if he hadn't died.

I left Moriarty at the hospital for overnight observation and came home with a pamphlet of information on substances toxic to animals. Who knew there were so many household plants that could kill a cat or dog?

I did now.

Lilies in particular, the vet told me, were so poisonous to cats that simply drinking the water out of the vase in which they'd been placed or licking pollen off their fur could prove fatal.

It wasn't very late, but I was dead beat. Jayne had driven Moriarty and me to the after-hours veterinary clinic. After

Moriarty had been rushed into the examination room, I insisted Jayne go home while I waited for news. She'd made me promise to call with an update, which I had.

They allowed me in to see Moriarty before I left. He'd been sleeping peacefully, looking very un-Moriarty-like, small and frail in his cage. I'd felt an unexpected tug of the heartstrings toward him.

I drank a few quick gulps of tea as I texted Uncle Arthur, knowing he'd want an update, no matter the time in London: *Moriarty in hospital. Ate something he shouldn't. He'll be fine. Picking him up tomorrow.*

The reply was instantaneous: *V & P all right?*

Me: *A cat problem only.*
Uncle Arthur: 👍

The temperature had continued dropping rapidly as night arrived. I finished my tea and then put on my heavy coat, scarf, hat, and gloves, and got down the dog leashes. I called to the dogs, clipped on their leashes and took them for a walk.

I had a lot to think about—Ashleigh's whereabouts, the death of Dave Chase, whether whoever had tried to pretend that Scarlet House was haunted was the same person who'd killed Dave. And why someone had tried to pretend the house was haunted in the first place.

In a past case, someone had tried to kill me and had poisoned Jayne by mistake. This time, I didn't need to worry that the poisoning of Moriarty was related to any of my other problems. Donald had bought the flowers with all good intentions, and neither he nor I had been aware of how dangerous they were to the cat. Why would we? Lilies are fully edible by humans, although I am not entirely sure why anyone would want to munch on one.

As we walked through the dark cold streets, and the dogs tried to head off in alternate directions in pursuit of what only they could smell, I tried to focus my thoughts on Ashleigh and Scarlet House. If only I thought hard enough, and long enough, I should be able to determine what had happened in both situations.

Instead, all I could see was a small black face with a pert black nose sleeping peacefully under the bright lights of the veterinary clinic.

* * *

First thing in the morning, I called the clinic for an update. Moriarty, they told me, had not been happy to wake up and find himself trapped in a cage in a strange place surrounded by other animals and checked on by people he didn't know. A substantial breakfast had not improved his mood any. He was ready to come home. Reading between the lines, I got the impression the veterinary assistant was ready for Moriarty to go home.

I'd not heard from Ashleigh overnight. After I collected Moriarty and opened the shop, I'd call Ryan and insist he start an investigation. Something was not right, and further delay might prove as fatal as delaying Moriarty's trip to the animal hospital would have been.

When I put the dogs out, I stuck my nose out to check the weather and quickly pulled it back inside. I made a cup of tea and drank it while I got ready for work. I bundled myself up against the cold, took the dogs for a short walk, and then had a quick breakfast. I was scooping up the last of my muesli when Jayne texted: *Any news from vet?*

Me: *Have to pick M. up soon.*
Jayne: *Great! Want a lift?*
Me: *Aren't you at work?*
Jayne: *Not too busy this a.m. Got lots of baking done last night.*
Me: *Can you bring the cat carrier? In storage room.*

The next text arrived as I was heading for the door.

Uncle Arthur: *Status?*
Me: *Patient discharged.*
Uncle Arthur: ☺

I was waiting at the end of the driveway for Jayne, stamping my feet to keep them warm, when the familiar ping sounded once again.

Ryan: *Any update on Ashleigh?*
Me: *No*
Ryan: *Not good. Call me later and I'll open a file.*
Me: ♥
Me: *Updates on Dave Chase?*

Jayne pulled up, and I hopped in. "Wow, it's cold," I said.
"They're calling for snow later. A lot of it. Did you hear from Ashleigh?"

"No."

We freed Moriarty from one prison and stuffed him into another—his cat carrier. I paid the hefty bill, and Jayne and I were soon back on the road while Moriarty informed us that he didn't care to be confined.

I twisted in my seat and looked into the back. "I saved your life, you know, buddy. I expect some gratitude."

He hissed at me.

Jayne laughed. "All he's going to remember is being put in that carrier. And that you're the one who did it."

The veterinary clinic was located in the north end of West London. We drove south on Harbor Road, heading for Baker Street. Not many people were out, and everyone who was had wrapped themselves up so warmly I only got a glimpse of the occasional nose. "Are you in a hurry to get back?" I asked Jayne.

"Not particularly."

"We're almost at Scarlet House. Let's see what's happening there."

A couple of cars were in the parking lot in front of the house. Police tape was wrapped from one tree to another, marking off the barn and barnyard, but I could see no one guarding the scene.

"Shall I leave the engine on?" Jayne asked me as she parked beside Robyn's SUV.

"Why?"

She gestured to the complaining cat in the back seat. "It's cold."

"We won't be long, but in case we're delayed, I'll bring him in. We shouldn't keep the car idling."

I opened the back door and lifted out the cat carrier. Moriarty snarled at me. I bent my head and peered inside. "I could leave you to freeze, you know."

He snarled again.

"He knows that's an idle threat," Jayne said.

The sign next to the door informed us that the museum would be open from noon to five today. Despite all my warnings and suggestions of precautions, the front door wasn't locked, and Jayne and I simply walked in.

A light buzz of conversation came from the rear of the house. "Anyone home?" I called.

"We're closed," Robyn yelled.

"It's Gemma and Jayne." I headed for the kitchen, carrying the cat. "If you're closed, the door should be locked."

Robyn glared at Sharon. Sharon said, "Wasn't me. I came in through the back door."

"Sorry," Mrs. Ramsbatten said. "I was struggling with my gloves and must have forgotten."

"See that it doesn't happen again," Robyn snapped. "We have to beef up security around here."

Mrs. Ramsbatten glanced at me and rolled her eyes. She then smiled at Moriarty. "Who do we have here?"

I put the cat carrier on the floor. "This is my shop cat, Moriarty. He spent the night at the vet's, and we made a quick stop here as we were passing."

Sharon dropped to her haunches and made cooing noises into the cat carrier. She pressed her fingers to the bars and a small black paw reached out. Sharon and Mrs. Ramsbatten were in costume: long brown dresses, white aprons, lace caps. The replica vintage brooch was pinned to Sharon's collar. My neighbor sat in the rocking chair, her knitting by her side. She hadn't yet picked up the needles and was incongruously sipping from a Starbucks cup. She lifted the cup to Jayne. "Robyn made a coffee stop on her way to collect me. Not nearly as nice as yours, dear."

Jayne smiled at her.

"I'll have proper tea and coffee ready in a jiff," Sharon said from the floor.

The fire had been lit and was roaring to life. An iron pot full of water was suspended from a hook attached to the brick chimney. Bags of flour and sugar had been laid out on the big pine table, but Sharon hadn't started baking yet.

The kitchen was warm, and I unwrapped my scarf, unbuttoned my coat, and peeled off my gloves while Jayne did the same.

"Houses of this era in this climate were built to keep heat in in the winter," Sharon said, getting to her feet with a bit of a struggle and a soft grunt. "In this weather, the kitchen would be delightfully warm, no need for central heating. In the summer, it could be stifling, thus many houses also had a summer kitchen that didn't directly join the main part of the house."

"I've worked in bakeries that might have been mistaken for the seventh circle of hell in a Boston summertime," Jayne said.

"What brings you here?" Robyn asked. Unlike the other two women, Robyn wore modern clothes. A brown wool trouser suit with bright gold buttons on the jacket and brown leather ankle boots. Diamond studs were in her ears, and a delicate gold and diamond necklace around her throat.

"We literally were passing, and I wanted to check in," I said. "I see the barn's still closed off."

"I asked the police to take that ridiculous tape down. My docents can be relied on to keep people away from where they're not supposed to go, but the police refused my perfectly reasonable request."

Robyn, I decided, was not in a good mood today.

"Did someone take the animals?" Jayne asked.

"They're still here. One of our board members found a farmer who agreed to help with them if needed. Craig Jones volunteered to keep up the feeding for now, although he balked at mucking out the stalls."

"No kidding," Jayne said. "Farming is fun. Until it isn't."

"You're opening the house today?" I asked.

Robyn threw up her hands. "We will if we have any visitors. We had a full schedule planned for yesterday, and the police wouldn't let us open. As for today, one school group has cancelled already. Concerned for the safety of their students, they said. Bunch of nervous nellies, if you ask me."

Mrs. Ramsbatten rolled her eyes once again.

"Good thing my baking keeps so well," Sharon said. "Without refrigeration or plastic containers, or even a twenty-four-hour convenience store to pop out to, our ancestors had to ensure that food lasted until it was needed, and they had no tolerance for waste."

"You keep telling yourself that, Sharon," Robyn snapped. "As though people didn't die of food poisoning, never mind malnutrition."

Sharon let out a huff of such indignity, the brooch pinned to her collar bounced. "*Not* in the Scarlet family."

"Is Ethan coming in today?" I asked.

Robyn groaned. "Another thing I don't need. I'm getting tired of him and his so-called research. The man's a pest. The history of the Scarlet family is well documented, and he's wasting his time trying to find out more. He doesn't ever ask if he can come. He just shows up, plants himself at a table, and uses his computer."

"He's in the way." Sharon sniffed in disapproval. "He's too old to be posing as a Scarlet child doing their schoolwork at home, never mind using a computer to do it. I asked him to at least put on something from our men's clothing selection, and he told me he doesn't play at history."

"I'm reconsidering my decision not to simply tell him to leave," Robyn said. "I didn't initially want to cause any animosity between us, but it's getting out of hand."

"As long as I'm here," I said, "I'm going to have a look around the house. Security check, you know."

I left the kitchen. Jayne followed. "You're still being a security advisor?"

"No, I'm being a nosy consulting detective. As long as we're here, I thought I'd have a quick look around, see if there's any evidence of our ghost coming back, although I don't think whoever's playing that role will return. With this business with Ashleigh and then Moriarty, I haven't been able to give this case the attention I'd like."

Jayne might have muttered, "Much to Ryan's relief, I'm sure," under her breath, but if she did, I pretended not to hear. As Dave's death had happened outside, the police hadn't needed to come into the house. Everything was neat and tidy and ready for a parade of history lovers. The dining room table was set for entertaining guests to dinner, the parlor prepared for afternoon tea service. Whiskers bristling, George Scarlet glared at us from the front hall, and we passed the row of portraits as we climbed the stairs.

"Do you suppose these people are Scarlets?" Jayne asked. "Or did the museum buy paintings just to have something to hang here?"

"The one by the front door's the only one with a card next to it, so I suspect the rest are bought. They're quite good, and hiring a portrait painter would have been a major expense. The Scarlets and their heirs might have been important people around this area, but they were still New England farmers, not Boston bankers or European aristocrats. As much as Sharon might like to think they were wealthy enough to make gifts of jewelry, like that ugly brooch, to their cook."

We checked the bedrooms and again found everything in its place. I stood at the window at the end of the hallway, looking out. The barn door leading to the pigpen was open, and I saw movement in the yard as the pigs shuffled around, no doubt wondering if one of the people who'd been here the other night had dropped anything to eat that they'd overlooked.

"If the museum wants to provide that authentic settler experience," I said, "they should have visitors help clean the pigpen."

"And the outhouse," Jayne said.

"Although there isn't one."

"They are offered Sharon's baking. That's enough of a pioneer experience for me."

I laughed as I opened the door to the back stairs and peered in. The light was off, and all was dark. Faint voices drifted up from the kitchen. I shut the door, and Jayne and I retraced our steps. As we approached the kitchen, I heard Sharon shout, "Stop!"

"Look what you've done now," Robyn yelled.

I ran the rest of the distance and burst into the kitchen, expecting to see the reappearance of the Ghost of Scarlet House. Instead, Sharon stood next to the cat carrier, her hands over her mouth, her eyes wide with shock. The door of the carrier, I noticed with a sinking heart, was open, and Moriarty's black tail was disappearing into the pantry.

"Uh-oh," Jayne said.

"Here kitty, kitty," Sharon called. "I'm so sorry. It was hard to get at that place under his chin to give him a good scratch, so I opened the door."

Moriarty, well I knew, was no fool. Like a prisoner probing for his jailer's point of weakness, he would have offered his chin for a scratch, keeping it just out of reach. And then, when the opportunity presented itself, he bolted. Sharon was lucky he wasn't big enough to lock her in the carrier while he made his escape.

The exit at the top of the staircase was closed, so he wouldn't be able to get too far. Then again, this was an old house, full of nooks and crannies, loose floorboards and gaps in the walls. Despite the prodigious amount of food he consumed in a day, Moriarty was able to make himself as thin as a mouse, if he so desired.

"Sharon," I ordered as I headed toward the pantry in pursuit of the fugitive, "you block off the means of egress."

"Huh?"

"She means stand in that doorway and don't let the cat past you," Robyn said. "If it gets into the rest of the house, we'll never get it back. I loathe cats."

"Why does that not surprise me?" Mrs. Ramsbatten said in a low voice.

This time it was Robyn's turn to pretend not to hear.

Sharon placed herself in the entrance to the pantry: back straight, fists held tight, arms outstretched, feet wide apart, her voluminous skirts stretched across the doorway.

"Can I get by?" I asked.

"Sorry," she mumbled. She wiggled an inch to the side, and I pressed past her. Jayne followed me, and Sharon took up her position again. To my infinite relief the door leading from the pantry to the servants' stairs was closed, although this room had plenty of places an intelligent, and willful, cat could hide.

To my further infinite relief, Moriarty hadn't sought any of them. Instead, he crouched in a corner of the pantry, his ears up, his attention fully focused on a crack in the baseboards near the rug. He reached out a paw and swiped at it. I gestured to Jayne, asking her to pick him up. He liked Jayne better than me. She stepped forward and snatched him into her arms. He emitted a squeak of protest, simply to make his point, but he didn't try to escape.

"You silly boy." Jayne tapped him on the nose. "What were you after? Mice in the walls probably."

"Mice!" Sharon squeaked. "There are no mice in my kitchen."

I studied the spot Moriarty had been interested in. After mice, almost certainly, and despite what Sharon might want to think, any building with walls and floors this old, situated on a farm no less, would be full of mice, particularly in mid-winter.

Floors this old.

Jayne carried Moriarty away, cooing to him softly. "Gemma," she called, "I need backup if he's going to go into the carrier."

"Just a minute." The rug wasn't an antique and was probably not original to the house. Some of the colors were still bright, although the edges were worn, and the surface marked by traces of ground-in dirt.

Moriarty howled.

"Gemma!" Jayne called.

"Let me help you, dear," Mrs. Ramsbatten said. "Now, Moriarty, we need you to be a good kitty. Oh dear, that hurt."

"Ouch!" Jayne yelled. "He's getting away. Sharon, get that door open." A chair fell over.

I continued studying the floor as the sounds of a pitched battle raged in the kitchen. I dropped to my haunches. The door of the cat carrier slammed shut.

"That was exciting," Mrs. Ramsbatten said. "I need to sit down and catch my breath." The rocking chair squeaked.

"I hate cats," Robyn said again.

"Sorry," Sharon said.

Moriarty howled.

"No harm done," Jayne said. "Ready to go, Gemma? Where's Gemma?"

I tugged at the rug, cursing myself for not having done so the first time I inspected the house. It was heavy and emitted a cloud of dust as I rose to my feet, pulling it after me.

A trap door lay beneath.

Chapter Sixteen

"Did you know about this?" I asked Robyn as the four women crowded around me, staring at the outline cut into the old pine planks that made up the flooring.

"No."

"I didn't either," Sharon said.

"Doesn't anyone ever clean in here?" Robyn snarled.

"Yes, we clean at the end of the day," Sharon replied. "It's part of our regular routine, as you well know. We don't lift rugs, though."

"You'd better start."

"I'm getting mighty tired of you thinking you're the boss around here, Robyn."

"Let me remind you that I *am* the boss. I—"

"Take it outside," I said. "Jayne, can you get me my gloves, please. They're in my coat pocket."

She soon returned with them, and I slipped them on. They were winter gloves, not suited to a careful examination of fine details, but the best I had at the moment. The wood was pitted and cracked with age, although less worn than the exposed flooring because it had been covered by the rug. At the top, near the wall, right about where Moriarty had been sniffing, a handle was inset into the wood. I pulled out my phone and snapped a couple of pictures, and then I leaned over, grabbed the handle, and pulled. The door lifted smoothly and easily, without so much as a squeak. The hinges had been oiled recently. And not by the resident ghost.

We leaned over and peered into the darkness. I switched on my phone's flashlight app and held it over the opening. It illuminated nothing but a packed dirt floor about three feet down. I dropped to my belly, stretched my legs out behind me, and peered over the edge. I could see nothing but stone and earth. I sat up and swung my legs over the space.

"Is it safe, Gemma?" Jayne asked.

"Only one way to find out." I dropped down, bent my knees, and landed easily. Scarcely a puff of dust rose at the impact of my feet. I shone my light around.

The underground room was about six feet by four, three feet high. The floor was hard-packed earth, the walls crumbling stone and packed rubble. The first thing I looked for was a second entrance, but I saw nothing like that. Wooden shelves, cracked and bent with age, lined three walls. They were empty of everything but mouse droppings, spiderwebs, a lot of dust, and a couple of shriveled and chewed objects I took to be long-forgotten apples. This had, almost certainly, been a root cellar long ago.

A metal pole, about five feet long, with a hook at the end, was propped against the wall. The hook would be just thin enough to fit through the crack between the floor and the hinged door, to reach up and pull the rug over the entrance when the door had been closed. Thus anyone who came into the pantry when the root cellar was occupied, wouldn't notice the rug out of place.

I shone my light down. The floor had none of the decades-long buildup of dust and mouse droppings that the shelves did, but in the light layer of dust, on either side of my own feet, lay clear evidence of footprints, the tread from a thoroughly modern set of trainers. I put my foot against one of the prints and took a picture. They were larger than mine, but not excessively so. An attempt had been made to wipe the detritus from a circle of floor and the portion of the wall next to it. A section approximately the right size for a person to sit on the floor, knees pulled up, and lean against the wall. Scuff marks in the light layer of dust next to the spot showed me where something had rested. A backpack or shopping bag possibly.

"What have you found down there?" Robyn called.

I didn't answer.

I studied the shelves in more detail. One spot had been swept clear of dust and droppings but there were no traces of what had been put there.

"You had no idea this was here?" I called up to Robyn and Sharon.

Four faces peered down at me. "No," Robyn said.

"No mention was ever made in the book where the volunteers leave notes and reminders for each other?"

"No. Is it a root cellar?" Sharon said. "How exciting! In the days before refrigerators and freezers, a farming family would have needed to store vegetables from the autumn harvest somewhere dark and cool in order for them to last over the winter months until—"

"I know what a root cellar's for," Robyn said.

"Well, pardon me for living," Sharon said.

"Should we call the police?" Mrs. Ramsbatten asked.

I popped my head through the opening. "Yes, I think you should. Someone has been here, and recently, and seeing as to how the entrance was concealed and the owners, meaning the Historical Society, didn't know about it, I'm going to say the reason for the visit was not entirely on the up-and-up."

"Is there an exit?" Jayne asked.

"Not that I can see."

"Why would someone have gone down there then?"

I keep promising myself to spend more time at the gym and sign up for yoga classes. Somehow that promise always seems to get away from me in attending to the business of the shop and the bustle of day-to-day living. I was regretting it now. A step or stool would be nice, but nothing like that was down here. I'm five foot eight, which gave me enough height that I could rest my forearms on the edge of the pantry floor.

"Do you need a hand?" Jayne asked.

"Let me try." I jumped and pulled and managed to flop onto the floor much like a fish being tossed onto the bottom of a boat. I wiggled my hips and pulled my legs out of the hole and tried not to grunt with the effort.

Any reasonably fit person could get out of the root cellar without aid. Mrs. Ramsbatten couldn't have managed, and probably not Sharon. Robyn was a good deal older than me, but she looked like a woman who visited the gym regularly.

"I think," I said, "we've uncovered the lair of the Ghost of Scarlet House."

* * *

I advised Robyn to call the police and tell them what I'd found. No point in my waiting around—the discovery of a previously unknown hiding place in an old building that wasn't even a private home wouldn't be a priority. I advised Robyn to contact board members and volunteers to ask if anyone had been in the root cellar lately or had noticed any signs of it being used.

We collected Moriarty and left while Sharon bustled about getting ready to begin her baking and Robyn started making calls. Mrs. Ramsbatten settled into her rocking chair, pulled her phone out of her skirt pockets, and sent a text. Her thumbs flew over the keypad with as much dexterity as those of a twelve-year-old. I couldn't help but notice that she kept the face of the phone turned from me. I wouldn't have paid any attention at all except that before focusing her attention on the phone, she gave me a big smile and a wave of her fingers. Mrs. Ramsbatten had begun volunteering at Scarlet House around the time the ghostly incidents started happening.

Coincidence? It had to be.

I hid a smile. She was hiding her texting because she didn't want me to catch her spreading gossip. I have nothing against gossip: a great deal of the things I learn about people come from overhearing gossip.

* * *

The Game Is a Footnote

Moriarty emerged from the crate as though he'd sprung off a trampoline or been shot out of a cannon. He flew across the room in a flurry of teeth, fur, claws, and hisses, to land on the top of the gaslight fiction shelf. And there he stayed for the rest of the day, eyes narrowed, tail twitching, watching my every move. He couldn't even be lured down when Lauren Tierney popped in to buy a stack of books shortly after noon.

"Why's he being like that?" she asked me.

"He spent the night at the animal hospital. He's letting me know he doesn't want to go back."

"Poor Moriarty. When Snowball went to the vet for her shots, she wasn't happy either. Mom said she didn't understand that we were doing the right thing and taking care of her. When we got home, she hid until dinnertime."

"I suspect Moriarty will come down when he hears the opening of the cat food can." I rang up Lauren's purchases. "Are these books for you or for a gift?"

"The Enola Holmes set's a birthday present for Madison. The other one's for me."

Business in the shop had been light all morning, so I had time to chat. "Do you ever go to sleepovers?"

"Sure. All the time. Madison's birthday party's going to be a sleepover. Why do you want to know?"

"No reason. How's school?"

Lauren gave me a big smile. "Good. I like it there. I thought I'd miss my old school, but the kids at the new one are nice, plus I'm still friends with Madison and some of the other girls from the old school."

"Glad to hear it," I said. Lauren's parents had recently had to scale down their lifestyle substantially, and one of the things that had to go was the private school for their daughter. That Lauren was happy in her new situation made me happy too. "Speaking of school, why are you not there? Today isn't a holiday, is it?"

"I had a dentist appointment. Mom took me, and she wanted to stop at Mrs. Hudson's to get a coffee to take into work, so she said I could run in here for the gift."

At that moment Lauren's mother came through the sliding door, take-out coffee cup and brown bag in one hand and a whipped cream–topped concoction for Lauren in the other.

I handed Lauren her books and said, "Good morning, Sheila."

Sheila Tierney gave me a nod. She didn't like me much, which was fine with me, as I thought she was a self-absorbed, self-obsessed mess who didn't deserve a daughter as curious and clever as Lauren. "Ready to go?"

"Yup." Lauren wiggled her fingers at Moriarty. "Bye. See you soon."

Some of the ice faded from his eyes, and his tail stopped twitching, but he didn't come down to see them off.

Sheila and Lauren were heading for the door when I remembered that high schools were hotbeds of local gossip, and Sheila taught at West London High. "Sheila, one moment, please."

She turned. "Yes?"

"Quick question: I've been trying to get in touch with a woman by the name of Bunny Leigh. Do you know who that is?"

"Oh yes. The pop star. Former pop star, that is. I heard she was in West London. I don't know her, if that's what you're asking."

"I want to arrange an event here at the shop, but no one can tell me where she's staying. I don't suppose any of your students mentioned it, did they?"

She shook her head. "Sorry, no. Bunny Leigh's way beyond the age for my students to have any interest in her. Some of the teachers were talking about her in the lunchroom last week, but I've heard nothing more."

"Thanks," I said.

They passed Ryan Ashburton on their way out. "Do you have time to grab a coffee?" he asked me.

"Sorry, no. I'm here by myself. Gale's coming in at three to work until closing."

Not for the first time, and not even for the first time that day, I reflected on how Sherlock Holmes hadn't had a business to run at the same time he was dashing about "the lowest and vilest alleys" and "smiling and beautiful countryside" on a case. I should be beating the bushes, searching for Ashleigh. I should be crawling over every inch of Scarlet House, looking for more hiding places. I should be speaking to everyone who'd ever had anything to do with Dave Chase or might possibly have encountered Bunny Leigh.

Then again, I was not a consulting detective, and the town of West London, Massachusetts had a perfectly capable police service. One member of which was standing before me, looking very handsome in a black leather jacket, gray wool scarf, and dark khakis. His cheeks were ruddy with cold, and he rubbed his ungloved hands together. He leaned against the sales counter. A couple of customers wandered in, and I called them a welcome.

Ryan spoke in a low voice. "I heard about what you found at Scarlet House this morning, and I sent an officer around to check it out. Do you think this supposed secret room has anything to do with the death of Dave Chase?"

"Not directly, as he wasn't killed in the house. But indirectly, it might. The root cellar has to be where the supposed ghost hid himself or herself." Robyn had reported seeing a ghostly figure on the upper floor, in the vicinity of the back staircase. The figure had disappeared, yet it had not gone through the kitchen, which was full of people at the time. A quick stop in the pantry and into the root cellar to wait until the coast was clear? A not very comfortable place to wait it out with a backpack of supplies? Almost certainly.

"Which brings us back," I said, "to the central question, which is why someone is pretending the house is haunted."

"When we know that, we'll be on our way to finding out who killed Dave Chase."

"Have you confirmed it's murder?"

"No, and unless—until we find someone who witnessed what happened, or who caused it, we won't know for sure. He fell and landed badly. The autopsy found no evidence of him having suffered a heart attack or an aneurism, or anything else that would have caused him to collapse. He was in generally good health. Whether he was pushed or not is the question, and so I'm still digging. We've found no signs he was in a fight, no signs of anything untoward happening in that hayloft. He was wearing a heavy jacket, so there was no bruising on his chest or arms that might indicate he'd been pushed."

"Change of subject: What's happening with Ashleigh? Did you open a file?"

He nodded. "Yes, I did. But I have to warn you, Gemma: all that means is our officers have been told to speak to her if they come across her, and ask if she needs assistance. It's her right not to tell anyone where she is if she doesn't want them to know, and without evidence of foul play . . ."

"I know. I do. It's just so uncharacteristic of her. Have you had any luck locating Bunny Leigh?"

"Again, Bunny Leigh has done nothing to warrant us searching for her. That you saw her watching Ashleigh isn't enough to have a police investigation opened."

"But—"

He lifted one hand. "But, considering it's you who noticed it, I'm giving the issue more weight than I would otherwise." He glanced up. "What's with Moriarty today? All he does is crouch up there and stare at me as though he's wishing he had enough weight behind him to land on me and pound me into the ground."

The only person Moriarty doesn't like, aside from me, is Ryan. "Don't ask." Last night, in our mad rush to the emergency vet, we'd taken the vase and flowers with us. I hoped Donald didn't come in for a few days and wonder where his flowers were. I didn't want to have to tell him he almost killed my cat.

"Okay," Ryan said. "I won't ask. I've started a few subtle inquires as to Ms. Leigh's whereabouts. Some not so subtle, as several women who work in the department, officers as well as civilian staff, were excited about her being in town. She's been spotted shopping on Baker Street, and I gather that was a thrilling occurrence. That happened a few days ago, and there've been no sightings since. It's not known where she's staying or if she's still in town. Rumor says she rented a house for the winter, so

I'm having someone make calls to realtors and renting agencies, but so far nothing. If she rented directly from the homeowner, or if the property was taken under another name . . . Not much more we can do. Not yet."

I didn't like the sound of that *yet*. What Ryan meant was he couldn't do more until he had evidence that Ashleigh had not left voluntarily, with or without her mother.

"Excuse me." A woman smiled shyly at me. "Do you have any books on the actor Jeremy Brett? I loved him as Holmes."

"We do," I said. "Be with you in a minute." I glanced at Ryan.

"I'll let you know if anything more comes up." He gave me a wink and his private smile, and then headed to Mrs. Hudson's for his coffee, and I went to help the customer.

* * *

Gale arrived for work at three. For some reason we had a rush of customers, and even with her help, I was kept busy behind the cash register. The shop was full at twenty to four, so I popped my head into the tearoom to tell them I wouldn't make today's partners' meeting with Jayne.

"Did you hear anything further about Bunny Leigh?" I asked Fiona and Jocelyn.

"Not a peep," Jocelyn said. "She hasn't been in here again."

By five thirty the rush had slowed. Moriarty still hadn't come down from his fortress, and I was thinking about the discovery of the trap door when an idea hit me.

"Things seem okay here," I said to Gale. "For now. Think you can manage if I go out for an hour or so? You have my phone number."

"Sure. Why's Moriarty sulking up there anyway?"

"Don't ask."

After leaving the vet and then Scarlet House, I'd had Jayne take me home so I could get my car rather than be dropped at the Emporium. If I heard from Ashleigh and she needed help, I wanted to be able to get to her quickly.

I ran upstairs for my coat and bag and then let myself out the back door into the alley. It was almost fully dark and the streetlamps had come on. The air was sharp and cold. I got into my car and pulled my phone out of my pocket. The battery was showing less than ten percent charge, so I plugged it into the car's power supply.

Cheerful yellow light spilled from the shops and restaurants along Baker Street and Harbor Road, but the boardwalk and the pier were wrapped in midwinter dusk. The lighthouse flashed its regular rhythm, temporarily breaking the gloom. Overhead, clouds covered the stars, and the ocean was a sheet of black velvet, punctured by the lights of the few fishing boats heading for harbor or passing freighters far out at sea. A handful of cars were in the parking lot in front of Andy's restaurant, and as I passed, I caught the whiff of something delicious wafting out of the kitchens.

Reminding me that as well as all the other matters jostling for attention in my mind, I was supposed to be helping Jayne plan her wedding.

I drove north on Harbor Road and pulled in at Scarlet House. No cars were in the parking lot, and although the light over the front door was on, the interior of the old house was dark, as was the barn. The lamp at the top of the tall post between the house and the barn threw a circle of light onto the ground.

I parked and reached into the glove box for a flashlight. I stood next to the car for a few moments, taking stock of my surroundings. I could hear the soft murmur of the sea in the distance. Muffled grunts, squeals, brays, and baas drifted out of the barn.

This afternoon, as I'd been waiting on customers, ringing up purchases, worrying about Ashleigh, and being glared at by a vengeful cat, it occurred to me that if I'd found a previously unknown hiding place in the house, something similar might be in the barn.

This wasn't the time for a thorough search of a place I didn't know my way around, but it wouldn't hurt to have a quick look. If I found anything at all out of the ordinary, I'd call for backup. Although, what constituted "out of the ordinary" in a working barn, I—city girl through and through—had no idea.

I switched on my flashlight and headed for the barn. The pigs heard me coming and set up a chorus of excited yips, squeals, and grunts. That got the chickens, the sheep, and the donkey joining in. The bright red door was secured by a metal latch, but no lock, and I let myself in. My flashlight's a powerful one, so I didn't bother trying to find a light switch. The main entrance led directly into the clean open space where the docents give demonstrations and the play-farmer talks to visitors about his day's work. The wide-planked floor was spotless, the few pieces of furniture—a couple of wooden stools, a three-legged pot suspended over a cold firepit—dusted, and the farm implements attractively arranged on the walls. No cobwebs hung in the corners, and no traces of the passing of mice could be seen. There were no rugs on the floor, or anything else that would conceal a secret entrance. A door, secured by the same sort of latch as was the main entrance, divided the demonstration area of the barn from the working farm part. I lifted the latch and stepped through. Now this, I thought, was more like the real thing. The rough wooden planks of the floor were marred by patches of dried mud and stray pieces of straw. A mouse trap—thankfully empty—was tucked into a corner. Bags of feed were stacked next to plastic tubs and galvanized iron buckets, cracked or rusted with age and thick with dirt. A jumble of tools was piled against one wall. I bent over and lifted one of the feed bags. Or rather I attempted to lift it. It was very heavy and I let it go. If a hiding place was under there, no one would be able to slip in and out quickly. I stood on my tip toes and peered over the five-foot-high partition into the pig enclosure. The sheep were kept next to the pigs, then the chickens, and the donkey was housed at the far end. The door to the outside was open, presumably so the pigs could come and go as they liked. They pushed their snouts against the wall nearest me and squealed, ordering me to toss some food their way. Four tiny curved pink tails quivered.

A plank creaked. I heard a puff of breath, and I turned as the door leading to the main part of the building swung shut.

I crossed the floor in a few quick steps and reached for the handle, only to find there wasn't one on this side. Instead, a string passed through a small hole drilled in the door. Presumably the string was attached to the latch on the other side. I tugged at it, and the entire thing slipped through the hole. I stared at the dangling end stupidly.

"Hello? Anyone out there?" I tried to listen for sounds of someone moving, but the pigs were beginning to get agitated, and their grunts and bellows were increasing. Something extremely heavy and extremely solid crashed against the rickety wooden wall of the pig enclosure. It was soon followed by another thump, and then another, as the pigs tested the strength of the barrier.

I slipped my hand into my pocket and it came up empty. I muttered a curse: I'd left my phone charging in the car.

I smothered a sense of rising panic, stepped back, and took stock of my situation. An interior door lay to my right. I opened it and peered in. More feed bags, coils of chicken wire, plastic tubs, and rusty tools. No exit.

A rickety wooden ladder led up into the darkness of the hay loft. I considered climbing it and jumping down into the yard, but then an image of Dave Chase flashed through my mind.

The two small windows on this level were big enough that I could probably force my hips through, but iron bars were inset into the frames. I gave them a solid tug, but nothing moved, not even a wiggle.

I stood on my toes once again and peered into the pig enclosure. They were below me, grunting and shoving their snouts against the wall. They knew I was here, and they knew I had access to their food supplies.

The door leading from their pen to the outside was open. The fence around the barnyard was made of wood rails, easy enough to clamber over. An electric wire ran through it, but I figured I could avoid that wire as I climbed over, as I had when I discovered Dave Chase's body. If not, a quick bolt of electricity wouldn't hurt me.

Much.

The pigs were getting louder, bellowing and squealing, sounding almost frantic as they tried to get at me and their food. The walls shuddered under the force of their substantial bodies. The sheep began chiming in, and then the donkey. The chickens called and flapped their wings. If I opened the door, the pigs would rush into the storage area. They'd tear the feed bags apart, but that couldn't be helped. I'd call someone to tell them what was going on once I got to the car.

The door into the pen opened inward, toward me. It was old wood, cracked and warped, secured by a thick bolt. I grabbed the handle of the bolt and pulled it hard to the right. It slipped easily out of its socket, and the door began to swing open. Before I could let out a sigh of relief, several hundred porcine pounds hit the door full on. I yelped and shoved at it without thinking. The door crashed backward and stopped before it broke into the pigpen, but it had gone past its resting place and the bolt was firmly embedded in the warped wood of the door frame. I pulled at it, to no avail. It was thoroughly stuck.

I pushed down my rising panic. The sound of the pigs trying to get at me (more likely trying to get at their food, but I hated to think what would happen if they thought I was in the way) was absolutely terrifying. Genuine horror movie stuff.

"Get a grip, Gemma," I said out loud. "They're farm animals. Not wild boars. They're well fed, comfortably housed, not starving in the forest in the midst of a Russian winter."

More weight crashed against the walls. Swine squealed. I trembled. I might be able to tell myself I was in no danger from them, but my primal instincts said otherwise. There had been a time when weak frail creatures such as me were nothing but food for the wild things of the world.

"This," I said in a good loud voice, "is West London, Massachusetts, and it is not those times." I thought my voice was firm. It might have come out more as a squeak.

I might not be pig food, not today, but danger could lie elsewhere. I pulled my mind back to more immediate questions. Had I heard someone outside moments before the door closed on me?

If so, they'd deliberately locked me in, and there was no point in yelling for help. As for hailing anyone: no one passing on the road would hear me. A dog might try to investigate the cries, but its owner would simply pull it back and carry on.

How long would it be before someone noticed I was gone and came looking for me? Would Gale worry when I didn't return to the Emporium in time for closing? Had Ashleigh told her I was a "scatterbrain" and always rushing off? Entirely possible. Uncle Arthur was away, and I had no plans to meet anyone tonight.

Presumably my absence would be noted shortly after opening time at the shop tomorrow. Whoever arrived to open the museum in the morning would see my car. Someone would come to tend to the animals first thing. I didn't fancy spending the night in here, but it was warm enough, and I had my coat. I had nothing to eat—save some pig food—and no water, but I'd be okay for one night.

What then had been the purpose of locking me in? If that's what had happened. I thought I'd heard someone approach the door, but I couldn't say for sure, not over the noise of the pigs.

I had another flash of panic. Not primal fear this time, but the sense of immediate danger. If whoever locked me in set the barn on fire, I'd be trapped. I took several deep breaths, but to my infinite relief, I smelled not a hint of smoke.

A practical joke?

Maybe. I did have a reputation for being a snoop. Robyn and Sharon were both on edge, and about to tip over. Ethan, the PhD candidate, didn't seem to care for me poking around. Was he genuinely concerned that my "ghost hunting" would interfere with his dissertation? Or was it something more?

The who or why didn't matter for the moment. I was trapped in a pig barn. I might survive having to spend a long winter's night in here, but I'd rather not. I also had to consider that they—whoever they were—might come back and finish the job. I pulled on the bolt and tugged on the door, but nothing moved. Both were thoroughly stuck. All I managed to achieve was to get the pigs riled up even more. I'd foolishly left more than my phone in the car. I kept a small screwdriver in my bag, intended for just such emergencies.

I eyed the ladder to the hay loft and shone my light up into the darkness. The ladder was steep and rickety and no doubt the wood would be full of splinters. I gripped the railings the best I could while still holding onto the flashlight and began to climb. My head emerged into the hay loft. Thick clouds of hay, dust, and desiccated insects swirled through the light. Once again I remembered Dave Chase, his neck broken. Surely I'd be okay if I judged the distance and jumped carefully?

If I didn't—how long might I lie there with a broken leg or worse? Down below me the pigs grunted. Pigs, so I've heard, aren't all that fussy about what they eat.

I climbed back down.

I kicked the door to the pigpen. It didn't move, but that gave me an idea. I eyed the plastic tubs, but they showed signs of cracks. I didn't trust them with my weight, and the bottoms of the iron buckets were rusty. I put my flashlight on a shelf, grabbed a bag of feed, and slowly dragged it to the half wall. For what felt like hours, I dragged bags across the room and heaped them on top of each other. When I'd built a wall about three feet high, I climbed up and looked down at the pigs. My activity had driven them into even more of a frenzy. They threw their bodies at the wall, they grunted and bellowed and paced back and forth. If I suddenly appeared in their midst, would they trample me underfoot or knock me over? Would they decide I'd do in place of the pig food I was keeping them from?

What can I say? I'm not a farmer. Only now, I did realize that I was surrounded by animal feed. It took me a while, but I managed to tear open one of the bags using the edge of a dull, rusty farm implement of unknown purpose as a makeshift knife, and I filled a bucket with the dry porridge-like contents. I clambered onto my hastily constructed platform and dumped the food over the wall. The pigs ran for it, pushing and shoving each other out of the way. They buried their noses into the feed.

Just to be safe, I tossed in another bucketful.

Pigs distracted, I threw the bucket to one side, braced myself, swung one leg over the wall, took a deep breath, and pulled the other leg up after it. I considered going back for my flashlight, but I needed the light to see my way over, and I didn't want it encumbering my hands.

I jumped.

The Game Is a Footnote

I landed in a patch of warm, wet straw and rolled. I didn't want to think about what made the straw warm and wet, as I leapt to my feet. A quick mental inventory showed me that I appeared to be unharmed.

A brown-and-beige-spotted pig lifted its head from the feast, and one small black eye studied me.

"Nice piggy?" I said.

She shoved a smaller animal out of the way and went back to her unscheduled meal.

I ran into the barnyard.

Next thing I knew, I was flat on my back, staring up into the night. As the temperature dropped, the mud had turned into a sheet of ice.

Taking more care, I slowly got to my feet and then carefully waddled across the yard. Keeping my eyes on the thin wire running between the wooden fence posts about a foot off the ground, I climbed carefully. I reached the top and jumped down without touching the live wire.

I took another deep breath, this time of relief.

That had been incredibly frightening.

Traffic moved steadily on Harbor Road. Lights shone from houses backing onto the museum property. A plane flew overhead, heading west toward Boston, perhaps having crossed the ocean from Europe. Maybe even dear old England.

The sounds from the barn had died down as the pigs happily stuffed themselves and the other animals were assured the excitement was over. Otherwise, nothing moved and all was quiet.

I gave myself a few minutes to calm my nerves. I doubted someone was out here, waiting to jump me. If that had been their intent, they would have had a far better opportunity to overpower me when I was straddling the wall to the pig enclosure. I went to my car, grabbed my phone, and switched on the flashlight ap. Then I went back to the barn. I shone my light on the ground, looking for signs of footprints placed on top of mine, but the ground was slick with ice and it was impossible to tell in the hardpacked, frozen earth what was fresh and what wasn't. I couldn't even distinguish my own prints. Inside the barn, there were no visible footprints on the clean floors of the display area. I studied the latch on the door to where I'd been trapped. It was in place, as I'd found it before I opened it. I'd stuffed the string into my pocket, and I took it out and studied it under the light from my phone. The string was old, the ends frayed but not cut. Impossible to say if it had been deliberately untied or had simply come loose. I considered going inside for my flashlight but decided against it. I had no desire to venture in there again.

I called good night to the pigs and headed for my car. I switched on the engine and cranked the heat up high. I didn't know who was caring for the animals now that Dave wasn't, so I called Robyn.

She answered and didn't sound at all surprised to hear my voice. Did that mean she hadn't hoped I'd be pig food by now? Impossible to say. I asked her to tell the farmer the pigs had had an extra meal today.

"What does that mean?"

I hung up and drove back to the Sherlock Holmes Bookshop and Emporium in time for closing. As I drove, my headlights reflected off the few drifting flakes of snow.

Chapter Seventeen

"Everything okay?" Gale asked when I came in, brushing snow off my shoulders and attempting to smile brightly. "Why wouldn't it be?"

"No reason. Before you ask, I didn't hear from Ashleigh. I'm getting worried, Gemma."

I dropped the smile. "So am I. Sorry to have kept you. Something unexpected came up. You can go and I'll stay until closing. Will you be able to come in tomorrow?"

"I'd be happy to. I like working here."

"You were hired for two days a week, but . . ."

"It's only until Ashleigh comes back, right?"

"Right."

I glanced around the store, taking a quick mental inventory. A few books had been removed from the shelves, but otherwise it seems to have been quiet. Then I noticed one thing in particular missing. The shelf above the gaslight section was empty. "Where's Moriarty?"

"He came down as soon as you left, but he must have heard your key in the back door. He ran up the stairs as though he was in hot pursuit of a mouse, and a moment later, you came in."

"Let me hang up my coat, and then you can go."

"If you don't mind my saying so, Gemma . . . you don't smell too good. Did you step in something, and how'd your coat get so dirty?"

"I had a tumble on the ice. No harm done. It's starting to snow."

She lifted one eyebrow but said nothing.

Upstairs in my office, I took off my coat and hung it on the hook behind the door. "Dirty" was an understatement. The front was covered with dust, cobwebs, splinters of wood, and whatever had rubbed off the feed bags. The back was worse— mud, the remains of rotting vegetable scraps, and whatever the pigs had left in their passing.

It was a nice coat too—a check pattern of brown and beige outlined with thin red lines, made of good warm wool. I hoped it could be saved.

I went into the washroom to check myself in the mirror. I didn't look much better than my coat, but at least I could be washed. I plucked strands of straw off my face, wiped away dirt, and tried to shake thawing mud out of the back of my hair.

Oh well. It was almost closing. I'd do.

It likely had been my boots Gale had smelled. They were thick with whatever had been the soft, warm stuff I'd landed on in the pigpen. I gave them a thorough rinse and scrub in the sink and managed to get most of the residue off. Feeling barely presentable, I went back downstairs and told Gale she could leave.

I then checked my phone for messages, hoping I'd have an update from Ryan on the search for Ashleigh, but nothing. I considered telling him about my adventures in the barn but decided not to. Not yet anyway. I couldn't be positive someone had locked me in, and I had come to no harm.

Which made me wonder what—if it had been deliberate—had been the reason behind it. I'd been momentarily frightened (okay, totally terrified), but that was all. I hadn't seen signs of anyone in the barn, or disturbed anyone in the house getting up to something they shouldn't. I hadn't finished searching the barn for a secret room, but that didn't mean I wouldn't be able to do so another time. I briefly considered returning to the museum to search for additional clues, but I decided discretion was the better part of valor. If someone had been up to something earlier, they'd be long gone now.

I considered that it had been nothing but an attempt to put a fright in me (a successful attempt at that) in order to discourage me from poking my nose into either the ghostly happenings or the death of Dave Chase. If so, that person didn't know me very well. I hadn't really been investigating anything. It was only by happenstance and because of an angry cat that I'd discovered the root cellar. Now, I was most definitely interested.

That reminded me, once again, that on another occasion Jayne had been harmed by someone trying to get to me. I called her, and she answered. I could hear a buzz of conversation and what sounded like banging pots in the background, and felt an instant sense of relief.

"Hey, Gemma. What's up?"

"Nothing much. Just checking in."

"Have you heard from Ashleigh?"

"No."

"That is worrying. I asked the staff here if anyone had seen Bunny Leigh, but they said no. Most of the people who work here don't even know who she is."

"Are you at the Café?"

A man shouted something indecipherable, and a woman shouted back, "Hold your horses, I'm on it!"

"Yup." Jayne giggled. "I'm helping Andy with dinner. Some people might not think that's a hot date, but we do."

It didn't sound much like a hot date to me either, but to each her own. "Will you do me a favor, Jayne?"

"Sure. What?"

"Stay alert, please."

"What does that mean? What happened? Something happened, didn't it—I can tell."

"Nothing happened." I lied, but it was for her own good. "Until I hear from Ashleigh and know she's safe, we need to be on guard, that's all. Let me speak to Andy."

"No."

"No? What do you mean, no?"

She lowered her voice. The sound of the busy kitchen fell away, and I assumed she'd taken herself out of Andy's hearing range. "I'm not going to let you tell Andy he has to guard me or something. He'll go way overboard. You have to admit, Gemma, you don't know Ashleigh all that well. Maybe she did simply decide she'd had enough of working at the Emporium and left."

"In the middle of her shift? I don't believe that and neither do you."

"I have to go. The pasta sauce needs stirring."

"Jayne—"

She'd hung up. I considered phoning Andy directly but decided not to. Jayne didn't often get angry, but when she did—watch out. She'd be furious if I worried Andy, and she was probably right. I didn't know if Ashleigh had been lured away or harmed, and I wasn't entirely sure my recent misadventure hadn't been an accident. I hadn't looked at the string on the latch to the door before going inside; it might not have been attached properly to begin with. A gust of wind (although it was an interior door) could have swung the door shut behind me.

I helped the last few customers and then flipped the sign to "Closed" and locked the shop. I ran through the usual end-of-day routines before going upstairs for my coat and bag. As I climbed the steps, I might have heard the sound of paws skidding across the floors, but I saw no sign of Moriarty. I filled his water and food dishes, cleaned the litter box, called a cheery "Goodnight," and took myself home.

*　*　*

I dug in the freezer searching for something for dinner. Uncle Arthur's the cook in our house, and he always prepares extra servings for me to have when he's away. I found a container of beef stew that I remembered being very good, and popped it into the microwave. While it heated, I threw together a quick salad.

Meal ready, I put my bowl on a tray, added a glass of wine and some cutlery and carried it into the den. Violet and Peony, replete with their own dinner, followed me.

I put the tray on a side table and crouched in front of the fireplace. Crumpled-up newspapers, used computer paper, and the usual assortment of unwanted advertising flyers were piled in a wicker basket next to the fireplace. Another basket held kindling, and thick logs were stacked to one side. I arranged the paper and kindling and struck a match. Nothing warms my English soul like a real fire on a cold winter's night.

The kindling caught quickly, and I laid two hefty birch logs on top. Then I settled myself in a comfortable chair and opened my iPad. I checked for recent news of Bunny Leigh, hoping someone would have seen her going in or out of a house in West London, but I found nothing. It had briefly crossed my mind that the incident in the barn might be related not to the goings-on at Scarlet House, but to the disappearance of Ashleigh, but I could see no connection between the two problems. Didn't mean there wasn't one, of course.

I didn't bother to phone Ryan for an update. If he had something to tell me, he would.

I placed a different call. "Good evening, Mrs. Saunderson. It's Gemma Doyle here."

"Who?" Ashleigh's grandmother's voice was full of suspicion.

"Ashleigh's employer? From the Sherlock—"

"Oh yes. You. What do you want?"

"I'm wondering if you've heard from Ashleigh since we last spoke."

"I told you, Ashleigh calls us on Sunday. Every Sunday. It hasn't been Sunday yet."

"Yes, but I thought that if she . . . uh . . . changed her plans, decided to look for a new job or such, she might contact you."

She lowered her voice. "Have you seen Leigh?"

"Leigh? You mean Bunny Leigh? No, I haven't. Should I have?"

"If she's in your town . . . bothering Ashleigh, I thought . . ."

"Mrs. Saunderson. If Ashleigh's mother wants to see her, I wouldn't consider that bothering her."

"She broke our hearts, that girl. Her father's most of all. Left us without so much as a by-your-leave and then showed up at our door years later with a baby in her arms. A baby she didn't have any interest in raising herself. She said hello, handed us the baby, and then it was goodbye once again."

A voice in the background demanded to know whom she was talking to.

"I have to go," Mrs. Saunderson said. "If Ashleigh calls, I'll tell her you're asking after her." The line went dead.

Whatever the history of the Saunderson family, it sounded like a sad one, but I'd learned what I needed to know: Ashleigh hadn't been in touch with her grandparents. Which meant absolutely nothing.

I settled back in my chair and switched my train of thought from Ashleigh to the people at Scarlet House. I hadn't asked Robyn who was looking after the animals in the absence of Dave Chase, and I decided to do that now. I called her, but she didn't answer, so I left a message. She might, or might not, call me back.

I next accessed the *West London Star* and the WLPD web pages, but neither had anything new to tell me about the progress of the investigation. I ran my fork through beef gravy and thought about the people involved with Scarlet House. I didn't know much about Ethan Evanston. Time to rectify that. I put down the fork and began to type.

From what I discovered, he appeared to be exactly what he claimed to be: a candidate for a PhD in American history at Yale. His BA was in colonial-era American history from the University at Albany, and he'd earned his master's degree at Cambridge in England, where his thesis had been on patterns of immigration from Britain and Ireland to North America over the seventeenth to nineteenth centuries. He'd grown up in Rochester, New York, second son of an insurance salesperson and a bank executive. He'd played shortstop on his high school baseball team and had done the same at Albany. I found plenty of pictures of him enjoying the pub life of Cambridge and at various Yale events. It was possible he'd decided his doctoral thesis needed an extra something, and he'd invented the ghost of Scarlet House to provide that, but I couldn't see it. Yale was, or so I'd heard, a staid, respectable institution. As he'd told me, whispers of ghost hunting would not be likely to advance his academic credentials in any way.

The dogs were snoozing in front of the dying fire. I was about to get up and put on another log, when Violet leapt to her feet, and Peony quickly followed. They set up a chorus of barking and ran out of the room. A moment later the doorbell rang.

I glanced at my watch. Ten o'clock. Late for a caller. If it were Ryan or Jayne, or even Donald or Irene, they would have texted to tell me they were coming.

I switched on the outside light and peered through the glass of the door.

The Game Is a Footnote

A woman stood on the step. She smiled at me and lifted a gloved hand in greeting. Behind her, the streetlamp caught the shape of a large black SUV disappearing into a sheet of swirling snow. I took a step backward, shook my head, and looked again.

She was still there. My eyes had not been deceiving me.

I opened the door and said, "What on earth?"

"You're pleased to see me, I trust," Phillipa Doyle said.

Chapter Eighteen

"I accompanied my boss to Washington for meetings, totally fruitless meetings, I might add. He's staying on for a few days and told me I wouldn't be needed, so I decided that since I was in the neighborhood, it would be fun to pop down and see you."

"Up."

"Up?"

"Washington is south of Cape Cod. Therefore you came up. Not down. Which is beside the point as I wouldn't exactly say we're in the same neighborhood."

"Not by U.K. standards, no, but the distances are so much greater in North America, aren't they?" My sister took off her cashmere camel coat and peeled off her fur-trimmed brown leather gloves. Her bright red carry-on suitcase was on the floor next to her high-heeled leather ankle boots. Her scarf and handbag matched the suitcase. I didn't think that was accidental. Her hair was slightly longer than when I'd last seen her and colored a shade lighter. It suited her. She'd put on a couple of pounds. Which definitely suited her better than her formerly skeletal frame.

She opened the closet door, found a hanger, and hung up her coat. She wore a navy-blue business suit consisting of a perfectly tailored jacket, knee-length skirt, and crisp white blouse that didn't show a single wrinkle. She took off her boots and then turned to me with a smile. "Are you going to invite me in?"

"Looks like you're already in. I'm surprised to see you, that's all."

We stepped toward each other and hugged awkwardly. That over, thank goodness, we separated. In true upper-crust English tradition, our family has never been one for visible displays of affection. On top of that, Pippa and I had never got on terribly well. She's seven years older than me and has always been inclined to look at the world and everyone in it as though from a lofty height.

She said, "I'm absolutely starving. Such an exhausting day and then the tedious journey here."

"I'm sure I can rustle up something. Come on in." I led the way down the hallway while Violet and Peony danced around our legs.

"I see you have dogs," Pippa said. "Two dogs. How . . . nice."

I opened the fridge and peered in. "Sandwich okay?"

She pointed to the open bottle of wine on the shelf. "Along with a glass of that, would be perfect."

I took out the bottle and poured. Pippa glanced casually around the kitchen. She appeared nonchalant, but I was well aware she was checking everything out, down to the finest detail.

"If I'd known you were coming"—I handed her a glass—"I'd have tidied up."

"Never mind the sandwich, this will do. I had something inedible on the plane, crammed into the middle seat between an overweight man and a restless teenager whose hideous taste in music leaked out of his earbuds the entire time."

"I doubt that," I said. "If you did fly from Washington, you were on a private jet to Hyannis airport, and once you arrived, you didn't bother stepping into the street and hailing a cab."

She raised one perfectly sculpted eyebrow. "What makes you think so?"

"That SUV that dropped you off? That was no airport limo or taxi, it was a government vehicle. High security, trying and failing to be incognito. Driver and bodyguard in the front."

She smiled. "I'm pleased to see living in America hasn't dulled your wits."

My father had said exactly the same thing when I was last in London. I wondered if they'd been talking about me. Probably.

"I didn't need the security, but my boss insisted. America can be so dangerous, can't it?"

"I also notice you didn't call ahead or worry about dropping by without notice and not finding me home. I might have gone out of town for a few days."

"Nothing high-level intelligence about that. Uncle Arthur told me you're in charge of the dogs, not to mention your businesses, in his absence." She glanced down. Violet and Peony sat at her feet, smiling up at her. "If you'd been out for the evening, I would have taken a seat on the doorstep and waited."

"Unlikely," I said. She would have tracked me down, and I had no doubt she would have found me.

She lifted her glass. "Cheers."

I lifted my empty hand. "Cheers. I was in the den. Come on through."

The Game Is a Footnote

I tossed another log onto the fire while my sister studied the comfortable room. "This is an interesting house. The design is most unusual."

"It's called a saltbox, a traditional Cape Cod plan. Uncle Arthur's suite's upstairs, and I have the section down the hall. We share the living room, den, and kitchen. The house was originally built in 1756."

"It's nice."

"We like it."

She crossed the room and stood in front of the painting hanging on the wall next to the fireplace. It was of a woman, lush black hair, wide dark eyes, full red lips, extravagant gown trimmed with red lace, spray of black feathers in her hair. "Maria Fernanda Garcia Gonzalez, I presume."

"You know her name? Uncle Arthur has never, in all the time I've been living here, said a word about it. Or about her."

"Father told me the outline of the story once. She and Uncle Arthur were engaged to be married. She was a Spanish opera singer of some renown. She died."

"Uncle Arthur never got over it."

"No."

I was quiet for a moment, thinking about the woman I'd never known, and then I said, "Speaking of one's true love, how's Grant?"

Pippa turned from the painting. Her smile was radiant. "Splendid. Absolutely splendid. He didn't come on this trip because it was a last-minute thing when my boss decided he needed my assistance."

"With road planning."

225

"The design of new expressways in urban areas can be highly complicated. So I've learned from taking the minutes at meetings." She took a seat. Peony sniffed at her skirt, and Pippa hesitantly held out one hand.

My sister told the few people who might be interested that she labored as the personal assistant to a mid-level bureaucrat in the Department for Transport.

I believed she ran the British government single-handedly. Once, I would have instantly suspected she would only have made this impromptu visit to me in pursuit of the interests of the British government. But the look on her face when she mentioned Grant, the way her eyes shone and her lips turned up at the edges, how something in the nature of softness replaced the usual no-nonsense lines, made me reconsider.

She had made this sound like an impromptu visit, but Pippa has never done anything impromptu in her life, and I didn't think she even knows what "fun" is. I pushed aside my suspicions: maybe being in love with Grant Thompson was making her slightly human after all, and I was happy for that.

But I still didn't think she'd been in Washington to discuss highways and decided to pay a social call out of the blue.

"Speaking of men," she said with a wink, "how is the delectable Detective Ashburton?"

"He's well. We're good. He's busy on a murder case right now."

"Is he indeed? That must be so interesting."

I settled back in my chair and asked after our parents.

* * *

My sister and I talked long into the night. Pippa had always been able to get by on a minimal amount of sleep, and the time change didn't seem to be affecting her. She leaned back into the cushions and curled her legs underneath her. After a few minutes of initial hesitation, she clucked and cooed to Violet and Peony, and gave them rubs behind their ears and scratches between their eyes. Her phone buzzed a couple of times, and she checked it without comment, her face expressionless. She did not reply.

I didn't tell her about the goings-on at Scarlet House, but I did mention that my shop assistant had disappeared and I was getting worried.

"You say that behavior's out of character for her? I scarcely remember being in my twenties, Gemma, but I do remember it was an impulsive time of life."

I stared at my sister. She didn't know the meaning of the word *impulsive*, never mind once having been so. "People can act in unexpected ways," I said. "I suppose it's possible, as everyone keeps telling me, that she met some guy and was completely swept off her feet, and they've run off for a quicky marriage and a few days of wedded bliss in Provincetown or something, but I have trouble seeing it. I thought I knew Ashleigh well enough to leave my livelihood in her hands. I thought I was a good judge of character."

"Everyone thinks they're a good judge of character," Pippa said.

The name Bunny Leigh didn't mean anything to Pippa, but when I'd finished telling her what I'd discovered about her relationship with Ashleigh, she said, "Instead of meeting a man, what if your clerk encountered her long-lost mother and became so overwhelmed with emotion she forgot common sense. That's the sort of occurrence that might cause someone to behave uncharacteristically, I would think."

"Maybe. But I'm still worried about her." I suppressed a yawn and felt my bed calling to me. "It's late and I have work in the morning. The spare room's made up. You're welcome but . . . uh . . . how long are you planning to stay?"

Pippa shrugged. "I thought a couple of days. See the sights. There are sights to see, I gather?"

"Yes. Although January isn't the best time."

"I'd like to see Jayne, such a lovely woman, and I'll pop into your little shop. I'm wondering what appeal it can possibly hold for you."

* * *

I woke to bright sunlight, the kind you only get after a fresh snowfall, streaming in through my windows. Violet curled into my back, Peony breathing into my face, and the sound of cupboard doors opening and closing in the kitchen. I shoved the dogs aside and went to investigate.

"I thought I'd dreamt about you," I said to my sister. "I guess it wasn't a dream after all."

"Here I am, in the flesh. Tea?"

"Thank you."

Pippa was as fresh-faced as though she hadn't recently crossed five time zones and sat up talking half the night. Her eyes were alert, her face scrubbed, her hair tied back, and she wore midnight-blue satin pajamas. She poured my tea. "Toast?"

"Not yet, thanks." I put the dogs out. The snow had stopped overnight; everything was pure and clean and brilliantly white, but a strong wind was blowing off the ocean, whirling flakes through the air.

I accepted a cup of tea. As I sipped the perfectly made cuppa, I checked my phone. No messages. I texted Ryan: *Of all strange things, Pippa arrived last night. Staying for a few days.*

"Warning your beloved to stay clear?" Pippa asked.

I was facing toward her, holding the phone in front of me. No way would she have been able to see what I was typing. She gave me a wink.

I finished my tea while Pippa rummaged through the fridge, searching for the jam. "I usually walk to work, so you're welcome to the car. Keys are on the hook in the mudroom. Don't forget that they drive on the wrong side of the road here. My neighbor comes over in the afternoons when Uncle Arthur's away to let the dogs out. I'll mention you're here before I leave."

"Your neighbor? I'd love to meet her."

"Since when are you interested in meeting random people?"

"I'm interested in people, Gemma."

"How'd you know it's a her?"

Something that might have been a flash of annoyance crossed Pippa's face. But then it was gone and she said, "An educated guess. No doubt she's fallen under the considerable force of Arthur's charm."

I had to admit that was a good guess. Most of the elderly ladies in West London and environs had made friends with Great Uncle Arthur. A good many wanted to be more than friends.

I stood up. "I'm going to get dressed. Can you let the dogs in when you hear them at the door, please? Make yourself at home."

I put my phone on the night table while I jumped in the shower. As I stood under the hot water washing my hair, I tried to decide what I thought about Pippa's visit. In all the years I'd been living in West London, this was the first time she'd come. As I've said, we'd never been close. She did seem to have changed since she met Grant—a bit more relaxed maybe, allowed herself to become a person capable of being happy. And that was a good thing. Maybe he'd been talking about West London and had put the sudden visit into her mind. I couldn't help being suspicious, but I could think of no reason to be distrustful. Nothing was going on in West London, Massachusetts, that would be of concern to topmost echelons of the British government.

I dried my hair and added a touch of lipstick and blush, and then I studied myself in the mirror. I hadn't said anything to Pippa last night about Scarlet House. I decided to do so now. Regardless of why my sister was here, she had the sharpest mind of anyone I knew. She might see patterns in the events at the museum I'd missed.

I dressed for a day at work in casual black trousers and a cashmere cardigan in a soft shade of blue over a navy shirt, scooped up my phone and headed for the kitchen. I heard the scape of dogs' nails on the kitchen floor and Pippa's low voice talking to them. I glanced at my phone as I walked and saw the phone message icon was on. I called it up, but I didn't recognize the number. Likely a blasted duct-cleaning salesman or someone informing me I was about to be arrested by the IRS for owing back taxes.

"Hey, Gemma. How's it going? Ashleigh here. My phone got dropped in a sink full of water, and it's toast, so I've borrowed

The Game Is a Footnote

this one until I can get mine replaced. Hope all's okay at the store and Gale's managing okay. Bye!"

"What is it?" Pippa looked up from the laptop she'd opened on the kitchen table.

"Ashleigh. She called when I was in the shower and left a message."

"That's good. Isn't it?"

"Yes, it's good that she's okay. She says she's okay."

"You think she's not?"

"No. Yes." I returned the call. I let it ring for a long time, but voicemail didn't pick up. "I don't know. I need to speak to her. No one's answering." I shook my phone and tried again. Still no answer.

"I'm sure shaking it is going to help." Pippa nibbled on toast and returned her attention to her screen. "Oh good. The visit's on again. I was worried that silly incident in the Sahara would put a kibosh on it."

I was aware of no recent incident in the Sahara, silly or otherwise, but I didn't care about that now. I replayed Ashleigh's message. Her voice was low, as though she was trying not to be overheard, but I didn't read too much into that as she was generally soft-spoken. I guessed she was outside. I heard the faint sounds of traffic in the background and something beyond that.

I put the phone on speaker. "Listen to this. It's Ashleigh for sure. What else do you hear?"

Pippa tilted her head to one side. "Cars. Traffic going at moderate and consistent speed. A city street, not a highway. But the sound is faint, meaning she's not standing in or immediately adjacent to the road."

"Anything else?"

231

"Again."

I played it again.

"The sea, I think. Waves hitting the shore." Pippa pointed to the windows. The bare branches of the trees in the yard swayed, and the sound of the wind howled through the bones of this old house.

"That's what I thought. She's probably still on the Cape. Possibly in West London."

"I'm going to give Grant a call. Check in. Do you want to say hi?"

"I need to find Ashleigh." I stared at my phone as though willing the location of the call to appear on the display.

"Can't you ask the Delectable Detective to trace it?"

"I try to limit my requests for his official services."

"How's that working out?"

"Not well, I must admit. If I ask, he won't do it. He's got his officers unofficially looking out for her, but there's no proper investigation as such as there's been no sign of foul play."

"Let it go, Gemma." Pippa's fingers flew as she typed. I noticed she didn't once have to press backspace or delete. "The woman let you down. Time to find a new employee."

"It might be related to something else," I said.

Her fingers stopped moving, and she lifted her head. The intense hazel eyes above the sharp cheekbones studied me. "And that is?"

"We can discuss why you're actually here later," I said. "Right now I need that phone traced."

"How are you going to do that?"

"I'm not. You are."

"Me?"

"Make the call, Pippa. When we're on our way to get Ashleigh, I'll tell you all about Scarlet House."

"Sounds intriguing. I'll remind you that we're not in the U.K. I have no authority here."

"You know the people who do."

She closed the lid of her laptop, picked up her own phone, and left the kitchen.

*   *   *

I don't know who Pippa called, but she returned ten minutes later, dressed in a smart beige trouser suit and carrying her small leather handbag. I'd amused myself while she was away by trying to hack into her computer, even though I knew that would be a useless endeavor, no matter how much time I had. The screen that appeared when I opened the lid showed the Union Jack. I pressed the enter key and the password prompt appeared. I ran my fingers across my right cheek as I studied it. No point in trying something as mundane as Grant's birthday or our parents' anniversary. *Password* or *123456* would be useless. If I did by some fluke manage to get in, I'd be presented with layers upon layers of security, but I'd like to have a peek at the document she had open. Out of pure, simple curiously.

"Find what you need?" Pippa said.

"Not even close." I shut the laptop.

"The call originated at a private home in West London, Massachusetts."

"Thanks."

"Don't thank me. I'll be expecting something in return. Are we going now?"

"Might as well."

She picked up a bag from under the table and slipped her laptop into it. "Perhaps I need to keep an eye on this."

"You can put it in the safe. We have a real safe in the den."

"Behind Maria's portrait. I noticed yesterday the painting is not entirely flush with the wall. Do you and Uncle Arthur have such valuable items on hand that you need a safe?"

I must be getting sloppy—I hadn't realized the painting was hanging badly. "It came with the house."

"Do you know the combination?"

"Of course."

"Then I'll keep this with me, why don't I?"

* * *

I'd recently installed, with the help of a lot of people, a life-size bronze statue in the back garden. It's of a young girl playing with a dog, caught moments before she throws a ball to her pet. Right now, covered in a thin layer of snow, it looked even more charming than usual. Pippa noticed it out the kitchen window and said she'd like to have a closer look while I let the dogs out for another romp and quickly tidied up the breakfast dishes.

I called the dogs in, checked their water dishes were full, and pulled on my second-best coat, boots, scarf, and gloves. Pippa wasn't admiring the statue, so I followed the sound of low voices down the driveway and around the hedge. My sister and Mrs. Ramsbatten were seated on the veranda of my neighbor's house, close together, their faces serious. Mrs. Ramsbatten had her winter coat thrown over a long, slightly tattered housecoat.

Her curly white hair stood up in all directions, and she hadn't applied the touch of lipstick she never faced the world without.

They broke off their conversation and turned to smile at me as I came up the path. A gust of wind shook the branches of the trees, and a flurry of snow blew into my face. "Rather cold to be sitting out, isn't it? You'll catch your death."

"I enjoy the invigorating winter air," Mrs. Ramsbatten said. "More snow in the forecast for later today. I saw your sister in your yard and took advantage of the opportunity to meet her. You look very much alike, did you know that?"

"No," Pippa said, a bit too quickly.

"Oh yes. No mistaking you two sisters. Perhaps you could pop by for tea before you leave, dear."

Pippa stood up. "I'd like that. Ready to go, Gemma?"

* * *

"I was rather looking forward to a ride in the Triumph," Pippa said, referring to Uncle Arthur's prize 1977 Triumph Spitfire 1500.

"It's in the garage. I'm allowed to turn the engine over if he's away for more than a few weeks, but otherwise, I've never driven it. I'd never dare. Even Arthur doesn't take it out in the winter. I'm afraid you're stuck with the Miata."

Pippa tossed her computer bag in the boot of my car, and we set off. The address to which she directed me was on Harbor Road, not far from Scarlet House. I glanced up the museum's long driveway as I passed, but I could see no activity, and no cars were in the lot. I wondered if the pigs had suffered from tummy aches last night after the excess of the unexpected snack.

"Scarlet House Historical Museum." Pippa read the sign. "You mentioned you know something significant about it."

"I was locked in the pig barn yesterday evening. Most frightful experience of my life."

"Worse than your short and not lamented early marriage?"

"Even worse than that."

"You obviously escaped unscathed, as you did from that marriage. What then might have been the intent? That's if you were deliberately locked in and the door didn't simply swing shut behind you?"

"I don't know, Pippa. There seems to be a great deal I don't know going on around here lately, and I do not like it. You went to Cambridge."

"An abrupt change of subject, but yes, I did."

"Have you paid a visit there lately? Maybe had some contact with foreign students over the past few years? You read Russian literature, as I recall, but you've always had an interest in history."

"Russian literature *is* history, so yes I have. I maintain contact with some of my fellows, and I occasionally keep up with their news."

"I'm sure you do. Did you run into a visiting American student of history by the name of Ethan Evanston while doing this keeping up?"

"Not," Pippa said, "that I recall. I meet a great many people, Gemma."

And, I was sure, she remembered the name of every one of them. But I had no time to press the point.

Our destination came in sight, and I slowed. The property we were interested in was located on the eastern side of the street, meaning ocean front. A tall hedge offering absolute privacy lined the road, and the gates were closed. Pippa hopped out and flipped the latch, and the gates swung open easily.

"Lax security," she said, getting back into the Miata.

"Security might not be an issue to the homeowner. This is a low-crime town in the off-season. Sleepy, actually."

"How's that working out for you?"

"Maybe it's not as sleepy as I might like." I drove onto the property.

"Impressive," Pippa said.

"Expensive piece of real estate," I said.

The house was white with gray trim and a steeply pitched gray roof, two stories in the center, with wings jutting out on either side. The gardens were tucked away for the winter—the flowerbeds overturned, the perennials cut back, the bushes wrapped in burlap. No cars were parked out front, but the two garage doors were closed, and no tracks marked the fresh snow.

I pulled up to the front steps, and Pippa and I got out of the car. Before leaving my house, just as a precaution, I'd texted my destination to Ryan, saying I'd heard from Ashleigh and was going to meet her. I didn't bother to inform him of how I knew where to go.

He'd replied: *Got it. Pippa's here?????? In West London????*

Large iron urns stood on either side of the steps, filled with golden magnolia leaves, red dogwood branches, and sculpted evergreens.

My hair blew around my face as I rang the bell. From one direction, I could hear the steady buzz of traffic on Harbor Road, and from the other, the sound of the sea, the waves pounding against the shore in the strong wind.

The door opened and Bunny Leigh stood there. She wore black yoga pants and a sleeveless blue shirt. Her face was clear of makeup and her hair brushed off her face. Her feet were bare, making her so short she had to tilt her head back to look at me. Without her hat, sunglasses, and full makeup, the resemblance to Ashleigh was striking. "Can I help you?"

"I'd like to speak to Ashleigh, please."

"You're her boss. From the store."

"I am."

Bunny's eyes flicked to Pippa, but they held no signs of recognition.

"Don't mind me. I'm just along for the ride," my sister said in a perfect Boston accent.

"Ashleigh and I aren't accepting visitors," Bunny said. "We're wanting some private time to ourselves." The door began to swing shut.

I stepped forward and pushed it back. "I need Ashleigh to tell me that."

"Don't bother trying to argue," Pippa said. "Gemma can be very stubborn that way. You know what the English are like."

Bunny studied me for a long moment. I smiled. Pippa smiled.

"I won't take up much of your time," I said. "But I do intend to speak to Ashleigh."

Bunny hesitated, and then she stepped back, and Pippa and I entered the house. Ashleigh was coming down the hallway, smiling. She wore a black blouse with puffy sleeves and a floor-sweeping multicolored skirt I hadn't seen before. A large brooch in the shape of a butterfly was pinned to her chest, and her feet were also bare. "Hey, Gemma. What brings you here? Isn't this a great house? Have you met Bunny? You won't believe it. The most absolutely fabulous thing has happened."

"Ashleigh," I said, "why didn't you tell me you were leaving?"

"Leaving? I'm not leaving. I'll be at work tomorrow. Didn't you get my message? I called you this morning."

"You called her?" Bunny said. "When?"

"Sorry, but I grabbed your phone when you went to the shower. The screen hadn't locked yet. I wanted to check in with Gemma, that's all." Ashleigh turned to me. "Bunny wanted us to have some together time, without interruptions. No phones, no disturbances, but I felt a little bit guilty about not checking in, so I snuck in a quick call. Bunny's looking for a house to buy in West London. Isn't that great?"

"I don't know about 'great.' Have I missed something? You left my shop without a word and walked away, leaving the place unlocked. I might have been robbed blind."

Ashleigh glanced at Bunny.

"Sorry about that," Bunny Leigh said, looking not at all sorry. "That might have been my fault. You're here now, might as well come in."

Chapter Nineteen

We settled ourselves in the ultramodern kitchen, covered with the debris of several days' meals and a substantial number of empty wine bottles. The large windows looked across the snow-covered lawn to the sparkling blue waters of the ocean in the distance. Bunny offered us coffee already made in the enormous coffee maker. I declined, but Pippa asked if she might have tea.

"Sure," Bunny said. When she headed for the fridge, rather than the kettle, I suggested Pippa might not want tea after all.

"You're Ashleigh's mother," I said. "You haven't seen her since she was born, and you've come to West London to try to build a relationship."

"How do you know that?" she asked. "No one knows."

"Gemma knows things," Ashleigh said with what, to my surprise, sounded like a touch of pride.

"If you'd requested the time off," I said. "I would have given it to you."

"I know that, but Gale said she could fill in anytime, so I figured that would be okay. It all happened in such a rush, and

Bunny . . . Mom . . . was in a hurry to be off. She didn't want anyone seeing where we were going. You know, fans and such."

"You didn't ask Gale."

"Sure I did. I mean . . . you saw me send the text, right, Mom? You said she'd replied to say she was on her way."

Bunny Leigh shrugged. "I might have been mistaken about that. Obviously, no harm done. Now, if you'll excuse us—"

I rolled my eyes to the heavens. "Do you know the police are looking for you both?"

Bunny shrugged once again. She seemed to do that a lot. Ashleigh appeared to be genuinely shocked. "What?"

Pippa chuckled.

I looked at Bunny in question.

"I preferred that no one," she said, "and that includes you, knows where we've gone. It's so tedious, being chased by chubby middle-aged women with gray hair and pictures of grandchildren, wanting to tell me how much they loved me *soooo* many years ago. A constant reminder that my career's long over. Not to mention paparazzi hoping to get a picture of me looking haggard and worn out, so they can do one of those 'unrecognizable' articles."

I thought Bunny looked anything but haggard and worn out. Having spent time with her daughter clearly had done her good. She turned to Ashleigh. "You sent the text to your coworker and went upstairs for your purse, leaving your phone on the counter. You'd put so many smiley faces into the text you didn't press 'Send.' I deleted it."

"Why'd you do that?" Ashleigh asked.

"So we wouldn't be bothered of course." Bunny laid a hand on Ashleigh's arm, giving the younger woman a look brimming with joy and love. "I wanted us to have this precious time all to ourselves, with no pesky interruptions." The joy disappeared and she glared at me, obviously considering me to be a pesky interruption.

"You said Gale replied to say she was on her way," Ashleigh said.

"A little white lie, darling."

"I gave you Gemma's number, and you said you called her to explain while I was getting my things."

Bunny shrugged. "Another little white lie."

"Sorry about that, Gemma," Ashleigh said. "Bunny explained that she wanted us to have a few days of private time to ourselves, so she popped my phone into her purse before we left the store. While I was settling in here, she accidently dropped it in the sink."

Bunny smiled at me. She didn't even try to pretend there had been anything "accidental" about it.

Pippa chuckled again.

"It's drying out now," Ashleigh said. "The advice on the internet said to leave it turned off for at least forty-eight hours."

"I told you I'll get you another one, sweetie," Bunny said. "A much better one."

I stood up. "You'll be at work tomorrow?"

"Yup," Ashleigh said.

"Let's go," I said to Pippa. I had more than a few words to say to my employee, but I'd wait until she was back in the Emporium. I couldn't imagine what suddenly meeting the mother she never knew would have done to any common sense Ashleigh might have had.

"Before you go, Gemma," Bunny said. "You've been helping out at Scarlet House. Maybe you can give me some idea of what's going on there. Is there any word about when it's likely to be put up for sale?"

That stopped me in my tracks. "You're the person who's been asking about buying it?"

"As nice as this place is," she lifted her arms to indicate the house we were standing in, "it belongs to a music producer friend of mine from the old days. He's spending the month in the Caribbean, so he offered it to me. I need a place of my own." She smiled at Ashleigh. "Of *our* own. We need to be near town because Ashleigh likes to be able to walk to work."

"Scarlet House isn't for sale, but if it were, it's going to be in the several million dollar range."

"I'm about to sign a contract with a studio for a biopic of my life. It's going to be a major motion picture. So exciting. Never mind the generous fee they're paying me for consulting on the movie, once it comes out, my records'll start zooming back to the top of the charts, and I have plans to release a new album."

I hadn't seen anything about this proposed movie in my search of info about Bunny. It was possible it was being kept under wraps until the deal was finalized. It was also entirely possible it would never happen.

"Are you sure the house isn't for sale? I was so hoping to buy it. Ashleigh would love to live on a farm and have horses. Wouldn't you, dear?"

"That would be wonderful."

"I could totally redo that stuffy old house. Put in a lovely modern kitchen, like this one. I'd be respectful of the historic

Vicki Delany

charm, of course. I asked a friend of my friend to talk to some of the neighbors about it. I want to keep it on the downlow that I'm the one interested in buying. I wouldn't want to push up the bidding if word gets out."

"What made you think it's for sale in the first place?"

"The chair of the board told me so."

"Robyn Kirkpatrick told you the house is for sale?"

"Not in so many words, but she told me the museum is losing money. I dropped in one day to have a look at it. It wasn't very interesting—just a bunch of old furniture and a horrid kitchen. Anyway, she followed me when I left, and asked if I had a moment to talk. She knew who I was, you see. I invited her to walk with me."

My head spun. Robyn knew all along where Bunny was staying? While I was telling everyone I knew to keep an eye out?

"I invited her in for a coffee. If I'm going to move to West London, I'd like to get to know the people. The important people anyway. I thought she was going to ask me about my career and my plans for the future, but she wanted me to invest in the museum. I mentioned I'm thinking of moving to West London, although I didn't say why. She told me the Historical Society, which owns the house, is on a shaky financial foundation, and it needs an infusion of cash. She offered me a position on their board in exchange for a donation. As if I'm interested in helping run some old house." She shrugged once more. "If her group needs the money, I thought maybe they'll have to sell the house. I wanted to get my offer in early."

"You wouldn't have been trying to accelerate the sale, would you?" I asked.

"I don't even know what that means. Are you on the board?"

"No."

"Too bad. I was going to ask you to put in a word for me. When I told Robyn I'd be interested in buying the house, she froze me out right quick and left. I tried to say if the Historical Society's short on money, they should sell the house and use the profits for their other projects, but she wasn't interested in hearing it."

"The only thing the Historical Society owns is Scarlet House."

"Really? Too bad for them. Does that mean they're not going to sell it?"

I decided on the spot that Bunny Leigh had not been attempting to pretend Scarlet House was haunted. She simply didn't have the guile. Likely she didn't have the intelligence to pull it off either.

"That's an interesting piece of jewelry you're wearing, Ashleigh." Pippa spoke for the first time. As we'd talked, she'd checked out the kitchen, wandered to the windows, peeked into the living and dining rooms. She looked the picture of total boredom and complete lack of interest, but she'd been listening to every word.

Ashleigh glanced at the brooch pinned to her blouse. Pippa stepped closer and studied it. The piece was large and ostentatious, a cluster of rhinestones formed into the shape and colors of a butterfly. "Do you like it?" Ashleigh asked. "Bunny . . . I mean Mom . . . gave it to me."

"Costume jewelry. Circa 1950s." Pippa turned away, having instantly lost interest.

"It's not worth anything," Bunny said, "but I like it. I bought it at an antique stall in L.A. when I first found out I was pregnant with Ashleigh, and I've kept it all these years to remind me of her. Did you get the significance of her name? Leigh. Ashleigh."

"Yeah," I said. "I got it. Thank you for your time."

"I'll show Gemma out," Ashleigh said.

Bunny wandered into the living room.

"You will be at work tomorrow?" I asked.

"Yes." Ashleigh lowered her voice. "I am sorry about that mix-up, Gemma. Bunny came into the shop and told me I was her daughter. I had no idea. She showed me pictures of her with Grandma and Granddad when she was a girl, and some of me as a baby that are the same as in the albums back home. I've always known my mom was out there somewhere, but Grandma and Granddad refused to talk about her. Ever. They said she'd disgraced them, abandoned me, and I was better off without her. I'm not giving you a sob story, Gemma. I had a good childhood. My grandparents were kind and generous, and I've always known they loved me. It's just, well, I guess their daughter hurt them so much they couldn't handle it."

"Why didn't you phone Gemma?" Pippa said. "She's been worried."

"It all happened so fast, I didn't know what to think. I was in shock, I guess. She asked me to come with her, right now. We needed time together to get to know each other without people from our everyday lives interfering. I didn't just walk out on you, really. I thought I'd texted Gale. I thought I'd sent the text, then I put my phone down and ran upstairs for my things and to visit the restroom. When I came back, my phone was gone. Bunny told me Gale had replied saying she'd be right over. She also said she'd called you, Gemma, and you were okay with it."

Pippa snorted.

"Okay. I shouldn't have let her have my phone. I should have called you myself to let you know what was happening. It's just . . . I was so excited, I forgot about everything else. I've found my mom at last. And she was famous! She wants to be with me and she is whisking me away to a life of celebrity and money and a house like this one. She said I didn't even need to go back to my apartment to get my clothes and things. She'll lend me what I need at first, and then we'll go out and buy all new stuff." She touched the brooch on her chest. "It's been great, really great, getting to know each other, but I'm starting to come back to earth." She gave me a soft smile. "I'm Ashleigh Saunderson, a store clerk. She wants to buy Scarlet House because of the barn and the farm. She wants me to have a pony and us to pretend we're farmers. When I was twelve years old, all I wanted in the world was a pony."

"Every preteen girl wants a pony," I said.

"I didn't," Pippa said.

"Why does that not surprise me?"

"Bunny's trapped in her idea of what a mother–daughter pair should be," Ashleigh said. "Not the reality of me being a grown woman with my own life experiences and my own dreams for the future. None of which involves having a pony. I'll stay here tonight and come to work tomorrow. She has the use of this house until the end of the month, and then we'll see what happens."

"You should phone your grandparents," I said.

"Why?"

"They might be worried. I called them, looking for you."

"They won't be happy to hear Bunny's now in my life. They've been holding a lot of anger for a long time, but I'll make them understand. I'm happy she's here, Gemma. That we've found each other after all these years. Thanks for going to so much trouble to find me. I won't let you down again. I've got my head back now."

"See you tomorrow then."

Pippa and I left.

"You're too soft," my sister said as she did up her seat belt. "If she were my employee, I'd fire her."

"Good thing she's not your employee then, isn't it?" I turned the engine on. "You paid a considerable amount of attention to that brooch she was wearing. What do you care about antique jewelry?"

"I have many and varied interests."

"You do not," I said.

* * *

Pippa accompanied me to the Emporium. She got her laptop out of the boot of the car and said she had some work to do and would use my office.

Moriarty greeted her at the door as we came in. She gave him one long look, and he ducked his head, lowered his body, and crept away to his bed beneath the center table. "I do not understand this modern habit of allowing animals into retail establishments." Pronouncement over, Pippa spent a long time examining the room. "So this is the Sherlock Holmes Bookshop and Emporium," she said at last. "It's . . . nice."

"Thank you," I said.

"Does it truly provide you and Uncle Arthur with a living?"

"It and the tearoom next door. We're half owners in that with Jayne."

"Such a small world you live in, Gemma," she said. "Oh well, to each her own."

Once a crack like that would have stung me to the core. Now, I brushed it off. My small world suited me very well indeed, as I'd realized when I'd last been in London, and Pippa offered me a job. She never said what the job was, but I suspected it didn't have much to do with the Department for Transport.

"Is Jayne likely to be in the tearoom?" Pippa asked.

"She should be."

"I'll pop in and say hi. I liked her very much."

"Bring me a tea when you come back, please. They make a proper cuppa there. They should—I taught them myself. I'll have a blueberry muffin too."

Pippa left, still carrying her laptop bag. I was pleased she liked Jayne. Pippa, I knew, had no friends. She had her "office" and she had "people," but no close women friends. No men friends either, until she unexpectedly fell head over heels in highly un-Pippa-like fashion with my friend Grant Thompson. I heard from Grant occasionally, chatting about enjoying his new life in London, where he'd established a trade in antique books, and life with Pippa. He sent us pictures now and again, of them enjoying dinner or pub nights out and walks by the river. They'd had a vacation in Wales (I had trouble accepting the very idea of Pippa on vacation) and had taken my parents to the Orangery at Kensington Palace for afternoon tea to celebrate my dad's birthday.

Pippa, I thought with a smile, was leading an almost normal life.

Before opening the shop, I texted Gale to tell her Ashleigh had been located and was safe and sound, and we'd be back to the regular staff schedule tomorrow. She replied with a thumbs-up emoji. I then called Ryan. He answered immediately, and I got straight to the point. "I've found Ashleigh. She's fine, just needed a few days' break, and we got our wires crossed."

"I'm glad to hear it. I'm sorry I couldn't do more, but you know how these things work."

"I do know and I understand. It would have been embarrassing to mount a full search for her, only to have her show up and say she'd lost her phone. Sorry."

His deep voice rumbled down the line in a chuckle. "Pippa's really here?"

"She showed up on my doorstep last night. She says she was in Washington and impulsively decided to pay me a visit on her few days off. I have my doubts about the veracity of that."

"Why?"

"Pippa doesn't do impulsive and she doesn't take days off like normal people do."

"Grant's changing her. You said so when he sent us those pictures from Wales of her in hiking gear."

"That's true. But still . . ."

"What are you up to today?"

"Just work. Anything happening with the Dave Chase situation?"

"Confidentially, not a lot. His son Kyle has arrived from California, but he can shed no light on what might have happened if the fall wasn't an accident. He himself was working a shift in the ER at the time Dave died. However—"

"I do love a however."

"Turns out Dave has a brother with pretty shady connections. Kyle Chase told me Dave and this brother have had almost nothing to do with each other for most of their adult lives. The brother lives in New York City, and I've asked the NYPD to do some checking for me. It's possible some of his underworld contacts were sending him a message."

"By killing his estranged brother?"

"Stranger things have happened. It's a long shot, but worth following up. Dave Chase himself was squeaky clean, far as I can tell. A widowed former veterinary surgeon wanting to keep active in his retirement. Exactly what he appeared to be. The major players at Scarlet House also appear to be exactly who they say they are."

"Speaking of Scarlet House . . ."

His voice changed instantly as he went on alert. "What?"

"Something happened that I should probably tell you about. I'm fine, obviously, but someone might have made a threat against me."

"Might have? You don't know?"

"That's the thing. I don't know."

"Tell me."

I quickly filled him in about the barn incident, glossing over how genuinely terrified I'd been. I admitted that I hadn't seen anyone in the vicinity and that nothing had come of it.

"I don't like it," he said. "Nothing else happened? No warning notes left on your windshield or rocks through the window?"

"No. Which is why I'm inclined to think it must have been an accident after all. The door simply swung shut behind me."

"A warning, maybe. From someone who doesn't know you can't be warned off. I don't have to tell you to be watchful."

"You do not."

"Because it doesn't matter what I say. I've got a lot on today, but I'd like to see you. How about dinner tonight? Just you and me . . . and Pippa."

"I'll invite Jayne, and we can go to the Café. Maybe I can persuade Andy to come out of the kitchen and join us."

His voice dropped. "I've been missing you."

"I've been missing you too. The shop closes at seven tonight. I'll make a reservation at the Café for seven thirty."

"Better let me do it. I'll take care of that soon as we hang up. You have a tendency to forget things."

I was quite offended at that. "I do not."

"I love you, Gemma."

"I love you too," I said.

* * *

Things were surprisingly busy in the shop for a Wednesday in January, and I was kept on the hop most of the day. Gale came in at one, full of questions about Ashleigh. I simply repeated the line about crossed wires. It would be up to Ashleigh to tell people where she'd been, or not.

Pippa returned from the tearoom, bearing two take-out mugs of tea and a muffin for me. She took her laptop upstairs and worked for less than an hour.

When she came down, she said she was going shopping. I wondered if "shopping" was a euphemism for something else, but she was back several hours later, laden with bags from the shops on Baker Street. "What a charming little town you have, Gemma. I might even come to accept that living here has its advantages. It would be a nice place for one to spend one's retirement years."

I introduced her to Gale as Moriarty fled to safety beneath the center table.

"Nice to meet you," Gale said, "I can tell you're sisters. You look so much alike."

"We do not," Pippa muttered. "Gemma, you might want to tell the owner of that shop across the street, her staff need to work on their public relations skills. The hatchet-faced clerk was downright rude when I told her I wanted a little memento of Cape Cod for my family in England. She doesn't seem to care for English people much." She sniffed. "Colonial resentment, I suspect."

"That was no employee," I said. "That was Maureen, and she owns Beach Fine Arts."

"Does she? The shop is ill named. I went in planning to purchase a piece of fine art for Mum's birthday. They had nothing of the sort. I didn't even bother to buy a postcard. Do you have time for a late lunch, Gemma?"

"I don't normally take a break. I'm having tea with Jayne at 3:40, if you'd like to join us."

"I'll try to make it. Keys?"

"What?"

"Car keys. You said I could use your car."

"Sure. Keys are in my bag, which is—"

"I saw where you put it. Thanks."

"You can leave your laptop here if you're going to be sightseeing."

"Nice try, Gemma," she said.

* * *

"I totally forgot," I said to Jayne as we gathered for our regular partners' meeting over tea and leftover sandwiches and pastries. "We're going to dinner at the Café tonight when the Emporium closes. Want to come?"

"Who's 'we'?" Jayne stirred a few grains of sugar into her teacup.

"Ryan, me, and Pippa."

"A date night," my sister said. "You included me. How nice. I was hoping to get the opportunity to see the Delectable Detective again."

"Will you stop calling him that," I said.

"I'm in," Jayne said. "I'd like you to meet my fiancé, Andy, Pippa. He's the chef at the Blue Water Café."

"That would be nice. You have a slight depression on the third finger of your left hand that wasn't there when you were in London, but I didn't like to ask. How are the wedding plans going?"

"We've set the date for this time next year. Other than that—"

"Don't ask." I helped myself to a ham-and-cheese-on-croissant sandwich. "Is that a real watch?" I asked Jayne. "I haven't seen it before."

She touched the timepiece pinned to her apron. It was an antique-looking silver pocket watch, about two inches across, with an ornately engraved surface, a silver clasp, and a short chain. "Isn't it cute? Andy gave it to me for my birthday."

She released the catch, and it opened to reveal the inside. The visible clockworks were colored gold, and black Roman numerals on a white surface displayed the correct time.

"It's gorgeous," I said. "Didn't he give you tickets to a play?" Andy had put on a party for Jayne at his restaurant, complete with more balloons that should have been able to fit in the space, a sit-down dinner, gaily wrapped presents, an enthusiastic round of "Happy Birthday," and a giant cake with candles that the blushing birthday girl blew out in one go. I'd been pleased Andy had fiddled with the date, choosing to close his restaurant on a Monday rather than the actual date of Jayne's birthday, which had fallen on a Friday this year. January sixth is also the date assigned to honor the birth of the Great Detective, although such an event is never mentioned in the Canon, and Donald had invited me to accompany him to a special Sherlockian celebration in Boston.

Jayne blushed and ran her fingers over the watch. "The tickets were his public present. This one he gave me when we were alone."

I laughed.

"Like Mrs. Hudson herself would have worn at 221B to know when to serve Sherlock Holmes and Dr. Watson their breakfasts," she said. "The case is a genuine antique pocket watch, although the clockwork's modern."

I froze with my teacup halfway to my mouth.

Pippa read my expression. "You've thought of something. What?"

"Antique watch. That vintage costume jewelry brooch A'shleigh was wearing. You showed a surprising amount of interest in it, Pippa."

"And . . .?"

I threw the strap of my handbag over my shoulder and stood up. "You and Mrs. Ramsbatten had a pleasant conversation on her front porch this morning despite the fact that she was still in her nightwear and the temperature was below freezing."

"She's a friendly neighbor," Pippa said.

"I suspect you went back there this afternoon to finish this conversation and make some phone calls. I also suspect you came to no conclusions and learned nothing new. You can come clean later. Let's go."

"Where are we going?" Jayne said.

"You don't need to come."

"Oh yes, I do. I recognize that look." She set her face into determined lines, untied her apron, and threw it on the table.

Pippa also stood up. Her eyes sparkled. "It would appear that the game is indeed afoot."

Chapter Twenty

I made a quick phone call and was pleased to hear that the person I needed to talk to was at home. I said I was on my way as I ran through the Emporium calling to Gale that I had to go out and asking her to lock up if I wasn't back by closing. Pippa and Jayne followed me. Moriarty fled at Pippa's approach.

"What's—?" Gale said as we ran out the back door. I held out my hand, and Pippa put my car keys in it. My Miata is a two-seater, a zippy little sports car not well suited for New England winter weather, and definitely not suited for three people.

It was coming up to four thirty, but the winter night had settled in early. The threatened next batch of snow had arrived, and the car was covered in a thin layer of fat flakes. I ran my sleeve across it, clearing barely enough of the window to see through.

Jayne eyed the nonexistent back seat, normally used only to take Violet and Peony for an outing. "Maybe we could take my car?"

"We're not going far."

Jayne clambered in, and I turned my windscreen wipers on to clear the falling snow. Pippa settled into the seat next to me.

Sharon Musgrave lives in the north end of West London, in a nondescript apartment building about two miles inland from Harbor Road. Traffic out of town was building as the snow continued to fall and people made their way home, and our progress was slower than I might have liked. Eventually I parked in a loading zone by the front door, and the three of us spilled out of the Miata.

"Fill me in, Gemma," Pippa had said as I drove. "At the very least on who we're going to see in such a rush we didn't even stop to get our coats."

"Sharon Musgrave is the bookkeeper for the West London Historical Society, as well as one of the volunteers who leads tour groups through Scarlet House. She's highly invested in the success of the house, to the point, I'd say, of obsession. She considers herself to be a history lover, but her idea of history isn't anything people of the times would recognize. She likes it wrapped nicely in a bow and airbrushed to be presented to polite, well-scrubbed schoolchildren. She gets herself overly wrapped up in her historical impersonations. If she offers you a biscuit—she'll call it a cookie—decline."

"Thank you for that tip," my sister said.

"Gemma likes to keep her speculations to herself," Jayne said to Pippa. "She thinks it's more impressive that way."

"I believe it's more like she won't tell you in case she's wrong and has to change direction at the last minute, which she will then ensure you understand was her plan all along."

I searched the panel by the intercom for Sharon's name and pressed the required button.

"Come in, Gemma. It's apartment 306," a disembodied voice said as the locks on the door clicked to admit us. The fabric on the single couch in the small lobby was faded; the coffee table, marred by water rings; the carpet, worn and tattered around the edges. I pressed the lift button for "Up," and the doors swooshed open immediately.

The three of us crowded into the confined space, and I pressed "3."

Sharon Musgrave stood in her doorway, watching as we exited the lift. She was dressed in modern clothes of baggy jeans, a many-times washed T-shirt, and a loose cardigan with a scraggly hem. "What's this about, Gemma?"

"You're not working at Scarlet House today?"

"I don't normally go in Mondays or Wednesdays. I keep the books for a few small companies, and those are my days for working on them." She stepped back and admitted us to her home.

The apartment was small and the furniture cheap, but everything was sparkling clean. Paintings of Cape Cod scenes hung on the walls, and photographs covered a side table. Many of the pictures showed a younger Sharon with people I didn't recognize but whom I assumed, judging by the similarity in features, to be her relatives. Other photos had been taken at Scarlet House. Sharon in costume, posing with similarly attired people. A picture of her with Dave Chase in his farmer getup, a lamb in his arms, had been prominently placed at the front of the display.

Sharon glanced at Pippa, but I didn't bother to introduce them, in favor of getting directly to the point. "You were wearing an antique brooch with your costume the other day. Where did you get it?"

Pippa's composure cracked, and her eyes widened. She threw me a look of something approaching approval before the expression was wiped away.

"The brooch?" Sharon said. "What about it? What concern is it of yours?"

"Do you own it?"

"No. It belongs to the house. I . . . I found it. I thought it was pretty, and as it belonged to a Scarlet, it's period appropriate, so I added it to my working dress. It's not worth anything, is it?"

"Where did you find it?"

"In a drawer in the desk in the study. You know that desk is one of the few pieces we have that's original to the house, right? I was dusting underneath the desk and must have pressed a hidden lever or something, and a drawer popped out at the bottom. It was full of mouse droppings, some yellowing, handwritten legal papers, and that brooch."

"Did you show the brooch to anyone?"

She ducked her head. "I might have . . . forgotten to. I gave the papers to Robyn and some of the others. It was a great find: land deeds from the mid-nineteenth century. The papers didn't tell us anything we didn't know, and they're not of any legal value, but it's exciting to have original papers with Jeremiah Scarlet's own signature on them."

"What were Jeremiah's dates?" Pippa tried to sound disinterested, but she failed completely.

"He died in 1863. His second son was George, whose portrait hangs by the entrance to the house. George was—"

"When was this?" I asked. "When you found these items?"

"September."

"You didn't show the brooch to anyone?"

Sharon lifted her head, her eyes dark with anger. "I'm getting tired of Robyn treating the volunteers like we're some sort of servants or farmhands, and she's the lady of the manor. I was in favor of her taking over the job when Kathy died, but it's gone straight to her head. I pinned the brooch to my dress, planning to tell her I'd found it when we met to go over the quarterly budget. She was in a foul mood that day and snapped at me as though it was my fault we had a shortfall in income, so I decided she didn't need to know about it. It's not as though it's valuable. The Scarlets were a prosperous family for the area, but they wouldn't have had the money or the inclination to buy frivolous baubles. No mention was ever made in any of their letters or papers about any jewels."

It wasn't Sharon's place to decide what the Scarlets had or hadn't done with their money, but I said nothing.

"Where is this brooch now?" Pippa said quietly.

"It's at the house, of course. I don't bring it home. It doesn't belong to me."

"Where in the house?" I asked.

"The volunteers' office, in my locker." She ducked her head. "I wouldn't want any of the other volunteers helping themselves to it. It might not be worth anything, but it is museum property."

Sharon didn't want anyone asking why she had such a thing and wondering where it might have come from. She wasn't as naive as she sometimes appeared. She had to have realized that any piece that had been left in a concealed drawer was of some significance, if not value. I suspected she got a great deal of pleasure out of wearing an item that she secretly knew had been important to the Scarlet family.

"I'd like to have a look at this brooch," Pippa said in a low voice that barely, but not quite, hid her excitement. "Can you describe it to me, Gemma?"

"Thank you, Sharon," I said.

"Why are you so interested in my—I mean the brooch?" she asked. "You won't tell Robyn I kept it from her, will you?"

We left the apartment. I was too impatient to wait for the single slow lift, so I took the stairs two at a time and sprinted across the lobby. Pippa beat me to the car.

"I don't understand," Jayne said. "I've seen that thing, and it's hideous. What's an ugly fake brooch got to do with anything?"

I unlocked the car and we piled in. Jayne squeezed herself into the back. "This isn't a legal seat, you know. I hope the cops don't pull you over."

"The cops," I said, "can follow me. Call Ryan, tell him to meet us at Scarlet House ASAP."

Jayne placed the call as I threw the Miata into gear and headed toward Harbor Road. He didn't answer so she left a message. "Should I try Louise?"

"Let's wait until I see exactly what's going on," I said.

"You mean you don't know?" Jayne said.

"It's more interesting this way." Pippa clapped her hands. "This is exciting. Go faster, Gemma. I haven't been involved in a good car chase for several years now. You don't know how dull it gets when one starts climbing the official ladder and is taken out of the field."

"You mean inspecting road works and subway tunnels?" Jayne asked. "Why would that involve car chases?"

"She's speaking rhetorically." I took the corner into Harbor Road on two wheels. Not a good idea, as the roads were slick with a dusting of fresh snow, but the Miata handled it well.

I needn't have taken the risk: all of a sudden the traffic screeched to a dead stop. I slammed on the brakes and pounded the steering wheel in frustration. An ambulance came down a side street, full lights and sirens, and up ahead I could see blue and red lights flashing in the falling snow. "Check the traffic app, Jayne—see if there's a way around that tie-up. As for you, Pippa, time to spill the tea."

"I have no tea."

"That's an expression we young people use. Your age group wouldn't know it. Give me the gossip, although in this case I want the facts, not the gossip. You are in America in general and West London in particular, in pursuit of an antique piece of jewelry, and I have not the slightest idea why anything like that would be of interest to Her Majesty's Government."

"It is not of interest to Her Majesty's Government, but it is very much of interest to my direct boss."

"Who's that?" Jayne asked.

"'A certain gracious lady'."

"Isn't that a Sherlock Holmes quote?" Jayne said. "Referring to the time he met Queen Victoria? I don't get it. I also don't see any faster route. Everyone's trying to get around that accident, so the side streets are blocked."

"Pippa, can you get us out of this?" The car edged forward an inch.

"Not in the absence of a place for a helicopter to land. Back to your question. If what your Sharon found in a hidden drawer is what I suspect it is, you deserve to hear the story. It would appear I have time to tell you. In 1840, the young Queen Victoria married Prince Albert of Saxe-Coburg and Gotha. As history knows, it was a love match, and when he died in December of 1861, she went into mourning for the remainder of her long life. As an engagement gift he presented her with a brooch. An emerald surrounded by diamonds."

"You think the one Sharon's been wearing is an imitation of that one?" Jayne said.

"No," I said. "We think it's the real thing. It's so dirty I didn't recognize the jewels as genuine. Obviously I also didn't expect Sharon Musgrave to be wearing a piece of that value, so I assumed it was costume jewelry. An assumption on my part I will attempt never to repeat. If Sharon hadn't been playing her little tricks and wanting to keep her find to herself, the museum board would have taken it to a jeweler to be evaluated. And had a considerable shock. More than likely, Robyn and the other docents thought it was an item Sharon had found at an antique sale and decided to add to her costume, so they never asked about it. Continue Pippa."

"As royal jewels go, it's not an expensive piece, but the historic and sentimental value is enormous. The brooch could not be found in the days following the sudden death of Prince Albert, who was only forty-two at the time. Because of its sentiment to Victoria, she was distraught at its loss. At first, it was believed one of her ladies had misplaced it in the confusion following the death of the prince and all the disruption, both familial and royal, surrounding that. The household plunged into deep mourning, the extreme formality surrounding a Victorian bereavement period and subsequent state funeral, the grief-stricken Queen, the vast extended family arriving for the funeral, politicians and dignitaries paying condolence calls, etcetera, etcetera."

"In short, it was never seen again," I said.

"No. Over all these years the royal family has wondered what happened to it. Its loss was reported to the police at the time but simply listed as a missing piece, without mention of provenance. It was a private item, meaning not the property of the state. As history, its theft is a minor footnote, and as far as jewels go, it's not particularly valuable, but the family would very much like to have it back. The current monarch got word recently of what might have happened to it. It would appear that a minor American diplomat—"

"A certain Mr. Scarlet," I said.

"Precisely. Mr. Edward Scarlet accompanied the United States ambassador for an overnight stay at Windsor Castle a few weeks before the death of the prince. You may remember that the Trent Affair, which threatened outright war between the United States and England, had been resolved in November 1861, largely due to the intervention of Albert. The prince was in ill health by then, but nevertheless, the ambassador was invited to visit in recognition of that diplomatic success. Shortly after the departure of the American guests, an upstairs maid was dismissed without reference for engaging in improper behavior."

"What's an upstairs maid?" Jayne asked.

"Not a kitchen maid or a laundress. Her responsibilities would be cleaning the upstairs rooms—the bedrooms and dressing rooms."

"I get it. She would have been in a position to snatch an attractive babble."

"Precisely. The queen discovered the brooch was missing several weeks later, in the days following the prince's death. A discreet search was made for the maid, but she was never located."

"Easy to disappear in the days before cell phones, social security numbers, CCTV cameras, and all the rest." I leaned out the window to see what was happening up ahead. Officer Stella Johnson was directing traffic, but there wasn't much directing to do as nothing was moving. The driver of the car behind me leaned on his horn. That would be sure to help, I thought.

"What does all this have to do with us, in the here and now?" Jayne asked.

"A few months ago, a doctoral student researching an apparently unexceptional middle-class New England family uncovered a letter written in November of 1861, from Edward Scarlet to his brother, Jeremiah, back home on the family farm, saying he was prematurely resigning his post and returning to the United States by the next available ship."

"Ethan Evanston."

"I believe that's the researcher's name, yes. He had done a previous degree at Cambridge and mentioned it in passing to one of his professors there."

"The Scarlet family died out in 1914," I said. "And the house sold. Surely their correspondence would have been disposed of."

"Only because Edward Scarlet traveled abroad in the service of the American state department was anyone interested enough to save any of his letters. He was involved in discussions concerning the Trent Affair, therefore is of interest to historians. Of interest to us is that his letter to his brother mentioned that he had married and would be bringing his new bride to America with him."

"The missing chambermaid," Jayne said. "Oh my gosh, this is so exciting."

"The name of this bride was not the same as that of the errant maid, but your Ethan is a dogged sort, and he wanted to know more about her. We are talking about purely academic research so far. The lady never made it to the United States. She disappeared from the ship in the middle of the Atlantic Ocean. The official record said she must have taken a midnight stroll on deck, slipped, and fallen overboard."

"Like that happens all the time," I said.

"Indeed. Fortuitously, Ethan's queries ran up against those of someone working from the other end, who'd managed to trace the maid who'd been dismissed from her post to her assumed name and then to the purchase of a ticket for a ship bound for America. The English researcher then hit a brick wall, as I believe you Americans say, Jayne, as there is no record of who this woman had been traveling with. Her ticket was not issued in the name of Scarlet, which would indicate that she and Edward hadn't married after all. I'm sure he made promises to her."

"The cad," Jayne said.

"Indeed he was. The English researcher realized that he might have come across a clue to the fate of the Queen's brooch, and he alerted the interested parties."

"Meaning you," I said.

"Eventually the memo landed on my desk, yes. As a result of his earlier research, Ethan knew that Edward Scarlet, the perhaps not grieving not-widower, had disembarked in New York City, traveled by train to West Barnstable, and from there hired a driver to bring him to West London. He should have delayed. A storm arose that night, the horse got a fright and bolted, and the carriage overturned, killing both driver and passenger."

"Was that truly an accident?" I asked.

"Nothing indicates it was not. A sudden thunderstorm combined with excessive drink on the part of the cabbie was mentioned in the official report."

I saw an opening between the car ahead of me and a lamppost. Good thing the Miata's a small car. I edged forward and squeezed between them, leaving barely an inch of space on either side. The driver glared at me, and I gave him a cheerful wave.

"Close one," Pippa said. "Edward's brother, Jeremiah—"

"Who kept papers in the secret drawer Sharon uncovered," Jayne said.

"We can presume Jeremiah claimed the contents of his dead brother's luggage."

"If the brooch was in it," I said. "He would have had a considerable shock."

"That he would."

"You think Jeremiah kept it?"

"We do." Pippa said. I didn't ask who 'we' was. "The Scarlet family didn't come into money around that time, as they would have if he'd sold the brooch. I've said it's of no exceptional monetary value, but I am talking in terms of royal jewels. It would have been a life-changing amount to a New England farm family. I suspect the poor man simply didn't know what to do with it. If he tried to sell it, people would naturally ask where it had come from. He would have been conscious of his brother's—and thus their family's—reputation. Remember, news of the theft didn't get much play in England and none at all in America. He wouldn't have known who it had belonged to and what they'd pay to get it back. So he put it in a secret drawer in his desk, and there it remained. Until your Sharon found it and thought it a pretty bauble."

"Around the time the brooch was hidden, the Civil War began, and Jeremiah's sons had joined the army. He might have thought it best to wait until things settled down again, and his sons were home, before deciding what to do with it. He put it in his secret drawer and died before telling anyone what he had."

Suddenly, I saw my chance and took it. I zipped nimbly around a police car and climbed half onto the sidewalk to edge past the accident scene. It appeared to be nothing but a fender bender, and two men were standing in the middle of the road yelling at each other while Officer Richter tried to calm them down. Officer Johnston stepped in front of me and put up one hand. The snow was falling faster now, and the shoulders of her uniform jacket were covered with it.

I rolled down my window. "I'm in a hurry, Stella. Police business. I called Detective Ashburton to tell him to meet me at Scarlet House. You can check with him."

She looked dubious, as well she might, but she stepped back, and I sped away, to the accompaniment of blaring horns.

"You can tell me the details of how all this came to light later," I said. "I presume that people other than you and your employer are on the trail of the brooch. What I'd like to know is why all the subterfuge around it."

"Because we did not know where the brooch was, until now, or who else is after it. It is also, as I may have mentioned, a family matter, not the concern of countries. My employer insists that it remain a private matter. Meaning, I have no official status here. It's been missing for over a century and a half, and although my boss is getting on in years, we were content to allow time for my contacts to locate it. Then your murder happened, and I realized the stakes were increasing, and a personal intervention might be required."

"There was no trip to Washington," I said.

"All this is way over my head," Jayne said. "But I do understand one thing. The brooch's value is mainly because of who owned it, not so much because of its innate worth. So why does someone want it? They can't sell it."

"There are wealthy individuals, as well as some less respectable governments," Pippa said, "who enjoy the possession of rare or important objects for the sheer pleasure of knowing no one else has it. They don't mind if they can't sell it or even publicly display it."

"Weird," Jayne said as I slowed to turn into the museum grounds.

It was shortly after five o'clock. Lights shone from the house and the barn, and a cluster of cars were parked in the lot. A pack of preteens fell out of the house and piled nosily into a yellow school van waiting for them. One of the kids scooped up snow and was about to make a snowball when the teacher snapped at her to get in the bus and make it quick.

By the time I'd parked and we'd reached the door, it had been locked. I knocked and we waited. I knocked again, and eventually it was opened by Craig Jones. "Hi." His eyes flicked from me to Pippa, to Jayne.

I pushed past him and walked in. "What's up?"

"They're meeting in the kitchen. Robyn arrived a few minutes ago, so Cassie and I came over, hoping there was news about Dave. I mean news of when they're going to have the funeral. We'd like to go."

"Have they heard?"

"No. The police haven't released the body yet. No one can say when that's going to happen."

Craig had stepped aside as we came in, and he stood against the wall, next to the portrait of George Scarlet. I looked at the painting. I looked at Craig.

"Guess you might as well come in, long as you're here." He turned and headed down the hallway, and we followed. Lights were on in the front hall, the parlor, and the dining room. Voices drifted from the kitchen. I let Craig go ahead and, turning to Pippa and Jayne, touched my finger to my lips.

I stopped just outside the kitchen door. Pippa stood quietly next to me. Jayne tried not to breathe.

"Now that pack of unruly kids have gone at last, let's get back to the topic at hand." Ethan's voice was sharp with anger. "You people are interfering with serious academic research. Edward Scarlet was a scoundrel and a wastrel."

"I won't have you impugning the character of one of our house's namesakes," Robyn replied.

"I don't care what you will or will not have. I intend to publish what I've uncovered."

"Get out."

"You can't—"

"I think people will be more likely to visit Scarlet House when they hear about it's real history," Cassie Jones said.

"I don't care what you think," Robyn snapped. "Why are you two hanging around here all the time anyway?"

"We call it helping," Craig said. "If you don't want our help—"

"We do," Leslie Wilson said. "Robyn didn't mean it."

But Robyn was on a tear now. "First ghosts and now insults and slander! I won't have it."

"See reason, Robyn," Leslie said. "We don't have any choice. The truth will come out."

"My point exactly," Ethan said. "You can't stop the truth."

"I don't want to stop—"

"Why don't we invite our visitors to come into the kitchen and get warm," Mrs. Ramsbatten's soft voice said.

I stepped into the kitchen and gave my neighbor a smile.

"I saw your shadow on the wall," she said.

"Hi," I said. "Don't let us intrude. Carry on with your discussion."

Leslie Wilson and Mrs. Ramsbatten wore their period costumes. Mrs. Ramsbatten sat by the fire, knitting needles in hand, the world's longest scarf trailing out of the basket on the floor. The fire was low, allowed to die down at the end of the day, and a chill was settling on the room. Shadows flickered across the walls.

Jayne stood next to me, but Pippa had moved silently to stand in the gloom by the cupboard.

"Not you again," Ethan sneered at me. "Still searching for ghosts?"

"I am seriously beginning to regret asking for your involvement in our affairs, Gemma," Robyn said. "You've done nothing but stir up trouble with all this talk of ghosts and hauntings."

I didn't bother to reply to either of them. I'd never said I thought Scarlet House was haunted.

"And then poor Dave dying," Craig said. "Tell me again, who was it who found him? Or claimed to have found him. It was you, Gemma. Convenient, don't you think?"

His wife watched me through narrow eyes.

I thought back to the night we'd spent on ghost watch. I remembered who had been where, and when. And at that moment I knew who'd killed Dave Chase, and why. Poor Dave, who'd simply made an observation he didn't understand the significance of. Unfortunately, neither had I, at the time. "Jayne. Try that number again, will you please. If no answer, call the other person we mentioned. If still no answer, call the public line."

She took out her phone.

"As long as we're waiting," I said, "I left something here the other day. In the volunteers' room. I'll go and get it now."

Cassie's eyes widened and flew to her husband. He sucked in a quick breath.

I caught Pippa's eye and gave my head a slight jerk to one side. She nodded.

"I'm calling an emergency meeting of the full board," Robyn said. "We can get an injunction against your thesis."

"Wow! Legal action to muzzle me," Ethan replied. "The stuff academic reputations are made of. Please go ahead—there's nothing I or my dissertation supervisor would like better."

I went into the small room tucked between the dining room and study that served as the volunteers' office. Cloaks and hats hung on pegs, lace-up boots beneath them. A row of lockers lined one wall, one of which was labeled "Sharon," and secured by a dime-store combination lock. I decided not to waste time trying to figure out the code, and dug in my bag for the small but sturdy screwdriver I keep there. I fitted it in the lock and gave it a strong twist. The lock broke.

I opened the locker door. All it contained was a deep blue velvet bag secured with a drawstring. The bag was dusty and tattered, the soft cloth creased and faded with age. I picked it up, balanced it in my hand, and felt something heavy for its size inside.

"Why don't I take that off your hands," Craig Jones said.

"I don't think so," I replied. "The police are on their way."

"They won't get here fast enough. I heard there's a traffic tie-up not far from here."

I turned. He stood in the doorway, a gun pointing directly at me.

I kept hold of the bag and called, "Pippa?"

"We seem to have a problem here," my sister replied.

Craig stepped aside and waved the gun, telling me to go ahead of him. I kept my grip on the bag.

In the kitchen, Cassie stood next to Mrs. Ramsbatten's rocking chair, brandishing a weapon.

"What on earth is going on here?" Robyn demanded. "This is outrageous."

"Sorry, Gemma." Jayne showed me her empty hands. "My phone was off, and by the time it booted up, I didn't have time to make the call."

I held up the bag. "Cassie and Craig, you want Craig's family treasure, but you're too late."

"How'd you—?" Craig began.

"Shut up," Cassie snapped.

"How did I know you're a Scarlet descendent? I didn't until a few minutes ago. Seeing you standing next to the portrait of George, the family resemblance is obvious. I would have noticed it sooner, but for all those whiskers covering his face."

"You talk too much," Cassie said. "About things that don't concern you."

"So I've been told on other occasions. What are you intending to do now? You can't kill us all, not without starting a heck of a big manhunt, and I doubt you have the resources to make your escape in time."

"My buyer's ready for us," Craig said.

"As are my police contacts. I told Detective Ashburton I was coming here. And why." That was a lie, but they didn't have to know that.

"Do you think your buyer will want anything to do with this if I'm harmed?" Pippa said. "Knowing whom I represent?"

"I don't know who you represent," Cassie said. "And I don't care."

"Your buyer will. Know and care a great deal indeed."

Cassie's eyes flicked toward me. She was looking, I realized, not at me, but at Craig. He stood a few feet behind me, and I could almost feel the strength of the gun pointing at my back. His breathing was heavy and ragged. He shifted his feet. He was getting edgy. That's never good.

Cassie, on the other hand, remained calm and still. She wasn't looking at Craig for encouragement, but to ensure he was keeping himself under control. Doing as she expected him to do.

"Put that bag on the table," Cassie said to me. "And we'll be on our way with no harm done."

I balanced it in my hand. "Over to you, Pippa."

"It's just an object," she said. "Even my employer would say it's not worth dying for."

"You have no right to it," Craig said. "It's my family property. Cassie and I will do with it what we like. Aunt Ellen told me Ethan was interested in it, and—"

"Be quiet," Cassie snapped.

"Will someone tell me what's going on?" Robyn demanded.

I caught Jayne's eye. She cleared her throat and touched her coat in the area of her pocket. She might not have been able to finish the call to Ryan, but she was telling me she'd started it and not hung up before putting the phone back in her pocket. At least I hoped that's what she was telling me.

I kept my eyes on Cassie's face as I took a slow step forward. I held out the bag. "I've figured most of it out, but what I still don't understand, and what threw my thinking off, is why you tried to get this the night we were in the house. You knew people were spending the night here and in the barn. Why the rush? Why not wait until a better time?"

Cassie's face tightened as she couldn't help taking a quick glance at Craig. Cassie was the one in charge here. That is, she wanted to be the one in charge. When Craig acted under his own initiative, things didn't go well.

The Game Is a Footnote

"Our buyer's getting impatient," Craig said. "That was the deadline for us to get a bonus. Today's—"

"Will you shut up," Cassie said. "She's stalling, and I'm not playing that game. Put that bag on the table."

No, Cassie was definitely not playing games. I placed the velvet bag on the scrubbed pine table.

The edges of her mouth lifted in a smile, and she said, "Thank you. That wasn't so hard, now, was it?" She gave Craig a nod of approval and then, eyes fixed on the bag, she stepped toward it, passing between the rocking chair and the dying fire. "Let's have a quick look and make sure she's not playing some sort of bluffing game here."

She extended her free hand.

Mrs. Ramsbatten drove her knitting needle into Cassie's hip.

Chapter
Twenty-One

Cassie screamed. The knitting needle fell to the floor as she whirled around, her gun pointed toward Mrs. Ramsbatten, sitting primly in her rocking chair.

Jayne, Robyn, and Leslie screamed. Ethan yelped and dropped to the floor, to crawl under the table. I hesitated, conscious of Craig's gun behind me. Pippa moved, but the table was between her and Cassie. If Cassie fired, Pippa wouldn't get to her in time.

But Cassie had been thrown off balance. As she turned, she staggered against the sudden pain in her hip, and her momentum failed. Her leg gave way, she stumbled, and as her foot caught in the loose tassels of the hearthside rug, she began to fall.

The fire in the huge fireplace was dying down, but it was not out, and the iron pot full of water just off the boil hung above it. Cassie instinctively reached for the pot to keep herself from falling into the embers.

She grabbed the pot, let out a piercing scream, jerked back, lost her footing completely, and fell hard.

"Cassie!" Craig yelled. I felt more than saw the gun behind me move, and I swung around. I lunged forward, grabbed his right wrist and twisted at the same time as I aimed a knee at his delicate parts. He turned to one side to save the family jewels, but let go of the gun. It dropped to the floor.

"I've got her," Pippa shouted. "Gemma, you take care of him."

Robyn and Leslie scrambled for cover. Ethan wiggled deeper under the table. Jayne pulled out her phone, and I could hear her yelling that we needed help and we needed it now.

Craig recovered faster than I would have liked. He'd lost his weapon, but I had not incapacitated him.

Abandoning Cassie, blocked from both the kitchen door and the velvet bag by Pippa, not to mention Mrs. Ramsbatten, wielding the second knitting needle, he turned and ran down the hall, heading for the front entrance. I took off in pursuit. As we passed the parlor, we could hear the sound of sirens heading our way. They turned into the long driveway, and red and blue lights washed the front windows.

Craig didn't hesitate. He turned sharply and sprinted up the stairs, taking them two at a time. I followed.

I've been told on previous occasions not to chase a suspect, to leave it to the police.

Wise advice, but I decided not to follow it. If the servants' staircase was unlocked, Craig could slip down that way and return to the kitchen. Pippa, I was sure, was more than capable of looking after herself. But Jayne, Leslie, and Mrs. Ramsbatten were there, not to mention the others, and they would have dropped their guard when Craig left and Pippa assumed control of Cassie.

I reached the first-floor landing. The lamps had been switched off, but the shape of the man ahead of me was outlined by emergency vehicle lights pouring through the single window at the end of the corridor.

"The police are here." My fingers felt for the light switch behind the philodendron, found it, and I flicked it on. Electric light flooded the hallway. "You can't get far."

Craig's eyes were wild, his breathing deep. "Our buyer's coming for us."

"You don't have what they want, Craig. They'll get rid of you as soon as they realize that. You can't save Cassie."

Below us, the door crashed open. Footsteps pounded in the hallway, and men and woman shouted.

"I won't leave without Cassie," Craig said. "I'll get her and we'll be on our way. We'll disappear."

"Gemma!" Ryan yelled.

"Up here," I replied. "Secure the kitchen."

He issued orders, rapidly and succinctly, and I heard his tread slowly, cautiously climbing the stairs.

Craig had no chance of escape, but he wasn't going to give up. He spoke to Ryan. "Don't listen to anything she says, Detective. My wife and I have done nothing, absolutely nothing illegal. I'll freely admit we came here hoping to find the lost jewel, but we didn't find it, did we? You can't convict a man for intent."

"Jewel?" Ryan said.

"I'll explain later," I said. "Craig's right that he didn't get his hands on the item he was intent on stealing, but he's no innocent. He killed Dave Chase."

A flash of fear crossed Craig's face. "Why would I do that? Dave meant nothing to me."

"You were afraid he'd realize, eventually, that you started the fuss in the barn to give Cassie cover as she sneaked into the kitchen in an attempt to continue the search. When we talked over the events of the night that Jayne, Andy, and I were in the house, and you and Dave were supposedly keeping watch out in the barn, Dave was about to remember that you'd stepped outside moments before the animals started panicking. You covered that up smoothly, suggesting Dave had been asleep and not aware of what exactly was going on. You glanced at Cassie when you said it, and I only realized the significance of that just now, when I saw her give you a nod of approval. You wouldn't have needed her to approve of what you were saying if you were telling the truth. You're not the one in charge here—she is, and you need her reassurance that you're doing the right thing."

His gaze wavered. "She's nuts, Detective. You're not going to listen to this crazy rambling, are you?"

"I'd rather listen to you," Ryan said calmly.

"You got the animals agitated in an attempt to suggest the house was haunted as a way of trying to explain why things were being moved during your nightly searches. Maybe you even enjoyed watching everyone tearing their hair out, suspecting a ghost was in the house. My theory is that you waved a lit torch at the animals, maybe accompanied it with a few prods with a pitchfork to the donkey's rear end, and that started the panic you needed." I didn't need to explain my reasoning, but I kept talking, hoping Craig would eventually give up and go with Ryan.

"As for what happened on Saturday, Cassie wanted to wait for a better night to try again, didn't she? One when people weren't in the house. But you got greedy. You'd been offered a bonus if you could hand the jewel over within some specified time frame, and time was up that night. You must have convinced her that you could get us to leave. She's come to regret that."

"Time was running out," Craig said. "Time is running out. Our buyer isn't going to wait forever. They're making noises about wanting the money back they've invested. Money we don't have."

"Why Dave?"

He spoke to Ryan. "Okay, I don't know how she knows, but she's right, although I didn't kill him. It was an accident. Cassie went home, but I wanted to talk to Dave. I followed him into the barn after the meeting. He went into the hayloft to get hay for the donkey. I only wanted to talk. I told him to forget about whatever he thought he saw that night. He was befuddled and confused when he woke up. He didn't like being told what to do, and he took a swing at me. He was an old man. I didn't want to fight him, but . . . he slipped and he fell out that window. It wasn't my fault. It was an accident. You have to believe me, Detective. My wife and I haven't done anything. Yeah, okay, we played a practical joke, but no crime in that, is there?"

"All this is getting too deep for me," Ryan said. "Let's join the others and talk it all over." He took a step forward to stand next to me.

Craig's nerve broke. He grabbed the door to the back staircase and wrenched it open. Just then, the bulb of the electric lamp in the hallway popped; the light died, and we were plunged into near darkness. Craig stepped through the door. I began to run after him.

The moment I started to move, a shape passed across the window. It was gossamer thin, the edges indistinct, the height of a human, but no visible feet touched the floor. Tendrils of icy mist drifted around it as though a fog had crept into the house. It slipped silently through the open door, following Craig. I was frozen in place. I willed my legs to keep moving, but they did not.

"Gemma, wait," Ryan yelled. A sudden burst of light almost blinded me as Ryan switched on his flashlight.

A scream came from the staircase, followed by the thud, thud of a of a body falling. With a jerk, I regained control of my limbs and ran for the stairs. I stood at the top and looked down into the pitch dark. The temperature in this stairway was cold. Icy cold. Something as indistinct as the footsteps of an ant brushed against the fine hairs on my arms. My heart stopped under the sheer strength of the cold. I couldn't breathe.

And then it—whatever it was—was gone. I sucked in cool, not cold, air. Ryan rested one hand on my shoulder and used the other hand to shine his light down. Craig Jones lay in a crumpled heap at the bottom of the steps, his left leg bent behind him at a bad angle. He groaned and struggled to sit up. Ryan slipped past me and ran down the stairs, shouting into his radio that the scene was secure and he needed a medic.

I turned to look back in the direction in which we'd come. All I could see in the doorway was the play of lights against the far wall as an ambulance drove up.

Chapter Twenty-Two

Cassie and Craig Jones had been taken away—Craig on a gurney with a broken leg—and the police had secured the scene, although I could have told them the couple had no accomplices. None who were willing to show their faces at any rate. While that was happening, Pippa had unobtrusively slipped the velvet bag into her coat pocket and smiled sweetly at Ryan. "How nice to see you again, Detective," she said.

He glanced between her and me, clearly suspicious, but said nothing.

"I demand to know what's going on here," Robyn said. "Where's that bag and what's in it?"

"What bag?" Pippa said.

"What bag?" Mrs. Ramsbatten said.

"What bag?" Jayne said.

"Bag?" Ryan said.

Robyn looked around the kitchen, gave her head a shake, and said, "I must have been imagining it. What do you suppose came over them anyway? What does this have to do with the death of Dave?"

"I heard Gemma accuse Jones of killing Dave Chase," Ryan said. "He didn't deny being there, and he did try to get away after I'd told him to remain where he was. We'll be charging them with murder, as a starter. It's going to be a long list, with public mischief somewhere near the bottom."

"I need you people to leave now," Detective Estrada said. "We'll contact you for your statements later, but right now we have a scene to process. Thank heavens," she added under her breath, "we don't have to go back to that barn."

I leaned toward my sister and spoke in a low voice. "You can't keep that a secret. The police will want to know what the Joneses were after, and Ethan and Robyn saw it."

"I have no intention of keeping anything secret. I simply don't want it disappearing into a police evidence locker, never to be seen again. After I've made a few phone calls, I'll show it to the Delectable Detective."

"Stop calling him that."

"What'd you say?" Ryan asked.

"Nothing," Pippa and I chorused.

We filed out of the house and left the police to their work. Ethan fell into step next to Pippa. "I knew Edward Scarlet had to have some reason for resigning his post so quickly after the success of the Trent affair, never mind the honor of an invitation to Windsor Castle. That little trinket in your pocket might prove helpful to my thesis. Want to tell me the story? Or shall I go back inside and suggest the police search you?"

"Threats are unnecessary," she said. "All will be revealed. Gemma?"

"Might as well come to my house." I gave them my address. "Robyn, it would be nice if you pick up Sharon and bring her."

"Why should I be nice to Sharon?"

"Because you want to keep this museum viable and functioning smoothly, and she's vital to that. All she wants is to be allowed to think she's important, not treated like an expendable kitchen maid."

"I don't—"

"Whatever. Leslie, can you drive Jayne and Mrs. Ramsbatten?"

"Happy to. My head's spinning. Like Robyn, I have absolutely no idea of what's going on here."

"All will be revealed," I said, "in the fullness of time. Stop and pick up Andy, if he can get away. He'll want to hear the story too. You should probably tell him we won't make our seven thirty reservation."

Once again, the parking lot and driveway of Scarlet House were crowded with emergency vehicles. Flashing lights reflected off falling snow. Neighbors gathered at the road, watching. The pigs called out, and the donkey brayed softly. A forensics van pulled up, and men and women began pulling on white overalls, hats, and booties.

Ryan had walked behind us. He spoke briefly to Stella Johnson, assigned to guard the door. "These people have all been given permission to leave. Don't let them back inside once they've gone."

He touched my arm lightly, and I walked with him into the darkness at the side of the house. He didn't touch me again, but studied my face closely. "You okay, Gemma?"

"I'm fine. Really I am."

"You're sure Craig Jones killed Dave Chase?"

"Killed him deliberately or caused it to happen. I'm positive. You heard him confess."

"A confession won't stand up in court, not if he withdraws it. Not on its own. Do you have proof?"

"Not a single scrap. He'll try to say you misunderstood him or he was just wanting to get rid of me, but you'll get it all out of him soon enough. He's weak; his wife's the power in that couple. Keep them separated, and he'll crumble."

"You said something about him wanting to steal something. Someone mentioned a bag. What is it?"

"I suspect, Ryan, you'll be getting a call from Washington soon."

He cocked his head to one side. I nodded.

"I also want to hear what's been going on," he said. "Craig Jones has been taken to the hospital. He's drugged up now, and that leg will be operated on tonight, so he won't be talking for a while. It'll do his wife good to spend some time brooding in a cell, wondering what he's saying. I'll check that Louise has everything under control here, and then I'm coming around to your place."

I smiled at him, and he gave me a long look. Then the edges of his mouth turned up. "Loving you, Gemma Doyle, is a challenge. But I wouldn't have it any other way." He lifted his hand, but conscious of all the people around, he didn't touch me. He turned and walked away, and I watched him go as snowflakes swirled around him.

When I got into my car, Pippa was putting her phone away. "That's that sorted," she declared.

* * *

Pippa held the brooch in her hand. Her gaze was reverent, full of awe as she stared at it. It needed a good scrubbing, but as not even Pippa was an expert in handling rare gems and antique jewelry, we didn't dare run it under the tap and apply a tooth-brush to the fine metalwork.

"It's going to look spectacular when it's cleaned up," I said. "Craig mentioned that he has a buyer for the brooch. Do you know anything about who that might be?"

"I do not. I intend to find out, however."

We were in the kitchen of the saltbox house, preparing for an influx of visitors. Pippa slipped the brooch into its bag, put the bag in her pocket, and went to answer the doorbell. I put the kettle and coffee pot on, laid out mugs, got wine and beer out of the fridge, and took glasses out of the cupboard while my guests streamed into the house and gathered in the living room.

Jayne came into the kitchen to help me. "Nothing like an impromptu party."

"There's some cheese in the fridge. Somewhere. Should I bring it out?"

"Don't go to any trouble, Gemma. You don't even need to bother with the coffee things. Everyone just wants to hear what's going on. *I* just want to hear what's going on."

Nevertheless, I put everything on trays, and Jayne and I carried the refreshments through.

The buzz of excited conversation stopped as we came into the living room. Everyone stared at me.

Pippa had taken a seat in a far corner. The velvet bag sat in her lap, and she idly stroked the soft old cloth. Her face had returned to its usual inscrutable expression.

Peony and Violet were overjoyed at the unexpected infusion of company and ran from one person to the other, accepting pats and scratches, and sniffing socks and trouser legs.

"Did you tell Uncle Arthur you have it?" I asked Pippa after I'd put my tray on the coffee table and our visitors began to serve themselves.

"Among others, yes. You appear to have figured out most of it."

"Did you doubt I would?"

"Actually, yes. I did. My mistake. It won't happen again. We won't know for sure, of course, that this is the genuine article until it's been properly examined, but I'm confident we have it."

"Can I get you something to drink, Pippa?" Jayne asked.

"A glass of wine would be nice. I have something to celebrate."

The front doorbell rang, and Violet hurried to answer. I heard Ryan's voice as he greeted her, and then he came into the room, followed by Louise Estrada. Ryan looked directly at Pippa. "I've just had the most interesting phone call."

"I thought you might."

Estrada stared at Pippa. Pippa gave her a broad smile and put on her most pompous English accent. "I don't believe we've been introduced, Detective. Phillipa Doyle."

Estrada stared at Pippa. She looked at me and then back at Pippa. She groaned. "Two of them."

"Can I get you a coffee?" Andy asked.

"Please," Estrada said.

"That'd be good, thanks," Ryan said. "We've got a long night ahead of us, so let's get started. Pippa, are you going to show it to us?"

"Show us what?" Robyn said. While I'd been in the kitchen, she'd arrived with Sharon, and both women perched on the edges of their seats. Mrs. Ramsbatten relaxed in an armchair, and Ethan paced the room. Leslie threw a questioning look at her daughter, and Andy helped serve the refreshments.

Pippa slowly opened the velvet bag and took out the brooch. She held it up. Thick with grime and neglect, it didn't look all that impressive at first glance. But in the bright light of the lamp next to her chair, several of the diamonds sparkled, and something deep within the emerald glowed red.

Sharon leapt to her feet. "That's my—I mean the museum's brooch. Give it to me."

"Sit down," Pippa said.

Sharon sat down.

"Is that the thing Sharon's been wearing with her costume?" Robyn sniffed with disapproval. "As though a farmwife or kitchen maid would wear something like that while bending over an open fire or lugging a bucket of slop out to the pigs."

"Well, pardon me for liking it," Sharon replied. "It was important to the Scarlets and thus important to me as a representative of the family."

"So important you didn't bother to tell the board about it? Where did you get it, anyway?"

I interrupted before they could start shouting at each other. "'Important' is the right word," I said. "People have been looking for this little trinket for a long time, but the main search was abandoned more than a hundred years ago, and the item assumed to be lost. Something happened quite recently, and the hunt was on again. Two somethings, I might say. Craig Jones is a direct descendent of the Scarlet family."

"He is?" Sharon said. "Why didn't he tell us?"

"He didn't tell me either," Ethan said. "It might have helped with my research."

"Why don't you start by telling us about that," I said.

"Happy to. When I started this phase of my project, I contacted scattered remnants of the extended Scarlet family, explaining my thesis and asking if they had old letters or diaries I might find of interest. Other than a handful of family recipes, no one had much of anything to send me. People don't keep family documents anymore, which is making research harder and harder and—"

Mrs. Ramsbatten cleared her throat.

"Sorry," Ethan said. "Back to the point. A woman by the name of Ellen Jones wrote to tell me her grandmother, whose mother had been Rose Scarlet, youngest child of Jeremiah, had always claimed that the family was in possession of some item of treasure. Something so valuable, it was kept hidden, the knowledge of its whereabouts passed from father to son, only to be used in times of great need. Such as if the farm would have to be sold otherwise. As with most tales of long-hidden family treasure, Mrs. Jones gave no credence to the tale. The farm was sold on the death of Jeremiah's sister, Josephine, in 1914, as we know, and no treasure appeared. Ellen Jones told me about it as an amusing story. Other than that, she had nothing to tell me about her Scarlet ancestors."

"Jones," Mrs. Ramsbatten said. "You didn't make the connection with Craig?"

"I never even knew Craig's last name until today. No reason I should. I don't think we were ever introduced. I don't know that we said more than hello to each other. Same for his wife. And even if I had known it, Jones is a mighty common name, and Ellen Jones's story didn't stick in my mind, as she didn't have anything to back it up."

"Rather than being handed down from father to son, the treasure was lost after Jeremiah's death," I said. "But the details don't matter—it's the stuff family legends are made of. Your letter started Mrs. Jones remembering the story, and she told it to Craig, who, judging by what he said in the kitchen, must be her nephew. He did take the story seriously, or his wife did. Meanwhile, Ethan, you had other lines of research to follow, whereupon you managed to discover that Edward Scarlet had caused a maid to be dismissed from her post in 1861."

"That's the Scarlet you called a scoundrel," Robyn said.

"And he was. He was on the verge of being fired outright and sent back to America in disgrace, under suspicion of robbing houses where he'd been a guest. Before that could happen, he tricked a maid into stealing from her employers, on the promise of taking her to America with him and marrying her. He didn't marry her, and he threw her overboard once they were out at sea."

"You don't have any proof of that," Robyn insisted.

"I don't need proof for my thesis," Ethan said. "I have plenty of circumstantial evidence."

"You didn't know from where this maid had been dismissed," I said, "but your research bumped up against someone searching for her from the opposite direction." I looked at Pippa. "Arthur Doyle."

"How did you arrive at that conclusion?" My sister had slipped the brooch into the bag and was running the drawstring through her long thin fingers.

"Arthur knows how to search shipping records. He has contacts, probably in the hundreds, in nautical historical societies, both civilian and military. Arthur has spent the last weeks in London, unable to travel. I suspect being confined to bed rest in my parents' house in a London winter made him restless. You gave him a task to keep him occupied."

She smiled at me. "And he accomplished it in far less time than even I'd expected. Yes, Arthur located the upstairs maid and traced her to her sudden demise one dark night in the middle of the Atlantic Ocean. Edward Scarlet of West London, Massachusetts, was on the same ship."

I turned to Mrs. Ramsbatten. "Whereupon Uncle Arthur asked you to get a position at Scarlet House and keep him informed."

She dipped her head. "You caught me sending him a message after we discovered the root cellar."

"That, plus Pippa knowing my neighbor was an elderly woman, and then catching the two of you chatting on your front porch, acting all innocent despite the cold."

"Okay," Ryan said. "As fascinating as this is, I haven't got all night here, and I've heard nothing I can use against the Joneses. I've been"—he shifted uncomfortably—"advised not to take that thing Pippa has into custody, even though it appears to be evidence in a murder case. I'd like to know what it is that has attracted so much attention."

Pippa leaned back in her chair and related the tale of Prince Albert's engagement gift as she ran her fingers over the velvet of the bag in her lap.

"Gemma's right that our uncle Arthur traced the missing upstairs maid to the ship bound for New York City, and discovered her unfortunate demise. The captain's log reported that the woman's death was considered highly suspicious, but as she was not known to be traveling with anyone, he had no lines of investigation to follow. He noted that she was traveling first class, but her accent and clothes indicated that she didn't belong there, and she kept mainly to her cabin on the voyage. When Uncle Arthur saw the name Edward Scarlet on the passenger manifest, his antenna twitched. Scarlet is, of course, an unusual name. He found out that this Scarlet was, in fact, the brother of the owner of West London's Scarlet House. He reported that information to me, and we decided to pay some attention to Scarlet House. I was reluctant to simply tell the current homeowners, the Historical Society, what we were looking for, and I assumed we had plenty of time to decide how to proceed. We were not aware, at the time, that the Joneses were also getting close. In retrospect, my delay was a mistake. A man died because of my hesitation, and I'm terribly sorry about that."

When she finished, the room fell completely silent. Even Violet and Peony had stopped snuffing around.

"Goodness," Sharon said at last. "You mean I've been wearing . . . all this time."

"If that's true," Robyn said. "The brooch belongs to the Historical Society. We bought the house and property, contents and all."

"I'd advise you not to try to make an issue of that," Pippa said sharply. "Provenance is of no doubt. The item was stolen from its rightful owner. The passage of years is irrelevant."

"But—"

"But you might find that if the item is returned to its current rightful owner, quietly and without fuss, she will be generous in her thanks."

For once Robyn was struck speechless.

"Craig Jones doesn't seem to me to be the sort to take tales of lost treasure all that seriously," I said. "But his wife is. She set about trying to find it. Ethan, when did you first hear from Ellen Jones?"

"Sometime last spring. I was just getting this phase of my project started."

"Cassie and Craig moved to West London in November. I suspect they spent the intervening months doing their own research. Cassie has written a couple of nonfiction YA books about pirates in the Caribbean, so she'd know her way around historical documents, plus it would seem natural enough that she'd show an interest in Scarlet House. They might have been waiting for that house they're in to become available for them to rent. They couldn't search Scarlet House in broad daylight so living as close as possible would be convenient. Cassie took a position as a docent. She was Sharon's substitute, wasn't she, on Mondays and Wednesdays?"

"Yes," Robyn said.

"Thus she never saw you wearing the brooch, Sharon. Somewhat ironic, come to think of it. It was there in plain sight, all the time. Yet Cassie never saw it." I thought back to when we'd gathered in the dining room, shortly before Dave died, to discuss what had happened the night Jayne, Andy, and I spent in the house. Cassie was there, and Sharon was in costume. But Sharon had thrown a shawl over her shoulders. I only saw the brooch when we went into the warm hallway, and she took the shawl off. "You told me you found the brooch in September, Sharon."

Sharon still looked stunned, having realized the value and importance of the little trinket she'd been wearing pinned to her historical costume. She nodded. "Before Cassie arrived. She would have searched the desk first thing, knowing it was an original piece of furniture. And she found nothing."

"We're very busy in December," Robyn said. "We do the full Victorian Christmas thing."

"My mince pies are particularly popular at Christmas," Sharon said. "I do them the way—"

"Cassie wouldn't have had the freedom to poke around where she wasn't supposed to be," Robyn said. "Some of the other docents complained about her. She didn't seem to be all that interested in showing the house to visitors. When Christmas and New Year were over, I politely informed her she wouldn't be needed again until the spring. It's hard getting rid of volunteer help, but sometimes it has to be done."

"All that nonsense about ghosts?" Estrada said. "You mean it was nothing but a cover for them searching the house? Seems a stretch to me. All that accomplished was to attract more attention. Leading directly to the death of Dave Chase."

I thought of what I'd seen, and what I'd felt, in the upstairs corridor as Craig headed for the stairs, but I said nothing.

Ryan put his coffee cup on the table. "Speaking of that, we need to be off. I've put in a request for a warrant to search their house and cars and bank accounts, and I have to call the hospital for an update. I'll interview Craig as soon as his doctor says he's able to answer questions."

Everyone murmured good night. Sharon said, "Any more wine in that bottle?"

Robyn said, "What degree of gratitude are we talking about, Pippa?"

Ethan said, "There had better not be an embargo on this story. It'll make my professional reputation."

Mrs. Ramsbatten said, "My, that was exciting. My old heart seems to be calming down at last. If you need any more help, Pippa dear, do let me know."

Leslie said, "Is Pippa telling us she was sent here by—?"

Jayne said, "I've learned it's better not to ask, Mom."

I walked the police to the door. Estrada slipped politely away, still muttering something about "two of them," leaving Ryan and me alone. When she was gone, he put his arms around me and pulled me close.

"Are you going to chastise me for chasing after Craig?" I said into his chest.

"I wouldn't waste my breath. Although I can, and will, think it. You are so very precious to me, Gemma. It frightens me sometimes when I think of what you get up to." He sighed, and his breath was warm in my hair.

I wrapped my arms tighter around him. We stood like that for a long time. Being together.

His phone buzzed and he pulled away. He checked it. "Louise. Telling me she's about to leave without me."

"When you search their house, have a look for something that could be used to drug a man. Craig brought the beer that night, and I suspect he also brought something to slip into Dave's drink to help Dave sleep and awake befuddled. But Craig panicked the next day, and he upped the stakes considerably. As he told us, he followed Dave to the barn after the meeting ended, while Cassie walked home. Dave went upstairs to get the hay, and Craig followed him. I don't believe for a minute that Dave attacked Craig, a man thirty years his junior. Dave might have said something that made Craig think Dave had figured it out, and Craig pushed him out the door. Cassie was furious at him for the killing. When I called on them after finding Dave, I thought she was genuinely upset at his death, but when I saw them together earlier tonight, I realized she'd been angry at Craig for killing him. She knew that would attract far more police attention than the theft that was their original plan."

"And they couldn't up and leave town without arousing suspicion."

"Exactly. If you get the chance, will you do two things for me?"

"What?"

"Search their house for a recording of kitchen items falling to the floor. And ask Craig why he locked me in the pig barn."

He touched the top of my head, and then he let himself out.

Chapter Twenty-Three

After our guests left, Pippa handed me the velvet bag and asked me to put it in the safe for the night. "Just to be sure. Too many people know where it is."

I took the bag and its precious contents into the den while Pippa gathered up the used glasses. I took Maria Fernanda's portrait off the wall and unlocked the safe. Before putting it away, I opened the bag and poured the brooch into my palm. I looked at it for a long time, thinking of the woman who'd worn and cherished it. I put the jewel back in the bag, popped it into the safe, spun the dial, and rehung the painting, ensuring it was flat against the wall. I then joined my sister in the kitchen, where she was washing cups and glasses.

"Why didn't you get me involved in this in the first place? Instead of Mrs. Ramsbatten, of all people?"

"I will admit, in retrospect that might have been a mistake. We didn't know who was after the brooch, remember, and obviously we never thought they'd go so far as to kill a man. Arthur had the idea of asking your neighbor to keep a quiet eye on the house. When strange things seemed to be happening, before we could even decide whether or not to involve you, the museum board approached you."

She finished rinsing a glass and turned to face me. "You have to admit, you do your best thinking when you don't have a clue what's going on."

I grumbled, and took myself off to bed.

* * *

When I got up the following morning, Pippa was gone. A hand-written note lay on the kitchen table, tucked under the salt cellar.

Had a fabulous time!! Simply must do this again!!!

I went into the den. The painting of the Spanish opera singer was on the floor, propped against the wall. The door to the safe hung open.

* * *

Louise Estrada came to the Emporium the following morning to get my statement about the happenings at Scarlet House, and she then went to the tearoom to speak to Jayne. After that, it was two days before I heard any more about Queen Victoria's brooch.

"Bunny's thinking maybe she doesn't want to buy Scarlet House after all," Ashleigh said on Friday afternoon after having served another happy customer.

Before the store opened, I'd cornered my assistant with the intention of giving her a good talking to. But that hadn't proved necessary. Ashleigh had been genuinely contrite about leaving without ensuring Gale was on her way and that I approved of her sudden departure. As I hoped no more long-lost parents would pop up, unannounced, I just asked Ashleigh to keep me informed—without relying on third parties—if her personal situation affected her work at the shop.

"Just as well," I said now, "as I have a feeling Scarlet House is not going to be for sale."

"Bunny says she's highly sensitive to the supernatural, and all this talk of ghosts and hauntings has put her off."

"Is that what you think?" I asked.

Ashleigh gave me a crooked grin. "Nah. She can't afford it. I get the feeling this movie deal she has her heart set on isn't going to happen. Which is probably better for me. It's mighty strange meeting your mother for the first time when you're twenty-two without the added pressure of fame and attention on top of it. She has to leave that house she's in soon, and she's looking for a moderately priced apartment in West London she can take for the remainder of the winter. We'll build our relationship slowly and carefully, and I'd like to keep a respectful distance between us while we do that. I have my life, she'll get on with hers, and we'll enjoy the time we can spend together. At the end of the winter, we'll decide what comes next."

"That sounds sensible to me."

"Besides, I don't want a pony."

I laughed.

"I'm trying to persuade her to come with me to Nebraska for a visit. She's coming around to the idea. She has her own parental relationships to repair. Oh, by the way, you were only half right."

"Only half? What was I half-right about?"

"Lisa."

"Who's Lisa?"

"Our customer, you remember? You said she'd reunited with her cheating husband or had found a new boyfriend. She came in in earlier when you were upstairs. She was here to buy a gift. She was blushing and giggling like a teenager, and she made sure I knew the present's for her new man's birthday."

"Good for Lisa," I said.

"She also told me her husband's girlfriend kicked him out, and he's had to move in with his parents. Speaking of the local gossip, the paper says they arrested some people for killing that guy at Scarlet House. Was that why Detective Estrada was in yesterday?"

"Yes. I had a minor role as a witness in the affair."

"Minor. Right. What's this about a valuable jewel being found in the house? Is that true?"

"I don't know anything about that," I said. "Excuse me, I need to get this."

I answered my phone, and Ryan said, "Hey."

"Hey yourself. I heard the news about the arrest."

"Yup. We've charged Craig Jones with the murder of Dave Chase, and Cassie Jones as an accessory after the fact, as well as for a slew of minor charges, including break and enter. I asked them your questions. How about I come around later to tell you about it?"

"I'd like that. Come for dinner at my house? It has to be late, though. Today's Friday and we don't close until nine."

"Late will be good. Still a ton of paperwork to get through."

* * *

Ryan arrived at nine thirty, a bottle of wine under one arm and a flat cardboard box under the other.

"You brought dinner," I said. "How nice. I was looking in the fridge to see what I could rustle up, and the answer is not much."

"Which," he said, bending himself around the box to give me a kiss, "is exactly what I figured."

Violet and Peony ran ahead of us into the kitchen. "Have you taken these two out yet?" Ryan asked me.

"I just got in. I had a customer who stayed long after closing. I pretty much had to manhandle her out the door."

"I hope she bought."

"Lots, which is why she wasn't manhandled at nine o'clock on the dot."

I got my coat and the dogs' leashes, and we set out. Ryan took Violet's leash in his left hand, and I had Peony's in my right, and he and I held hands. It was a nice night, cool and crisp, with no wind, the sky a blanket of stars.

"As you expected, Craig started singing like a canary almost right away. He fell all over himself making sure I knew Cassie had nothing to do with the death of Dave Chase."

"Surprisingly loyal of him."

"She didn't return the favor. She's happy enough to stick him with it. It went down pretty much as you guessed."

"I never guess."

"So you say. They freely admit they were after Queen Victoria's brooch, which according to Craig is his family's property and thus rightfully belongs to him."

"Good luck with that one."

"As they never did get the brooch, we can't charge them with the theft of it. As for murder—he's sticking to his story pretty much as he told it to us. He tried to say he intended to apologize for playing a trick"—here Ryan made air quotes—"on Dave by disturbing the farm animals, but I didn't buy that, and he changed his story to say he wanted to ensure Dave didn't remember precisely what was going on when he'd woken up. Guy's not all that bright, and without his wife to tell him what to say, he's digging himself into a deeper and deeper hole. He's being somewhat unclear about who took the first swing, but he insists Dave lost his footing and fell. Craig ran down to check on him, but he was obviously dead, so Craig panicked and ran home."

"Do you believe that?"

"Do I believe it was an accident? No, I believe Craig shoved Dave in a fit of anger. But it's not up to me to believe it or not. A court will decide that. Cassie's testimony, however, contradicts what Craig said. She says she saw you arrive at the house minutes after Craig got home. You told them that Dave had died—"

"I didn't. She figured it out easily enough when the ambulance didn't leave in any hurry and the police stayed, searching the barnyard. In the short time between leaving the meeting and Jayne and me arriving, Craig had changed his clothes. He got them dirty in the barn, probably in the barnyard. He would have had to kneel or crouch next to Dave when he checked on his condition. In fairness—and this is just my guess—if Dave hadn't broken his neck, I don't believe Craig would have finished him off. He didn't have it in him. Cassie, on the other hand . . .

"She's a tough one. She has her story and she's sticking to it. Craig arrived home, filthy and all in a panic. He told her Dave had had a fall and was dead. She says she didn't want to "get involved" and she told Craig they didn't need to contact the police, as there was nothing anyone could do for Dave now. I can get her for accessory after the fact, at the least, as she didn't bother to tell Louise that when she was interviewed. We found a half-empty bottle of sleeping pills in the bathroom cabinet at their house. Craig says he added some to Dave's beer when they were supposedly keeping watch in the barn, so he could get the animals riled without Dave realizing. He was, he says, playing a practical joke."

"Most amusing. Again, without Cassie to tell him what to do, Craig misjudged the dose, and Dave woke up at exactly the wrong time. Why'd he lock me in the pig barn?"

"That, Craig says, was another practical joke."

"Ha."

"Cassie had complained to him that you were interfering in things that were none of your business. He saw you drive up and go into the barn, and so he followed you and had the idea of locking you in. No harm done, right?"

"Except to my dignity."

"You could have been hurt trying to get out, so I'm recommending he be charged with willful endangerment on that score."

We passed under a streetlight. The strong lights showed the shadows under Ryan's eyes, the thick stubble on his jaw. Violet had been trotting at his side at a sedate pace, but she suddenly broke off and attempted to charge into a neighbor's yard, almost jerking Ryan off his feet. I would have laughed except Peony caught the same scent. He didn't weigh much more than ten pounds, but he could be mighty strong when he put his mind to it. When we'd wrestled the protesting dogs back onto the sidewalk and continued on our way, I said, "The supposed haunting?"

"Cassie spent a short spell as a docent in the house in December, but she wasn't able to do the sort of searching she needed to do, not in the daytime when people were around. And then Robyn said they wouldn't need her any more. She was not, to put it mildly, happy about that.

"She'd made herself a copy of a key to the house, so she started coming in at night. It wasn't originally her intention to pretend a ghost was in the house, but things got moved around and people—Sharon Musgrave most of all—started talking ghost. She decided to play on their fears. You'll be pleased to know that she says if she knew that would lead to you poking your English nose in, she would have thought better of it. At some point she found the root cellar in the pantry and made it into a bolt hole in case someone came in unexpectedly and she had to hide."

"Did you find the recording I asked about? Kitchen stuff falling over."

"Yes, we did. It was on her phone. Much clanging and clattering of pots. Cassie Jones is a ruthless woman, but she's not a very smart one, and her husband even less so. They were starting to get desperate. They'd been searching for a month and finding nothing, and their buyer was threating to pull out of the deal."

"They'd been offered a bonus if they produced it by Saturday night. Greed got the better of them."

"I'm not sure why they continued to be so convinced the brooch was in the house."

"It was a fair assumption in light of the rumors of family treasure," I said. "If we accept that Edward Scarlet had the brooch in his possession when he disembarked from the ship, minus the hapless upstairs maid. His brother would have taken ownership of his possessions on his death. The brooch was never sold; the Scarlets didn't unexpectedly come into money around that time."

"When you and Jayne and Andy were in the house, Craig disturbed the animals, and Cassie let herself into the kitchen in the uproar."

"Using a key she nicked when she was a docent. I told Robyn to get those locks changed. If she had, a heck of a lot of trouble would have been avoided. And poor innocent Dave Chase would still be alive."

"Yup. When Cassie heard Craig at the front door, she screamed and played that recording before hiding in the root cellar to wait for you to leave. She expected you to run screaming into the night, never to return."

"As has been said before, not very efficient criminals those two. They didn't bother to check into who they were dealing with before acting."

Ryan chuckled. "Yup. Instead of fleeing, you called the police. And, even worse, you intended to stay put the rest of the night. When Cassie realized you had no intention of leaving, she came out of the root cellar, ran around to the front of the house, and joined the rest of you."

"She overplayed her hand," I said. "Why did they start the original uproar in the barn? All that served was to focus attention on what was going on at the house."

"She claims they didn't do that. But it did give them the idea of trying it the night you were there, to cause a distraction. We'll have no trouble getting Craig for killing Dave, and I'm hoping we can get Cassie as an accessory. The details are up to the courts and the lawyers to sort out."

"Are they saying anything about this buyer? The one who's actually trying to get his, or her, hands on the brooch?"

"They never met him. All arrangements were made over encrypted correspondence. That's been passed on to the FBI, but the people who have money to collect such items have ways of keeping themselves under the radar."

"Pippa, and most of all her boss, have substantial resources also."

"I have no doubt about that. Otherwise, it's over. Pippa has her brooch and is taking it back to where it belongs."

Was it over?

I had one last question, but I had to ask myself: *Did it matter?*

If Cassie had been searching Scarlet House for the brooch, things would have been moved around, but she wouldn't have put candlesticks into the airing cupboard or notebooks into the flour bin. Why would she have gone to the trouble of putting on a period dress and flitting around the upper level so Robyn could see her when she'd been leading her tour group? When Cassie'd been in the kitchen, screaming and playing her recording, had she knocked the rolling pin off the shelf?

And what about the first night the animals had been disturbed? Craig and Cassie claimed they hadn't caused that, and I could see no reason for them to lie.

But most of all, what I didn't know was what had happened in that upstairs hallway after I confronted Craig Jones. What had I seen—or thought I'd seen—slipping through the door after him? Had Craig tripped on the stairs? Or had he been pushed? That sudden overwhelming cold I'd experienced and the feeling of being unable to move.

A chill ran down my back. What did it mean if Cassie Jones hadn't been the Ghost of Scarlet House?

Everyone says that over its long years, there'd never been so much as a whisper that Scarlet House was haunted. Might that be true only because the ghostly resident had never felt the need to show itself? Had it come out of the darkness to protect its home? Its property? Had it been moving random objects in an attempt to attract attention to the nightly goings-on?

I shook my head. Stuff and nonsense. All of this would have a perfectly logical explanation. Cassie herself didn't seem entirely stable, not considering the lengths she went to in an attempt to get an object that might have been nothing more than a family rumor. If I got a chance, I'd ask her why she'd done those things.

I quickly changed my mind. Better not to think about that. Not ever again.

"Cold?" Ryan said.

"Yes, I am. Enough of a walk. Let's get back."

We did a little dance to avoid getting tangled in dogs and leashes, and headed back the way we'd come. We walked in silence for a long time, enjoying the night and each other's company.

When the lights of my house came in sight, I said, "Tomorrow morning, first thing, I'm going to call Andy's mom and Leslie Wilson and set a date to get together so we can get on with this wedding planning. Jayne's counting on me, and I dare not let her down."

"You don't want me to do anything, do you?" He didn't wait for an answer before saying, "Good."

"You need a vacation."

"I just had a vacation. I went fishing in Florida with my dad, although honesty forces me to admit I'd have preferred to spend the time with you."

"I'm thinking a few days up the coast. A bed and breakfast with a big fireplace and ocean views. Restaurants with even bigger fireplaces and better ocean views. Long deserted beaches and woodland hikes."

"I'm thinking that might be a good idea," he replied.

I let us into the house. While Ryan played with the dogs, I opened the bottle of wine and served up the pizza, now going cold. We took our dinner into the den. I lit the paper and kindling I'd earlier laid in the fireplace and curled up next to Ryan while the fire caught, and Peony and Violet made themselves comfortable on the hearth rug. I hadn't turned on any lights, and we sat in silence and watched the flames chew through the logs.

My cursed phone beeped with an incoming text. I wouldn't have bothered to answer, but it was the signal for Uncle Arthur.

Now that's sorted, I'm off to Palma De Mallorca. And not a moment too soon—your mother's kicking me to the curb.

Me: ☺

"All okay?" Ryan asked.

"For now." I sighed happily and tilted my head back against Ryan's chest. Maria Fernanda Gomez Gonzales was watching me. A burning log fell in the fireplace and flames leapt, and for the briefest of moments, I thought she'd winked at me.

Enjoyed the read?

We'd love to hear your thoughts!

crookedlanebooks.com/feedback

Acknowledgments

Many thanks to Luhana and Zack Littlejohn of Littlejohn Farm in Prince Edward County for asking me to help look after their pigs for several months. The pig incident that happens to Gemma, actually happened to me and I knew right away (after I was freed from the barn) that it would make a great addition to the story. Fortunately, in real life, I had my phone on me so all I had to do was call for help. Yes, a hungry pig is a terrifying creature.

To Alex Delany who talked over many of the ideas for the plot of this book with me. Also to Cheryl Freedman, who brought her keen editor's eye, and love of mystery novels, to an early draft, and Sandy Harding, who as always did a marvelous job of helping sort out some of the tricky plot points.

Thanks to Mike Ranieri, Myers of the Bootmakers of Toronto, for the title, and to members of the Sherlock community for answering my questions and for accepting Gemma and Jayne in the spirit in which they are intended.